"You're turning me down, aren't you?" Maddy said in amazement

"I can't believe it," she added, gazing up at Nate, too surprised to be embarrassed. A moment ago they'd both been at the point of no return.

"Temporarily," Nate soothed, touching her cheek. "Until we go to Carmel. I want to make love to you slowly and gently, Maddy. I want the excitement to build between us." His eyes searched her face. "The first time . . . shouldn't be rushed."

She felt weak inside again. "You've really thought about this, haven't you?" she murmured, wanting to lighten the atmosphere. How was she going to wait thirteen days . . . and nights?

He laughed as he was meant to, then pulled her close. "When we're together I don't want *any* distractions—kids, work, phone calls. . . ."

"Until Carmel then," she agreed with a sigh.

"Carmel," he echoed. It was almost a commitment.

ABOUT THE AUTHOR

It was Margaret Chittenden's son who first suggested she create a chiropractor hero. A chiropractor himself, he even offered to help with the research! Meg took him at his word, and handsome, freewheeling Nate Ludlow was born. This talented author has over one hundred short stories, seventeen books and numerous articles to her credit. She also writes as Rosalind Carson.

Books by Margaret Chittenden

Until
October

MARGARET CHITTENDEN

Harlequin Books

TORONTO • NEW YORK • LONDON
AMSTERDAM • PARIS • SYDNEY • HAMBURG
STOCKHOLM • ATHENS • TOKYO • MILAN

Published August 1989

First printing June 1989

ISBN 0-373-70366-X

For my dear son,
Stephen J. Chittenden, D.C.,
and for Susan Pettigrew,
his friend and mine

CHAPTER ONE

NATE LUDLOW SLUMPED into his office chair, gazing gloomily at his own reflection in the rain-drenched window. The wavering blur of dark curly hair, craggy features and white shirtsleeves made him look like some lost creature in the process of drowning. No doubt about it, December was the pits, even in San Francisco, the best city in the world. The only bright spot on his horizon was the fact that today was Wednesday, which meant that the young woman in the safari jacket should be showing up in the parking lot at three twenty-five.

"Is that any way for a chiropractor to sit? What kind of example is that for your patients?"

Nate swiveled his chair around. His office manager was standing in the doorway, frowning at him, her plump arms full of medical records.

Emma Fieldstone looked almost as gloomy as he felt, though usually she was the cheeriest of women. December doldrums must be affecting her, too.

Sighing audibly, he hauled himself off his tailbone, ran a hand through his always unruly hair and straightened his tie. "What patients, Emma?" he asked. "This is the deadest afternoon we've had in months. I even gave Jamie the afternoon off to do her Christmas shopping. She didn't have anything else to do." Jamie was Nate's chiropractic assistant.

"Don't fret, Nate," Emma said soothingly. "We'll get back to our usual frantic pace as soon as the holidays are over. I expect everyone's busy being jolly."

"Everyone *I* know is busy being jolly in Waikiki."

With one hand holding her place in the filing cabinet, Emma studied his face. "What's wrong? The playmate of the month leave town?"

"Teddie and I have been seeing each other for four months," he protested.

"A new record."

He scowled at her, then sighed again. "It doesn't make any difference, I guess. Teddie went off to Hawaii for the holidays with a group of friends that just happened to include one Paul Duval, whom she thinks is *divine*." He shrugged. "It was winding down anyway, right on schedule."

"Your schedule, or Teddie's?"

"Both. Teddie doesn't believe in long-term stuff, either."

"So where will you go for Christmas?"

"If Sea-Tac airport doesn't get socked in, I'll go home, I guess."

"Why so glum then? I thought you enjoyed going home, now that you've grown up and decided your stepdad isn't such an ogre, after all."

"Home's okay. It's just that my stepsisters are both new mothers."

"What's wrong with that?"

There was an unusually sharp note in Emma's voice. Nate studied her profile as she went on with her filing, then shrugged again. "I've nothing against motherhood, Emma, as long as I'm not involved in it. Trouble is that if they aren't fighting with their husbands, which they do a lot, all Tess and Renny talk about are their two babies. My stepsisters used to be fun to be with, once they reached college age, anyway. Tess was in journalism and Renny in vocational education, and their conversation was *interesting*. Now it's either Ben didn't sterilize the bottles when he was supposed to, or Wade forgot to buy Pampers, or else it's teething and diaper rash and whose infant can crawl fastest."

Emma slammed a cabinet drawer shut and pulled out the one below it. "Don't lean over, bend your knees," Nate cautioned automatically.

She grunted, but obeyed. "Wait until *you* have a child," she said. "You'll find yourself boring everyone with tales of your offspring, too. If you ever stay in love long enough to get to the altar, that is."

"Fat chance."

"Not all marriages are miserable, Nate."

"The ones I've encountered have been. It's no use, Emma. You know I decided years ago that it's far safer to flit from flower to flower than to land feetfirst in the mud."

Emma laughed, as he'd intended her to, but the laugh was distinctly shaky and Nate looked at her more closely. She was as neat and rounded and sweet looking as always in her white cotton suit and sensible shoes, her straight dark hair brushed tidily behind her ears. But as she turned her head to examine the tab on a file folder, he saw that the tip of her nose was pink, which in Nate's extensive experience indicated a crying jag somewhere in her recent past. Yes. Her eyelids looked suspiciously shiny, too. "Hey, Emma, what's wrong?" he asked gently.

The sympathy in his voice was evidently her undoing. Pushing the drawer closed, she stood up, folded her arms on the top of the filing cabinet, put her face down and burst into tears. Nate grabbed a handful of tissues from the box on his desk, jumped up and went over to her. Pulling her into his arms, he started rubbing her back comfortingly.

Emma was a comfortable armful, a nice, round, comfortable, homey woman. Looking at her, you thought of cozy fireplaces and braided rugs and an apple pie, redolent of cinnamon, baking in the oven. A couple of years older than he and a foot or so shorter, Emma had mothered him ever since she came to work for him. He was very fond of her and hated to see her upset like this. It happened periodically. Usually the cause was the same.

"Love life giving you trouble again?" he asked, when the tears slowed and she was wiping her eyes with his tissues.

"When didn't it?" she asked resignedly.

"What did Lawrence do this time?"

She squirmed out of his arms and blew her nose. "Lawrence is out of the picture, Nate," she said indignantly. "He turned out to be married, remember?"

He did remember. Lawrence had taken the money Emma gave him to book a Caribbean cruise, and had bought his wife a diamond ring instead.

"Sorry, I get confused." He gave her an encouraging smile. "So if Lawrence is history, what's the problem?"

"Gary. Gary Conrad."

"The old school chum? I thought you were happy to see him."

He must have missed something. Emma had told him the previous week that Gary was once her closest friend. Evidently she and Gary had been misfits in high school and had formed an alliance against the rest. She hadn't seen Gary since graduation, but he'd turned up in San Francisco recently, selling some kind of burglar alarm system.

Nate walked over to the coffee maker, filled a couple of cups and handed one to Emma. "Correct me if I'm wrong, but didn't you say Gary was handsome and successful now? And staying at the Fairmont, no less? Wasn't there a suspicion that you'd finally found a man who wouldn't take you to the cleaners? What happened?"

He and Emma had no secrets from each other. Four years earlier, when Emma had been frustratingly in love with a compulsive gambler rather tritely nicknamed Chance, and Nate was trying to break away from a woman named Leonie, who had developed jealousy into a fine and terrifying art, Emma and he had gone out to dinner together, agreeing that everyone needed a friend to confide in. Someone who would sympathize and empathize, but not sit in judgment. Though sometimes it was difficult not to pass judgment on Emma's men; for an otherwise sensible and intelligent woman of thirty-four, she did so unerringly pick losers.

"He brought our old high-school yearbook over last night," she said gloomily.

"And?"

Emma set down her coffee cup and busily started filing again. "I told you Gary and I didn't fit in when we went to high school, but I didn't tell you why."

She took a deep, obviously painful breath. "We were fat, Nate. Not just overweight. Fat. Both of us. Gary overate to compensate for an abusive father, I did it because the pattern was set early in my life. When people teased us, Gary responded by acting the school clown, making jokes about himself before anyone else could do it. My defense was to do as much as I could for everyone, so they would like me."

She sighed, resting her hands on the top of the filing cabinet, a faraway look in her soft brown eyes. "When the yearbook came out our senior year, there was a picture of us sitting on a bench side by side, holding hands. At first we were pleased, we hadn't expected anything but the regulation student photos. But we couldn't understand the caption—PDC." She sniffed and pushed her hair back behind her ears, not looking at Nate. "A classmate enlightened us, with great glee. It meant Pillsbury Dough Couple. That's what everyone called us. I'd never realized how Gary and I looked together. I was devastated."

"It was a long time ago, Emma. Kids are often cruel."

"I know, and I thought I'd adjusted. I've lost all that weight, or most of it anyway, but I guess inside I still feel like a fat person. Seeing the yearbook again brought back all that old insecurity. Gary thinks it's funny. He keeps talking about it. And calling me pumpkin like he used to, which makes me feel like one. And that's not all. He's pressuring me."

"To do what?"

"To buy one of his damned security systems. Maybe that's all he's seeing me for, Nate. Maybe he just looks upon me as another customer. Sucker number three hundred and twenty."

"Tell him to get lost," Nate advised.

"I couldn't do that. He's an old friend."

"Old friends don't pressure old friends." He was really waxing profound today. "I'm sorry, Emma," he said. "I'm not being much help. I know you like Gary, but you must see that you tend to choose losers every time.''

"I don't know they're losers when I meet them," she said mournfully. "In any case, I don't choose them, they choose me. I didn't go after Gary, he came here. I didn't go after Lawrence either, or Chance.''

"Men know Earth Mother when they see her. Momma will forgive anything, take care of anything, lie down and let you walk all over her, if that's what it takes to make you happy. You have to learn to be more assertive, Emma. You have rights, too. The women's movement gave them to you.''

"I don't exactly have my pick of the crop, Nate," she said with an acerbic note he was happy to hear. A little acerbity, a little healthy cynicism, might protect this softhearted patsy from the leeches of the world.

"Being assertive can leave a woman all alone in a hurry," she pointed out before he could comment. "I don't want to be a liberated woman. I want to get married and have babies and live happily ever after.''

She laughed as Nate shuddered dramatically. "I know it's not *your* dream, Nate. But it is mine. I was *meant* to be a wife and mother. I like nothing better than keeping house and cooking. I don't even mind doing windows.'' She shook her head and closed the file drawer, then looked at Nate in a sweet troubled way that made him want to hug her again. "As far as choosing losers goes, Nate, I have to pretty well take what I can get. In case you haven't noticed, I'm not one of your long-legged American beauties. Men's heads don't exactly swivel when I walk by.''

He bit back the soothing platitudes that came to mind, knowing Emma wouldn't appreciate them. She was right, anyway. Most men did tend to look at the packaging first and the contents later. Some didn't even bother with the contents at all.

Before he could think of anything to say, Emma laughed in her usual no-nonsense manner and blew her nose once more. "Thanks for the coffee and sympathy, Nate. I'll be okay. I'm certainly not going to buy Gary's burglar alarm system, anyway. Twenty-five hundred dollars is too rich for my blood. Maybe Gary does like me for myself, after all. He sure seems to want to—" She broke off, blushing slightly, then glanced at the wall clock and managed a smile. "Speaking of long-legged American beauties, it's three-twenty-five, Nate. And this is Wednesday."

So she had noticed his miniobsession. Hardly surprising. Emma didn't miss much.

Once again he took up his post by the window. The rain had dwindled to a drizzle, so when the silver-gray 280Z arrived, he could see it from some distance away. Frowning in concentration, he followed its progress until the driver slid it competently into a diagonal parking slot between two larger cars.

The woman didn't bother with an umbrella to protect her hair from the rain. She wasn't wearing a raincoat, either. Her outfit was the same as always: tan pants, a matching safari jacket, sturdy walking shoes. Not exactly a feminine style of dressing, but it somehow suited her tall, slender body. Her one concession to femininity was her long, straight brown hair. He liked the way it lifted behind her as she walked rapidly toward the building's entrance. She carried her head high, chin up as though she were ready to take on the world. Such posture she had. As a chiropractor he always noticed posture. He strained his neck to catch a last glimpse of her, as she disappeared under the porte cochere.

"She's really quite gorgeous, isn't she?" Emma said softly. "I wonder how she gets her bangs to go up and over like that. God, she even has cheekbones. I hate women who have cheekbones."

He had forgotten Emma was in the room, hadn't noticed that she'd joined him at the window.

"That must be some kind of uniform she wears, don't you think?" he asked. "Or are safari jackets in this year?" He went on before Emma could comment. "She always looks worried. What do you suppose she's worried about? And she's always in a hurry, coming in or out. She doesn't run ever, but there's an impression of haste...."

"How long have you been watching her, for heaven's sake?"

He hoped he didn't look as shamefaced as he felt. "A few weeks, I guess. Every Wednesday. Wherever she goes, she's very prompt." Emma's brown eyes held a familiar teasing glint. "There's something intriguing about her," he said defensively.

"Obviously." Emma chuckled. "Why don't you check up on her then?"

"Check up how?"

She made an exasperated sound. "There are only six clinics in this building, Nate. She has to be in one of the other five."

It had never occurred to him to look. Usually he was too busy to even think about tracking down the young woman. Besides... "I'm not sure I *want* to meet her," he said slowly. "She'd probably turn out to have bad breath or rotten teeth or a voice like a cheerful chipmunk. Maybe I should just preserve the fantasy of an intriguing stranger. My mystery lady."

Emma laughed.

"On the other hand," Nate murmured, "we don't have anyone scheduled until four o'clock...."

SHE WAS in the second place he looked...way down the hall in Casey Dixon's waiting room, sitting beautifully upright on one of Casey's overstuffed sofas, a magazine held in both hands. *Newsweek*. She glanced up as he poked his head around the door. So did everyone else in the room. Evidently Casey's patients weren't off, being jolly. More difficult to postpone dental problems, he supposed.

"Hi," he said generally, feeling stupid.

A chorus of greetings answered him. The young woman's voice was not one of them, but she did smile tentatively. Nothing wrong with her teeth, as far as he could see. He was willing to bet she didn't have bad breath, either.

Close up her skin was perfect. A sheen left by the rain gleamed on her face, like dew on a fresh peach. More raindrops sparkled in her long brown hair. "Hi," he said again, directly to her.

"Hello." Her voice was low, well modulated, slightly husky, charming. A fleeting frown had shadowed her smooth brow and dark, dark eyes. He could almost hear her wondering if she was supposed to know him. He could also sense the interest of the other people in the room. Feeling more stupid than ever, totally unable to think of anything intelligent to say, he nodded and withdrew his head, closing the door softly behind himself. His heart was hammering against his ribs.

"HER NAME IS MADELEINE SCOTT," Casey said.

Taken aback, Nate stared at the back of his friend's head. The young black oral surgeon was lying face-down on the treatment table, so Nate couldn't see his expression, but there was definitely a smug note in his voice.

It was Friday. Meeting Casey in the foyer that morning, Nate had been appalled to see that he was barely able to stand up straight. "I put my back out last night," he complained. "I'll be in to see you as soon as I get a break."

"What the hell did you do?" Nate asked.

Casey had looked sheepish and hadn't answered right away. "Karen and I got to playing around," he'd finally admitted on the way up in the elevator.

Nate raised his eyebrows. "Tell me more."

"She dared me to carry her off to bed." Casey groaned, pressing one hand into the small of his back. "Man, it sure isn't as easy as Clark Gable made it look in *Gone with the Wind*. We ricocheted all over that damn staircase."

Remembering Karen Dixon's generous curves, Nate had winced.

"I suppose Emma told you I was interested in Miss Scott," he said resignedly as he checked Casey for any restriction in motion of the pelvic bones around the sacroiliac joint.

Casey turned his head over his shoulder and grinned. "Only when I asked. I saw you gawking at Madeleine on Wednesday," he added when Nate looked at him questioningly. "I was in my receptionist's office, saw you through the glass divider." He chuckled. "Something to see."

"Pretty dumb," Nate agreed. "For some reason, the instant I opened the door and saw her, I was tongue-tied." Lifting Casey's shirt, he gently palpated the area around his spine, looking for tight muscles and any change in temperature. "The X rays are okay," he added. "I'm going to give you some galvanic muscle stimulation first, to help ease the muscle spasms." He tucked the pads into the back of Casey's pants, added a hot pack on top, then switched on the machine.

Casey groaned. "That feels terrific."

"What exactly did Emma tell you?" Nate asked.

Casey chuckled. "That you've been moping over this woman for weeks, but didn't have the courage to speak to her. Didn't sound like the cool dude we all know and envy."

"Emma would never say I was moping," Nate said indignantly. "And it wasn't a matter of courage."

"So I dressed the story up a little. Sue me. Though you'd better be nice to me if you want more information. I could plead patient confidentiality."

"Madeleine," Nate murmured, liking the sound of the name. He roused himself, when he realized Casey had turned his head again and was regarding him with amusement. "Put your head down," he ordered. "Relax."

A few minutes later he helped Casey to a sitting position, had him cross his arms in front and went behind him to palpate once more the area of his spine that was restricted. "On your face again," he said. "I'm going to do some soft tissue work." For a while he probed with his thumbs in silence, then asked in what he hoped was a casual voice, "Are you going to tell me about Madeleine Scott or not?"

Casey laughed again. "Not much to tell," he said lightly. "She's a very private person. Twenty-six, -seven, in there somewhere. A little on the shy side, I'd say. Serious. Nice though. Lives in the Richmond area, near Golden Gate Park. She prefers to be called Maddy, by the way. I'm treating her for TMJ syndrome."

Nate pictured the temporomandibular joint, the hinge between skull and lower jawbone, wincing as he mentally traced the path of the dull aching pain to the angle of the jaw, the temporal region, the back of the skull.

"On your side," he said automatically. "Bottom leg straight, other leg bent." He pulled down Casey's left arm to straighten his shoulder, then adjusted his spine. "Okay?"

"So far, so good."

As Casey rolled carefully to his other side, Nate asked, "Is her TMJ syndrome psychophysiologic in origin?"

"Yep. She clenches her teeth in her sleep. Some kind of stress affecting her, though she denies it." Casey frowned. "I'm using diathermy, fitted her with a bite plate, of course, soft diet, aspirin. But she's not responding as well as I'd hoped."

"You could recommend chiropractic," Nate said innocently, as he took Casey to tension, then applied thrust in the direction he wanted the joint to open.

"As a matter of fact, I was considering doing just that," Casey said with a sly smile. "Which is why I've allowed you to pump me." He grinned up at Nate before rolling onto his front, so that Nate could check for any remaining imbalance. "Maybe I'd better send her to Jason Ross instead," he added, his voice muffled by his head-down position. "If she got involved with a decadent bachelor like you, she'd end up with more stress than ever."

He chuckled as Nate made a threatening gesture with cocked thumb and forefinger. "Okay, I surrender. How about you come over next Wednesday, and I'll introduce you in a nice, ordinary way?"

Nate shook his head and helped Casey to a sitting position. "It's Christmas next week. Anyway, knowing you, you'd say something to embarrass me."

"I didn't know it was possible to embarrass Nate Ludlow," Casey said, a glimmer of interest showing in his narrowed eyes. "What's with this woman, anyway? She's hardly your usual type. She's attractive, yes, striking even, but certainly not flamboyant about it."

Nate shrugged. "There's something about her...."

Casey eased himself to his feet. "I do believe I can walk," he murmured. "It's a miracle." He glanced slyly at Nate's face. "Can this be love?" he demanded. "Should I alert the media? Call in the troops, kidnap the woman? Tell me, old friend—now that you've cured me, I'll do anything, anything!"

"How's Karen?" Nate asked hastily, sitting down and starting to write on Casey's chart. He'd find his own way to meet Madeleine Scott, he decided. *If* he made up his mind that he *wanted* to meet her. After all, after Christmas everyone would be back in town again. Wendy and Teddie and Leslie and Ellen—well, maybe not Teddie.

Casey was successfully distracted. He loved talking about his wife. "She's terrific," he said, leaning against the table. "You realize we've been married six years?"

Nate shook his head in amazement. "Beats me how any man can promise to be with one woman forever. There are so many wonderful women out there. And so

many marriages that go kaput with disastrous conse-
quences to all concerned. Half the guys I went to school
with got married out of college or during college and
had their 2.5 children right away. Where are they now?
They've had their assets split fifty-fifty, and they see
their kids on Sundays if they're lucky. Some of them are
even supporting a second wife. Confirms my belief that
my method's best. Six months, seven at the outside and
the newness is off, the excitement's gone, doubts creep
in and the nagging starts on both sides—each wanting
to change the other person into something they're not.
Makes sense to break off while you're still ahead."

Casey chuckled. "I know your feelings on marriage,
man. You don't have to preach to me. I'm not even
going to argue with you. I've seen too many marriages
go on the rocks myself. I felt the same way until I met
Karen. I'll still admit marriage isn't easy. You have to
be prepared to work at it. Work, Nate. And time. It
takes a lot of time to build a successful relationship."

He laughed again. "I'll also admit there are times
Karen and I could cheerfully kill each other, but we'd
never leave each other. Never." He smiled reminiscently. "Lord, that woman is beautiful when she's
pregnant."

"She's pregnant?" Nate exclaimed. "You were tot-
ing around a pregnant woman? What's she doing pregnant again? She just had the last one."

"Time passes, my friend," Casey said good-
humoredly. "David is two years old already. Melanie's
five. She just had her birthday, as a matter of fact." His
face lighted up with a fatuous expression. "I do believe
I have some pictures with me," he added, reaching into
the breast pocket of the suit jacket he'd draped on the
back of a chair.

Nate groaned.

It wasn't until Casey was leaving that Nate thought to ask about Madeleine's job. "That's an unusual type of outfit she wears," he commented as Casey shrugged warily into his jacket. "Is she a park ranger or something?"

"Close," Casey said, smiling broadly. "She works at the zoo. I'm not sure what she does, except sometimes she drives the zoomobile—she visited Melanie's day-care center last week."

His dark eyes narrowed again. "Come to think of it, working in a zoo just might be the right preparation for an affair with a ladies' man like Nate Ludlow. If Madeleine can face up to apes and elephants, she ought to be able to handle Nate Ludlow." He ducked his head to avoid Nate's mock punch, then winced. "Hey, watch it, Doc. I don't want to lose the adjustment. What do I do now, anyway? Heating pads, hot bath, hot tub with hot wife?"

"Ice pack," Nate said firmly. "Ten minutes every hour. Come back tomorrow, so I can check up on you. I'll be in all morning. And no shenanigans with Karen. That's an order."

Casey sighed with mock exasperation as he headed through the doorway. "Party pooper," he called back over his shoulder.

He'd forgotten to ask Casey if Madeleine Scott was married, Nate realized as he went to greet his next patient. In the brief glimpse he'd had of her in Casey's waiting room, he had managed to note that she wasn't wearing a wedding ring. That didn't necessarily mean she was single, of course. But Casey would have told him, surely, if she was married. Wouldn't he?

MADDY HAD THOUGHT the rain was over for a while. It had rained all through Christmas and New Year, then the sun had come out, and San Francisco had sparkled until today. Of all the bad luck, to have it rain and prevent her from using her car.

Standing at the bus stop outside Dr. Dixon's building, she peered in the direction the bus should come from. She must have just missed one, for she'd been waiting quite a while. The rain had begun dribbling down the back of her neck—her hair was a sodden mess. One of these days, she'd have to get over her prejudice against umbrellas. She just hated having things to carry around—she usually had enough to keep track of, as it was. She hoped the children were inside the house. Of course they were, she chided herself; Kat was a good baby-sitter.

Huddled into her upturned collar, she didn't see the red Audi with the rack on top until it slid to a stop in front of her and she heard the buzz of its electrically operated window. The dark-haired male driver leaned across the front seat, smiling at her, his teeth startlingly white against his tanned, craggy face. "Can I give you a ride home?" he asked.

She recognized him instantly. He had peeked into Casey Dixon's waiting room several weeks ago. Dr. Dixon had talked about him afterward. Nate somebody? Supposedly he'd questioned the dentist about her.

She took a step backward, directly into a puddle. "Thank you, no," she said firmly.

"I'm perfectly respectable, Madeleine. You'd be safe, believe me."

He certainly looked respectable. He was wearing a gray suit that must have been custom-made for his powerfully built body, a white on white shirt, neat dark tie. He had smiling eyes with expression lines that radiated outward, a wide mouth that quirked up at one corner in an appealingly crooked smile. Obviously a practiced charmer, sure of himself and his attraction for the opposite sex. She knew the type and had no patience with it.

"I spoke to you in Casey Dixon's waiting room," he said. "Shortly before Christmas."

"I remember," she said. "Everyone thought you were Tom Selleck. You created quite a stir. But then Dr. Dixon came out and told us you were a friend of his, a chiropractor with an office in the same building. He thought you'd probably entered the wrong clinic by mistake."

"Well, it was something like that," he said ambiguously. "My name's Nate Ludlow," he added, then grinned. "You should have known I wasn't Tom Selleck, I don't have a moustache."

She couldn't help laughing, but didn't move any closer to the curb. He raised both dark eyebrows in a very cajoling manner. "I do wish you'd come in out of the rain, Madeleine. You look awfully wet."

"I'd drip all over your beautiful upholstery."

"I don't care." He smiled encouragingly. "The Richmond area's not out of my way, I have a condo down by the marina. And I'm not an ax murderer, honestly."

"You'd hardly tell me if you were an ax murderer, would you?" she said tartly. "How do you know where I live, anyway?" She answered her own question before he could respond. "Dr. Dixon, I presume."

She studied his face a few moments more, and decided it would be pretty dumb to refuse his offer of a ride on such a lousy day. "Should I turn on some heat?" he asked as she got into the car.

"Better not, I'd probably steam up all the windows. I'll just sit very still and try not to leak." *And make sure to keep Nate Ludlow at a distance,* she added to herself. "Dr. Dixon told me you were interested in me," she said as he pulled away from the curb. "What exactly did he mean?"

Her straightforward question obviously surprised him. "Well, you know," he said awkwardly, "me male, you female."

"I was afraid that's what he meant."

He frowned and was silent for a while. Then he said, "I really am interested, Madeleine."

"You don't even know me," she said, without trying to conceal her exasperation.

He had a very boyish grin. Chilled as she was, she found herself warming to that grin, softening. Nate Ludlow also had dangerous eyes, she informed that softer part of herself, hazel eyes that seemed to change color according to the light—kind eyes, but sexy eyes. He knew how to use them, too.

"I know you are Madeleine Scott," he said. "Your nickname is Maddy. You work at the zoo? You like animals, I take it?"

She nodded. That was a safe subject. "I love animals and I love zoos," she said with enthusiasm. "My dad is an engineer, so as long as I can remember, we traveled all over the world, while he worked on various projects. Sometimes it was hard to make friends—" She broke off, aware that indirectly she was telling this man more than she usually told anyone.

"It was sometimes lonely, and a zoo was a familiar place," he said, finishing for her.

His insight surprised her. "Exactly," she said. "Zoos were havens in unfamiliar territory. So when I was going to college, it seemed natural to take a part-time job at the zoo. That led to my decision to work there when I graduated. I'm the children's zookeeper."

"Casey told me you drove the zoomobile." He frowned. "I'm not sure I know what a zoomobile is, but I imagine it's some kind of van you cart animals around in? To schools, hospitals, nursing homes?"

She nodded. "I don't do it all the time—we mostly use volunteer help, but I pitch in when necessary, and even sometimes when it's not necessary. I like getting away once in a while for a change of pace. At the moment, I'm helping out a lot. We have several volunteers out with that horrible flu that came up from L.A."

He groaned in sympathy. "We had it in our building. We called it the Martian Death flu."

Again she had to laugh, but she was waiting to see what else he'd have to say about her. "You usually drive a silver-gray 280Z," he went on.

She nodded.

"It's out of commission today?"

"Somebody stole my T-tops over the holidays," she said shortly, still angered by the act. "It's taking a while to find replacements. I can't drive without T-tops when it's raining."

"Tough," he said sympathetically, then added, "I also know you have TMJ syndrome. Did Casey tell you it affects twenty million Americans?"

Startled and suddenly furious, she forgot she'd meant to sit completely still, and squirmed around in her seat to face him, just as he stopped the car at a red light. Several drops of water ran from her bangs down her nose, and she wiped them away with her fingertips.

"Dr. Dixon had no right to tell you that," she said indignantly.

"He was thinking of sending you to me for a consultation," Nate explained hastily. "I could show you an exercise that might help."

Before she could gather her wits, he had reached over with one hand to cup the side of her damp face. "Open your mouth a little," he ordered. "See if you can exert pressure against my hand."

Startled, she obeyed without question.

"You could do it yourself," he informed her. "Make your hand resist the pressure of your jaw. It's called active stretching. You could also hold a cork between your teeth when you're just sitting around." He laughed softly, intimately. "Best to do it when nobody's around."

Because of the rain it was almost dark outside. Lights from cars driving through the intersection shone in through the windshield and were reflected in his eyes, turning them as green as a cat's. His hand on her face was big and steady and warm. A tingling sensation started low inside her body and quickly spread upward, warming her in spite of her wet clothing.

And then the traffic light changed, he released her and gave her a sexy smile and turned back to the steering wheel. She looked at his hands on the steering wheel. They were very competent-looking hands, sprinkled with dark hair, nicely shaped, with long strong fingers. She could still feel the imprint of those fingers on her face and the impact of his touch all through her body. No doubt about it, Dr. Nate Ludlow was a very practiced charmer. He could be quite dangerous to someone who didn't have her wits about her—

especially someone who was determined to keep her life as simple as possible.

"I'm not sure I believe in chiropractic," she said shortly.

His sidelong glance was amused. "I'm right up there with the tooth fairy, huh? I'm real, I assure you, Maddy. Feel." His hand touched her knee briefly, startling her. "Chiropractic is a perfectly respectable science, Maddy. I'm surprised a woman of your intelligence wouldn't know that."

"My father had a bad experience with a chiropractor," she said defensively. "He had back trouble and ended up in more pain than he started out with."

"So he ran into a not-so-good chiropractor. Or else didn't stay with the treatment long enough."

Remembering her father's impatient nature, Maddy thought it entirely possible Nate Ludlow had a point, but decided not to concede it.

"I'm not sure I like you knowing so much about me," she said evenly as they entered Golden Gate Park. Traffic was as heavy as usual at this time of the day, but at least it had stopped raining. "I value my privacy."

He grinned. "So Casey told me. Would it help if I reciprocated?"

"What do you mean?" she asked warily.

He laughed. He laughed a lot, this man. Didn't he ever take anything seriously?

"I mean I should in all fairness tell you about me," he explained. "I'm really a very trustworthy person. I was born in Seattle. Nobody dangerous was ever born in Seattle, Maddy. I'm thirty-two years old. Single and likely to remain so. I'm gun-shy when it comes to marriage, but otherwise I'm fairly sociable."

Gun-shy. Was that supposed to be a warning? Was he really conceited enough to think all women were panting to take him to the altar?

"I didn't start out to be a chiropractor, by the way," he went on cheerily. "Like your father, I was going to be an engineer, but somewhere along the road, I decided I'd rather work with people than machines. About the same time a friend invited me to go skiing in the Cascades, where her uncle lived. Her uncle happened to be a chiropractor, as well as a very enthusiastic and convincing man."

He grinned at her again. "How am I doing? Are you getting the idea I'm a solid citizen?"

"Is a solid citizen usually gun-shy about marriage?" she asked dryly.

"This one is," he said, then continued as if that subject were closed. "I work at least five days a week, Maddy, sometimes six. I love my work. I love seeing people respond to treatment. I'm a *good* chiropractor. However, I also believe in having a good time. All work and no play do make people dull, you know." He gave her a humorously wistful smile. "To be honest, I was really meant to be a full-time sailboarder, but it doesn't pay well."

Maddy had watched sailboarders in action many times, when she'd taken the children to the marina. The children were always entranced by the sight of the colorful sails skimming across the water, especially when the water was running high and some of the more daring young people performed acrobatic leaps and turns. She was willing to bet Nate Ludlow was one of those.

"Have you ever tried sailboarding?" he asked.

"No. I'm not really a physical person."

Amusement flashed in his eyes.

"I mean I'm more interested in mental pursuits," she added hastily. "Reading, the theater, music."

"Do you swim?"

"Of course."

"That's physical," he pointed out.

"It's also good exercise."

"So is sailboarding."

"I've always been too busy for..."

"Frivolity?"

"Unnecessary activities."

"Well, *I* also play golf and tennis," he continued after a brief silence. "And so you'll know that I'm being completely honest and open, I'll admit I'm also what is quaintly known in some circles as a ladies' man."

"Dr. Dixon told me that part." She hesitated, then glanced at him once more. "Actually, what he said was that you were a real killer, where women were concerned."

"With friends like Casey, I don't need enemies." He grinned complacently, then added, "I almost forgot. I do have one mental hobby—I'm crazy about old movies."

She stared at him in utter amazement. "I'm a movie buff myself," she exclaimed, forgetting that she had meant to keep him at a distance. "The older, the better." She smiled. "I've never met anyone who felt the same way. People think it's an old-fashioned hobby to have. Most of the men I know prefer Rambo in all his incarnations. What kind of old movies do you like?"

"All kinds, especially black-and-white. Not colorized," he added with a shudder she could certainly relate to. "Drama preferably. Musicals. Older comedies if they aren't slapstick."

"*Wings*?" she suggested, bringing up one of her own favorites.

He flashed a delighted grin. "Exactly. The flying sequences in *Wings* were terrific."

"So was Clara Bow."

"How about Ingrid Bergman in *Intermezzo*?"

"And *Casablanca*."

In no time they were deeply involved in a discussion of the relative merits of Bogart, Charles Boyer, Jean Harlow, Valentino, Ronald Colman...Bette Davis as Queen Elizabeth.

Maddy was so engrossed that she almost forgot to give Nate directions and at the last minute had to yell, "Left here! It's the gray house with the white trim," she instructed him.

He appeared surprised. It wasn't too unusual for a single woman to live in a house in San Francisco, of course...though most of her friends and colleagues lived in apartments or condos. But none of them had her special set of circumstances.

"That was fun," she said, turning to him, deciding that even if he was full of cocky male confidence, he was still quite likable. "Thanks for the ride and the great conversation."

"It was my pleasure," he said. "It's not often I meet someone who shares my passion." It was a suggestive word, but there was nothing she could legitimately object to in his tone. All the same, the word seemed to echo in her mind as they both climbed out of the car. Passion wasn't something she had thought about for a long, long time.

Did Nate Ludlow expect her to invite him in? she wondered as he joined her on the sidewalk. "I have a pretty good print of *Abraham Lincoln*," he said. "The

1930 biography directed by D. W. Griffith. Have you ever seen it?''

There was an additional, unspoken question in his voice. He wanted to prolong the discussion. He probably *was* expecting an invitation. A confident man, Dr. Nate Ludlow. She supposed that in return for the ride home, she could at least offer him a cup of coffee or a glass of wine. But she was soaked through, and what she really wanted to do was jump into a hot shower. The children would be waiting for their dinner anyway; she was already later than usual....

The thought had barely formed when the front door of the house crashed open and Hannah and Adam tumbled out. Eight-year-old Hannah was yelling something, but she was so excited that her words were totally incoherent. She had something brown and fuzzy clutched in one hand. Pookie, could it possibly be Pookie? Hannah's sharp little face was flushed, her single blond braid coming unraveled. Adam, younger by a year than his sister, looked even more worried than usual.

Her stomach coiling itself into a tight knot, Maddy gathered rapidly that whatever Hannah was shouting about was not good news.

As she wrestled with the gate latch—it always stuck—she happened to glance at Nate Ludlow's face. He was standing stock-still on the sidewalk, staring at Hannah and Adam with an expression of absolute horror on his handsome face. "You have children?" he exclaimed.

Not surprisingly, he had jumped to the conclusion that she was Hannah and Adam's mother. Totally turned off by his horrified expression, she decided she wasn't going to enlighten him. In any case, she couldn't say, "They aren't mine," in front of Hannah and

Adam, not when she was the only person they could completely rely on. Let Nate Ludlow think what he liked, she decided. She wasn't going to waste time or explanations on a man who didn't like children.

CHAPTER TWO

"POOKIE'S ALL DROWNDED!" Hannah yelled, thrusting her Winnie-the-Pooh bear into Maddy's hands.

The bear, which usually slept with Hannah, had been missing for a week. His discovery should have been greeted with joy, for he was Hannah's favorite thing in the whole world. Puzzled, Maddy frowned down at the stuffed animal. Pookie was certainly soggy.

"Where did you find him?" she asked, making her voice as deliberately calm as possible. "Was he out in the rain?"

"He was under your bed." Hannah had grabbed Maddy's hand and was pulling her toward the front door. "Kat was playing hide-and-seek with us and she found him. He's drownded, isn't he?"

"Under my bed?"

Adam pulled at her jacket on the other side. "Is Pookie dead?" he asked. His cornflower-blue eyes looked so worried that Maddy wanted to pull him into her arms, but Hannah wouldn't stop tugging.

"He'll be fine," Maddy promised. "There's water under my bed?" Twisting her head as Hannah dragged her into the house, she called out, "Thanks for the ride, Dr. Ludlow. Sorry I couldn't—" She left the sentence unspoken. Nate Ludlow was still standing outside the gate, still looking stunned. He probably hadn't heard a word since the children appeared.

Maddy grabbed a towel from the children's bathroom and wound it around her head, slung her wet jacket over the towel rail, then dispatched the children to the laundry room with instructions to place Pookie in the dryer, with a towel and a tennis ball to fluff up his stuffing. Taking a deep breath, she reluctantly approached her ground-floor bedroom.

Kat had pushed Maddy's queen-size bed and nightstands over to the doorway, and was mopping the floor in the center of the room. "I dived under your bed to hide from the kids—straight into a puddle with Pookie in the middle of it," she explained. "It's a mess, isn't it?" She was smiling. Kat was always cheerful, impossible to faze. Somewhat strange-looking with her spiky punk haircut, sprayed orange or green or magenta as the mood struck her—orange today—and her studded leather outfits and bone and feather earrings, she was a loving, good-natured, friendly teenager, and the best baby-sitter of the three Maddy had hired since her sister Georgia had left home and family.

Tucking in the end of the towel at the back of her neck, Maddy edged around the bed to survey the damage. Several blocks of parquet flooring had come up like a pack of cards. Judging by the stains on the surrounding blocks, water had been slowly seeping under there for some time. The house was built on a concrete slab, so the leak had to be coming from one of the pipes that fed water to Maddy's bathroom. Unable to leak downward, it had taken the path of least resistance. The hot-water pipe, she realized. Her showers had been turning chilly for a month or so. She'd meant to talk to Brennan about getting a new hot-water tank, only he was never home.

"Did you turn the water off?" she asked faintly.

Kat nodded. "At the tank. It's stopped oozing, but there's still an awesome puddle under the flooring. I called Brennan. You'd already left the zoo. He said he'd call the insurance company and get a plumber. You suppose he'll remember?"

"Probably not."

Turning, intending to reach for the telephone on top of one of the nightstands, Maddy almost collided with Nate Ludlow. He put a hand on each of her shoulders to steady her, and her adrenaline reacted with a rush of activity. He'd startled her, of course, she told herself.

Abruptly she pulled away, and he looked apologetic. "I thought you'd gone!" she exclaimed, embarrassed by her overreaction.

He shrugged. "I gathered someone had 'drownded,' and thought I might be able to offer CPR. I take it Pookie isn't in critical condition, after all?"

"Pookie's in the dryer. He's a stuffed bear."

"That's a relief." He looked at the floor and grimaced. "Anything I can do?"

He'd evidently recovered from the shock of seeing the children, but Maddy hadn't forgotten his horrified expression. She was also feeling guilty for enjoying herself so much in his car, while the children and Kat were coping with something she should have handled. "Everything's under control now, thank you," she said briskly.

He raised his eyebrows, nodding at the floor. "It doesn't look too controlled. Will your husband be able to take care of it?"

"Husband, what husband?" Maddy asked. She had pulled the telephone directory from the bottom of the nightstand and was leaning over the bed thumbing through the book, holding the towel in place on her head and distractedly trying to remember the name of the plumber she'd called when the kitchen sink had sprung a leak several months ago. She had completely forgotten that she'd allowed Nate to think the children were hers. "What would I be doing with a husband?" she muttered. "I've got enough to contend with. Craig?" she queried, looking at Kat. "Was that the plumber's name?"

Kat shrugged. "Who knows about plumbers?"

Maddy went into the hall and called to Hannah. Hannah always remembered names. "Greg," the little girl yelled back over the pounding of the dryer, where she was evidently standing watch. "Greg Simpson."

Nate was eyeing Kat rather warily when Maddy returned. Kat was beaming at him, tossing her head to make her feathers and bones bounce. "Don't I know you?" he asked.

She nodded vigorously. "Kat Caley. You treated my boyfriend after he crashed his horse into a wall down on Jefferson Street."

"His horse? Oh, his motorcycle? I remember. Whiplash, wasn't it?"

"He swears by you, Dr. Ludlow. Tells all his friends they should go to you."

Nate Ludlow was looking a little bemused, Maddy thought. He was probably imagining what Rocko's friends looked like. Rocko himself was two hundred pounds of very hairy male, the despair of Kat's ultraconservative parents, who judged him by his barbaric appearance, rather than taking the trouble to get to know his remarkably sweet nature.

Maddy had found the plumber's name in the yellow pages. About to reach for the telephone again, she paused. "Thank you for coming in to check on us," she said to Nate. "It's too bad you aren't a plumber."

This time he obviously understood the dismissive tone in her voice. "I guess I'll get out of your way," he said. He looked at her, raising his eyebrows. "You should probably take off those wet clothes pretty soon."

"I will."

Hannah and Adam were blocking the doorway. As she moved out of his way, Hannah's blue eyes watched Nate suspiciously. She didn't do well with strangers.

"Hi," Adam said brightly. Adam was a friend to the world.

"Hi," Nate responded a little awkwardly. "Pookie okay?" he asked Hannah.

"Of course he's not okay," Hannah said shortly. "He's still thumping around in the dryer."

"Oh. Well..." Nate hesitated in the doorway. He looked back at Maddy, then at Kat and the children, hands in his pants pockets, car keys jingling. He seemed unsure of what to do.

Maddy just wanted him to leave, so that she could make her call. She picked up the telephone. "Thanks again for the ride home," she said.

He nodded, shrugged and smiled vaguely around the room, then he left. He certainly was a good-looking man, Maddy thought, an interesting man. Be honest, Maddy, she told herself sternly—he is an extraordinarily sexy man. She felt a momentary pang of something or other—regret?—but dismissed it immediately and dialed the plumber.

NATE WASN'T SURE if he was more relieved or disappointed as he climbed into the Audi and started the engine. So much for his miniobsession. No bad breath or chipmunk voice; instead a sweet aura of something old-fashioned, like lavender drying in the sunshine, backed up by a slightly musky odor of jungle, due to her work at the zoo, no doubt. She also had a pleasantly husky voice that had seemed to him the most tantalizing he'd ever heard. And she had appeared even more attractive close up than from a distance, in spite of her drenched condition.

Those wonderful eyes of hers, so serious, so dark that it was hard to tell where the iris ended and the pupil began. Eyebrows like birds' wings. Those cheekbones. And her skin, browned by the sun yet soft as rose petals, soft as satin, soft as every cliché he'd ever heard. She didn't wear much makeup, just enough to accent her marvelous eyes. No lipstick on the sweet curves of her mouth. Miss Natural.

She hadn't thought too much of him at first, that was obvious, but she'd warmed to him when they'd discussed movies. What a marvelous smile she had, starting slowly in her eyes, moving forward to light her face as her lips curved. Imagine her liking old movies!

However, there were serious complications—those two very lively children and someone named Brennan, who wasn't a husband, but evidently belonged to the household in some way. He remembered Kat Caley telling him proudly that she baby-sat for a scientist. Brennan? Was Brennan the children's father or an innocent bystander?

The little girl had looked definitely hostile. The little boy was friendly enough, but Nate was never quite sure how to act around children. They made him feel uneasy, as though they were plotting against him. Leftover paranoia from his teen years, he supposed. Those stepsisters of his...

He shrugged and forced himself to concentrate on his driving. Traffic was still heavy and the rain had started again. It was too bad, he thought as he drove toward the marina. He had liked his mystery lady. More than liked. But whatever Maddy Scott's domestic situation was, it wasn't anything he wanted to get involved in. To think he had almost asked her for a date, the moment before the children came boiling noisily out of the house. He'd really had a very narrow escape.

BRENNAN DIDN'T COME HOME. He was, no doubt, caught up in some exciting project at the Lowther Institute, Maddy thought resignedly after the children were in bed, a fully restored Pookie warmly tucked in beside Hannah. Half the time Brennan became so immersed in his research into children's diseases that he forgot he had children of his own.

It didn't matter, she told herself as she gazed unseeingly at a wildlife documentary on PBS. She had coped as she always coped. The insurance company would pay for the removal and replacement of the damaged parquet flooring. There was a deductible, of course, and for some reason that was impossible to fathom, the insurance company wouldn't pay for the actual repair of the hot-water pipe, but money wasn't one of Brennan Malone's problems. The flooring company would send someone over in the morning, and she'd left a message for the plumber on his answering machine. She and Kat had moved all of her bedroom furniture into the living room. It was pretty crowded, but they could manage for a couple of days. Luckily she had the next two days off. She just wished she could have had a shower before the hot-water tank gave up.

She wondered if Brennan would come home at all tonight. He often stayed at the institute. If he did come and happened to notice the excess furniture in the living room, he'd just think vaguely that Kat had rearranged things again. What a dear he was. Exasperating, though. Sometimes—not often, but sometimes—she could understand how her sister Georgia had come to leave him. She could never understand, however, how Georgia had brought herself to leave her children.

"YO, NATE, HOLD IT!" Casey yelled, just as Nate pushed the elevator button.

Nate held the door until Casey was inside. "Back still okay?" he asked. Casey had come in for a couple of adjustments, then stopped as soon as he felt better. Typical patient behavior. Nate could rarely convince anyone that regular chiropractic care would strengthen resistance to injury. Most people preferred a pound of cure to an ounce of prevention.

"Great," Casey said. "Nice day, huh? Feels warm enough to be spring."

"Winter will be back tomorrow," Nate said gloomily.

"Cheerful thought." Casey slanted a glance at Nate's face as they left the elevator. "You get anywhere with Maddy Scott yet?" he asked.

Nate swung around to face him. "You didn't tell me she had two children," he said accusingly.

"Aha, you did get somewhere! I might have known." Casey's black eyebrows drew together. "*Two* children? I've only met Adam. Nice little boy. Polite. Had to take out a couple of teeth. Small mouth." His face cleared. "Oh, yeah, Hannah. She came in once with Adam. She mothered him, I remember—odd little girl."

"You might have warned me," Nate said.

Casey grinned. "They aren't Maddy's, birdbrain. They're her sister's."

Nate suddenly noticed that sunlight was shining through the skylight above. It felt warm on his head, like a blessing.

"You mean Maddy's just taking care of them temporarily?" he asked.

Casey frowned. "I don't know about that. I got the impression the arrangement was pretty permanent. The sister took off somewhere, dumped the kids on Maddy. Father's Brennan Malone. He's a research scientist...a biologist, I think. Yeah. Director of research at the Lowther Institute. Little Adam told me that. Nice little tyke. Friendly. Proud of his daddy."

"Brennan is Maddy's brother-in-law?" Nate asked as Casey turned away.

Casey nodded, but kept on going toward the end of the hall.

"Then he's not...?"

Casey shrugged. "Who knows? They all live under one roof." He waved a hand and disappeared into his clinic.

The sun had gone behind a cloud. Nate's scalp felt cold again as he wandered into his own clinic. "Tough weekend, Dr. Ludlow?" Jamie asked.

He grunted at his pretty assistant, then managed a smile. "Maybe I've got a cold coming on," he offered as an excuse for his bad mood.

"Vitamin C and zinc lozenges," Jamie advised with a toss of her curly blond hair.

"I thought I was the doctor here."

"Then heal yourself, Doctor."

He grinned, feeling a lot better for the exchange. Not a whole lot better though, he conceded as he picked up the first patient chart of the day. Those children might not be Maddy's, but they were evidently her responsibility. And as long as he didn't know where the brother-in-law fitted in, he'd be well advised to stay away from his mystery lady.

TWO DAYS LATER he was standing once more at his office window. It was three twenty-five. Wednesday. In the parking lot below him, Madeleine Scott was walking toward the building, dressed in her usual safari outfit, her chin up, her long straight brown hair lifting behind her as she walked.

She looked worried.

At least he knew now why she always looked worried. He'd look worried, too, if he had to cope with hostile Hannah. He'd probably gnash his teeth a lot and develop TMJ syndrome, as well. If he tapped on the window, would she look up and smile that slow smile of hers? *Stay away,* he advised himself again.

"Are you going to spend the rest of your life watching that young woman?" Emma asked from the doorway.

"She gets to me," he said, turning slowly from the window. "I'm not sure why, but I'm still intrigued by her." He grinned. "I gave her a ride home last week in the rain, by the way. She works in the zoo, that's why she wears such sensible clothing. She's the children's zookeeper."

"Obviously perfect for you," Emma said with a grin. "Not your usual type, though. You've always gone for lots of glamour."

He sighed. "She's very attractive. Straightforward. Different. Appetizing. She even likes old movies."

"But?"

He sat down heavily in his office chair and ran a hand through his hair. "She's rather irritating in some ways."

"She didn't fall at your feet?"

He ignored the jibe. "She has two serious flaws," he said flatly. "Her sister's kids. Some kind of permanent arrangement, Casey thinks."

"Her sister died?" Emma's voice was soft.

He shook his head. "Not that I know of. But for some reason, Maddy has evidently inherited the kids *and* the brother-in-law."

"Complicated."

"Too complicated for me."

"Well," Emma said briskly, "perhaps you'd like to do some work around here instead, then. We just happen to have every room full."

She made an exasperated sound as he reluctantly stood up and ambled toward the door. "I like you better when you're your usual enthusiastic self, Nate," she told him. "You need a change of pace. Some nurturing maybe. Tender loving care. How about a bowl or two of chili at my place after work? I made a huge pot yesterday."

He grinned at her from the doorway. Emma was a terrific cook, and her chili made a man's ears smoke. "You're on, Earth Mother," he said, feeling cheerful once more.

EMMA LIVED in one of the older parts of town in a second-floor walk-up apartment that she kept scrupulously clean. Even the long flight of wooden steps leading to the upper verandah shone as if it had been polished. Emma probably scoured the steps weekly on her hands and knees, Nate thought as he followed her. She was always dusting or mopping up after the janitorial service he employed at the clinic. Cleanliness is next to Godliness was one of her mother's favorite maxims, she had told him once.

He looked around as Emma fumbled through her purse for the keys she'd put away after parking her car. Most of the small houses in the area were embellished in gingerbread fashion, and judging by the small but flower-bright gardens and the profusion of window boxes, many of the residents were senior citizens with time on their hands. It was a quiet neighborhood, apparently without children, at least none that Nate had ever seen around. A settled neighborhood. Peaceful. Very little traffic. Nate could even hear the leaves on the trees rattling in the slight breeze.

Startled, he flinched as Muggsie, Emma's elderly cockapoo, barked a shrill welcome from behind the apartment door, then he winced again as a blaring siren shattered the air above his head. Both he and Emma instinctively covered their ears against the godawful sound, which was several decibels above bearable level, then Emma began frantically clawing through her purse, still searching for the elusive keys. Why could women never find things in those huge bags they carried? he wondered, his hands still clapped to his ears. It was one of their more irritating traits. For that matter, why couldn't they hang onto the keys between car and house?

"What the hell is going on?" he exclaimed, as Emma finally flourished a cluster of keys, attached to what looked like a baby's teething ring.

She didn't hear him, of course. Nothing could be heard over that earsplitting din. He discovered the source at the same moment that Emma finally fought her door open and disappeared inside. Protruding from the eaves above Emma's front door there was a large horn. Entering the apartment hurriedly, turning to close the door against the horrendous racket, he saw that several cars had stopped in the middle of the street, their occupants peering upward. Some of the neighbors had emerged from their houses, along with a few from other apartments in Emma's complex, all standing stock-still, looking like the mechanical figures that pop out of cuckoo clocks to check the weather, except that they all had their fingers in their ears. Nate waved at them reassuringly.

Closing the door didn't help. The noise was as loud inside as outside. Emma was on her knees, fumbling around behind a fair-sized wooden box that stood on a lamp table in her small living room. The box was emitting the mind-numbing blare. Nate wondered if he'd ever hear anything again.

And then Emma found the switch. Abruptly there was silence—blessed, wonderful silence. Her eyes closed, Emma slumped against the edge of the sofa, and Muggsie crawled out from under an overstuffed armchair, her shaggy gray body shaking uncontrollably. Opening her eyes, Emma gathered Muggsie into her arms and murmured comfortingly to the dog. After a minute or two she looked apologetically at Nate, who was standing, arms folded, in the doorway.

"You bought Gary's burglar alarm, didn't you?" he said accusingly.

"He brought it over last night." She buried her face in Muggsie's soft hair, so she wouldn't have to meet his gaze.

"And charged you twenty-five hundred dollars?"

"Plus tax," she muttered.

He laughed ruefully. "Emma, Emma, Emma."

She stood up, still holding the little dog in her arms. "I can't use a complicated security system," she said defensively. "I didn't want wires all over the place, and anyway, old Mr. Rosini next door comes in several times a day to let Muggsie out. I don't think he could manage any kind of coded system. This one just consists of the monitor and a few sensors here and there. It's electronic. It doesn't go off unless someone breaks a window or tries to force open the door. You can actually leave it on all the time, without worrying about it going off accidentally."

"*Something* set the damn thing off."

Emma sighed, set down the cockapoo with a last reassuring pat and led the way into her kitchen. "I guess Muggsie's bark must sound like breaking glass," she said gloomily. "She only barks when I come home. She's almost completely deaf, but she seems to sense when I'm on my way in. I had no idea she would set off the alarm. I'm sure Gary didn't think so, either."

"She's not so deaf. She heard the alarm okay."

"Who wouldn't?"

Nate laughed. "Your love life's going to be the death of you one day, Emma Fieldstone," he said.

"Listen to who's talking," she said briskly, burrowing into a cabinet for pans.

An hour later they sat at the round oak table in Emma's kitchen. Emma was the kind of woman, Nate reflected fondly, who would always have a round oak table in her kitchen.

They were feasting on chili loaded with chopped onions, a huge tossed salad, and garlic bread, with some Henry Weinhard's Private Reserve to extinguish the heat of the chili. There were two bright spots of color on Emma's round cheeks, caused either by the chili or residual embarrassment—Nate wasn't sure which.

"So what are you going to do about the alarm?" Nate asked. "Your neighbors aren't going to appreciate that factory siren going off every time you come home."

The spots of color deepened. "I don't know what I'm going to do," she said miserably.

Nate took too large a mouthful of chili, spluttered, and reached immediately for his glass of dark beer. "God, this chili is fantastic," he said when he got his voice back. "You should leave a pot out for any potential burglar. He'd forget what the hell he came for. Probably hang around and ask you to marry him. I'm tempted to forget my vows and ask you myself."

Emma snorted. His attempts to cheer her were obviously futile. "You could call him, Emma," he said softly.

"What good would that do?"

"You can make him take it back, get your money back."

"But I *need* a burglar alarm. Two houses on this street were broken into, just last month."

"Well, maybe Gary can adjust it, change the frequency or something."

Her face brightened. "You think so?"

"Call him, Emma."

NATE DISLIKED Gary Conrad on sight, for no reason that he could determine. The man had turned out to be as tall as Nate, broad-shouldered, every bit as muscular, bright-eyed and clear-complexioned, with just enough gray in his dark hair to give it distinction. Somehow Nate had expected Gary to be something of a wimp, but he oozed confidence in himself. Maybe "oozed" was the operative word. He was just too determinedly macho. When Emma introduced him to Nate, he shook hands with a grip that left Nate counting his fingers. He had looked a little suspicious when he first arrived, but Emma's introduction: "This is my boss," had evidently reassured him that Nate wasn't competition.

"The monitor just needs a little adjusting," he told Emma, flourishing a screwdriver, sounding a little too patronizing for Nate's taste. "I've brought you a gift," he added.

"You have?" she breathed.

Were those stars in Emma's eyes? Nate wondered, then decided he was just feeling disgruntled, because he'd been promised some tender loving care and now he felt like a third wheel. He'd thought Emma might advise him on how to handle the odd tightness in his throat he experienced whenever he saw Madeleine Scott. Instead, she'd deafened his ears with sound, paralyzed his vocal cords with hot chili, and was now subjecting him to Gary Conrad's unpalatable brand of charm.

The gift turned out to be a rectangular block of white plastic with a black disc in its center. "Your very own panic button, pumpkin," Gary said fatuously.

If there had been stars in Emma's eyes, they blinked out now. Emma was looking at her old school friend with an expression of exasperation on her face. "What good is that going to do?" she demanded.

By way of answer, Gary pressed the disc once; that activated the alarm. He allowed it to blast out a couple of raucous hoots, which sent Muggsie scooting under the chair again, then pressed the disc twice to turn it off. "There you go," he said, presenting the thing to Emma as if it were made of precious metal. "One tap and you can activate the alarm from your bed, if you hear funny sounds in the night, two taps and you can switch it off from your car, before Muggsie has a chance to sound off."

"How much is it?" Nate asked suspiciously.

Gary waved a hand in an expansive gesture. "Usually they run around twenty or thirty dollars, but I'll throw it in for nothing. Least I can do for the other half of the PDC." He looked brightly at Nate. "Emma tell you we went to school together?" he asked. "She tell you about them calling us the PDC?"

Emma looked stricken as she heard the term again, and Nate could cheerfully have throttled the unfeeling oaf. "She told me," he said grimly. "I wouldn't think it would be something you'd want to remember."

"Water under the bridge," Gary said with a shrug. Then he smiled charmingly at Emma and said he'd work some more on the monitor, to see if he could lower the sensitivity just enough to put it out of Muggsie's range.

"Thank you, Gary," Emma said softly, looking genuinely grateful, and Nate decided he was being too judgmental. Emma was his friend, as well as his office manager, and if she liked this guy, that should be enough for him. *I don't exactly have my pick of the crop,* she'd said in such a forlorn voice. Pick of the crop. For some reason, the phrase reminded him of Madeleine Scott.

"Are you going to see Madeleine again?" Emma asked, a few minutes later when Nate was leaving.

Nate hesitated, conscious of Gary behind them in the living room, playing with Muggsie and an old white sock tied in a knot. He loved animals, he'd told Nate. He'd started out to be a veterinary assistant, but there hadn't been enough money in it. He'd also tried being a wine rep and a realtor and a medical supplies salesman. "Working my way up," he called it. "Now I've got it made. Electronics, that's where it's at. I aim to retire when I'm forty."

"I'm not sure," Nate said finally. "Two kids, after all." He shook his head. "Probably I'll leave it up to fate. If I'm meant to see her again, I will."

"You really believe that?" Emma asked, looking interested.

He frowned. "I guess I do. My mother's influence, I suppose. She's big on that kind of stuff. I don't go along with everything she says, though—she laid out a hand of tarot cards at Christmas that said I was going to get married this year. Wishful thinking on Mom's part there, I'm afraid. Anyway, Mom believes that if someone comes into your life, there's a reason. If they take off, there's a reason for that too, and if they come back, then it's definitely meant to be." He grinned. "At least that was the explanation she gave me when she married Joe."

"Your stepfather?"

"She met him at a party when she was sixteen. Then she didn't see him again until she was thirty-five or so. A few years after my dad died, Joe came knocking on the door, looking for directions to some day-care center. His wife had recently died, leaving him with Tess and Renny to take care of. Fate? It's possible, don't you think?''

Emma didn't answer. She was looking thoughtfully toward the living room, where Gary was still playing tug-of-war with Muggsie. "Fate," he heard her murmur—and wished he'd kept his big mouth shut.

Emma hugged him good-night in the doorway. "Take care, Nate," she cautioned, then added with a sly grin, "it will be interesting to see if Madeleine Scott does come back into your life, won't it? Of course, you can always waylay her on her way into Dr. Dixon's office and *tell* yourself it's fate."

He shook his head in mock solemnity. "You shouldn't mess around with fate, Emma. It's best to let fate hit you with an unmistakable wallop."

CHAPTER THREE

THE LAST STOP on the zoomobile's Valentine's Day run was at Maddy's favorite nursing home, one of the best run in the state. Maddy hadn't driven the zoomobile for a while and she usually enjoyed it, especially when everything went smoothly. Unfortunately this wasn't one of those days.

To begin with, after putting on her waterproof apron, a zoo issue imprinted with animals, she took the rainbow boa out of his pillowcase and found that the new volunteers, Lisa and Derek, had put a hot-water bottle underneath him in the carrying case, instead of putting it alongside.

An overheated boa was a lively boa. When Maddy was showing him to the group of senior citizens in the recreation room, he insisted on curling himself around her arm and poking his head under her apron and into her shirtfront, much to the delight of the men in the audience. Then Dora Duck startled her by coming up behind her and rattling her bill between Maddy's knees, which made her jump. That in turn scared Dora into relieving herself onto the linoleum. After Maddy had cleaned up the slimy green mess, she decided it was time for something safer, so she and Lisa and Derek took some of the smaller animals to visit patients who couldn't leave their rooms. It had been proven that an opportunity to pet animals was excellent therapy for shut-ins, and Maddy loved to see old faces light up when she came through a door. For safety's sake, she decided not to push her luck today. She took Annie Rose, a sweet-natured Holland lop-eared rabbit that was timid enough to stay out of trouble.

All went well until Maddy entered Barbara Oates's room. Barbara was one of Maddy's favorite people, an acidic old lady who always insisted that by the age of ninety-two, a person had earned the right to say what she pleased.

Cupping the little rabbit to her chest, Maddy pushed open Barbara's door with her elbow, sailed right in and stopped dead. Barbara was sitting upright in her wheelchair, her head turned sideways. Looming over her was Nate Ludlow, in dark pants and a white shirt with the sleeves rolled up, looking larger than ever. Both of his hands were wrapped around Barbara's thin neck. As Maddy watched, frozen with horror, his hands moved and there was the weirdest sound Maddy had ever heard.

"My God!" Maddy exclaimed.

Startled by Maddy's voice, Annie Rose leaped out of her hands to Barbara's bed, bounced off Nate's hip and landed on the floor, where she made a dash for the large metal locker in the corner of the room. A second later, she had disappeared under it.

"Just as I told Emma!" Nate exclaimed. "Fate has to hit you with a wallop."

Maddy stared at him. She had no idea what he was talking about.

Barbara gave her a toothless grin. She always refused to wear her dentures except at mealtimes, insisting they made her look like a car salesman. "Hey,

Maddy, that was a cute rabbit," she said cheerfully. "Why did you throw it away?"

Nate laughed. "It was a rabbit? I thought she was throwing a hamster at me. Couldn't think why. A rabbit now, I can understand *that*." He laughed again, then evidently couldn't stop laughing. His laughter triggered Barbara's, and they were both soon resting against each other, chortling like crazy people.

Maddy closed her eyes momentarily. Her heart was still beating like a trip-hammer from the shock of seeing Nate apparently throttling Barbara. Her jaw had begun to ache, and a second trip-hammer was banging away over her right eyebrow. When she looked again, Nate was preparing to adjust the other side of Barbara's neck. He grinned at her and quirked his eyebrows, probably amused by the way she looked in her animal-printed apron. Maddy was prepared for the sound this time, but even so it made her wince. "Is that how it's supposed to sound?" she asked faintly.

Barbara snorted. "Feels terrific," she said. "Don't knock it if you haven't tried it." She craned her neck from side to side. "Look at that—I can almost see behind me. We got a good release, huh, Doc?"

"That we did." Nate smiled at her and started massaging the back of her neck.

"Give you all day to stop that," Barbara told him. Her eyes were closed now, and she had the most blissful smile on her lined old face.

Maddy took a deep breath, feeling utterly foolish, then dropped to her knees and peered under the locker. Two bright eyes gleamed at her from far back against the wall. Maddy extended her arm as far as it would go, but she couldn't quite reach the rabbit. The locker wouldn't move; it was evidently bolted to the wall for stability.

"You need a carrot," Barbara said. "Pity I don't have any. We had some for lunch, but I ate 'em all." She snorted. "They were canned carrots, anyway. Mushy. Didn't even need my teeth."

"Would a coat hanger work?" Nate asked.

"No way," Maddy said indignantly. "I'm not going to risk hurting her."

"I meant a padded one, of course," he said. "Barbie's got some in her closet there."

"Scented," Barbara added.

Maddy was willing to try anything, but she felt pretty stupid, lying flat out on the floor, poking at a poor defenseless rabbit. Annie Rose wasn't about to cooperate, anyway. She simply shifted from side to side as the coat hanger skimmed her. Maddy would just have to wait until Annie Rose decided to come out.

She checked to see that the room's door was safely closed, then settled herself on the floor in front of the locker, so that the rabbit couldn't escape. She wished she'd brought along some food pellets. Looking up at Nate, she murmured, "I guess I made a fool of myself. You've no idea how awful that looked when I came in."

"I told you I wasn't a murderer," Nate said in a reproachful voice.

"You two young things go ahead and flirt," Barbara said. "Just so Dr. Ludlow's fingers keep doing the walking."

Now he had started working on Barbara's shoulders. Maddy watched him for a minute, until she realized she was remembering how his hands had felt when they touched her face.

"Pretty warm down there?" Nate asked.

Her face did feel hot. "I'm not having a good day," she said hastily and told him about her problems with the boa and the duck.

"Maybe I can help," he suggested, squatting beside her. He was suddenly so close that she could have reached out and touched his hair if she'd wanted to. He smelled very clean. Her mind filled with images... dune grasses swaying in a summer breeze, gentle waves splashing a sandy shore, shower water drumming on firm masculine flesh.

Nate was emitting a high-pitched squeaking noise, she realized. As she stared at him in surprise, wondering if he'd gone mad, Annie Rose popped out from under the locker and started sniffing at his fingers.

"I raised rabbits in junior high as part of a school project," he explained as he picked up the little rabbit and stroked her gently before handing her to Maddy. "I learned to speak rabbit then." His fingers twined themselves with hers as they made the transfer. His eyes were smiling directly into hers.

"First you pick an oral surgeon in my building," he murmured. "Then you wait for a bus in the rain at the precise moment I'm going to drive by. Now you come here. Too much for mere coincidence. My mother taught me all about this sort of thing. It's called fate."

He grinned. "Question is, what are we going to do about it?" He was still stroking Annie Rose. Maddy could feel his touch vibrating through the tiny rabbit's body directly into her hands. She felt almost mesmerized by the smiling eyes only inches from her own. Something very constricting was happening in her chest.

"What you two doin' down there?" Barbara asked. "I said you could flirt, not make out."

Maddy hastily got to her feet and held the rabbit so that Barbara could pet it. Nate rose more languorously, pulled on his suit jacket and looked down at Barbara, who was making cooing noises at the little animal. "How's your bedroom floor?" he asked Maddy.

Barbara chortled, obviously reading significance into the innocent question. Maddy felt herself blush. "All fixed," she said tersely.

He hesitated. "Could we have coffee, do you suppose?"

"I have to take the zoomobile back to the zoo," Maddy said. "This is a workday for me."

He nodded. "I've a couple more patients to see, too. I was thinking of after work. I still have that videotape of *Abraham Lincoln*."

"I don't have time for Abraham."

"Dr. Ludlow's a good guy, Maddy," Barbara said, glancing up. "He comes over here whenever he can, just to make people feel more comfortable. Nobody pays him for it. Least you can do is have a cup of coffee with him. For charity's sake."

"Thanks for the vote of confidence, Barbie," Nate said with a rueful grin. His eyes held Maddy's. "I do make a great Irish coffee."

"I bet you have great etchings, too."

Barbara laughed. "Got him there, Maddy."

Nate pretended to be offended, but those laughing eyes of his spoiled the effect. "You're very direct, Madeleine Scott," he said. "I like that. Be a little more direct and tell me why you don't trust me."

"It's not that I don't trust you," she said, then paused.

"Doesn't trust herself," Barbara murmured, still stroking the rabbit. "Good-looking guy like you, Dr. Ludlow, women get all unnecessary, just thinking about being alone with you."

"Barbara!" Maddy exclaimed. She looked up at Nate. He liked her directness, he'd said. So she might as well lay it on the line. "I have a full-time, very demanding job and I have my sister's children to care for. You don't like children, so..."

"You don't want to mess with me."

"Not my choice of words, but that's the general drift, yes."

"Couldn't we at least discuss it over a cup of coffee? At the Buena Vista Café," he added as she opened her mouth to refuse again. "They invented Irish coffee, so it's almost as good as mine. Shall I pick you up at seven o'clock or so?"

His confident, boyish grin was her undoing. What harm could it possibly do to go to the Buena Vista with him? The café was always crowded, and she could certainly use a break after a day like this one. Nate Ludlow was entertaining company, even if he didn't take life seriously. "Maybe I could meet you there for a short time," she said, only partially surrendering. "Better make it six o'clock, though. I can't keep Kat too late."

"Oh, yes, the children."

Now there was a resigned note in his voice. Maddy hesitated, about to call the whole thing off. But it had been so long since she'd been anywhere without the children, so long since she had agreed to meet a man. There was something about Dr. Nate Ludlow, she had to admit, that made him almost impossible to resist.

THEY ARRIVED at the same moment outside the Buena
Vista Café, even though it had taken Maddy twenty
minutes to find a parking spot.

"Definitely fate," Nate said with a grin. To Maddy's surprise, he was wheeling a mountain bike. He
looked even more attractive in blue jeans and a white ski
sweater. The evening had turned cold and damp, and
Maddy had dressed almost identically, except that her
sweater was an ivory-colored Irish knit.

"I needed some exercise," Nate commented as he
padlocked the bike. "Since you wouldn't let me do the
chivalrous thing and pick you up, I figured I'd get it this
way."

As usual, there was standing room only at the Buena
Vista Café, three deep at the bar. Maddy watched the
bartender pouring coffee into a row of glass mugs,
sweeping over at least twelve of them just fast enough
not to spill any of the liquid. Of necessity Nate was
standing very close to her. When he reached for the two
mugs the barman passed to him, he brushed against her,
and she felt a wave of yearning that she didn't want to
analyze too closely. She was relieved when Nate spot-
ted a small table way at the back and shouldered a path
for the two of them.

Two women hailed him on the way—a stunning red-
head in acid-washed denims and a willowy blonde in a
business suit with a large red plastic heart pinned on the
lapel. I'll Be Your Sweetheart, the legend read. A ro-
tund little man wearing a white golf cap called, "What's
up, Doc?" to Nate and leered at Maddy.

Nate smiled serenely and equally at them all. He was
obviously a regular here.

"It's not that I dislike children exactly," he said as
soon as they sat down. He obviously wanted to clear the

air between them. "I just feel uneasy around kids. They don't seem to like me."

Maddy clasped her coffee mug in both hands to warm them. She felt chilled after the long walk from the parking lot. "Why not?" she asked.

He grinned. "I've no idea. What's not to like?" He shook his head. "I really don't know, Maddy. I guess children are like animals—they sense when a person doesn't quite know how to treat them. I acquired two little stepsisters when I was ten, and they were always playing tricks on me. Especially when I was in my teens. They delighted in embarrassing me, which is easy to do to a teenage boy. They used to hide behind the sofa when I brought a girl home, then jump out at strategic moments. They also used to put their pet frogs in my sock drawer."

"You looked horrified when you saw Hannah and Adam."

"Terrified," he amended. "And you must remember, until Casey Dixon enlightened me, I thought they were yours. I thought I'd been wasting all my worshiping from afar on a married lady."

"What exactly did Dr. Dixon tell you?"

He frowned, drinking his coffee. It was very noisy in the café, but their small table seemed separated from the crowd, like an island, or an oasis, perhaps.

"That your sister took off and dumped the children on you."

"She didn't *dump* them," Maddy protested abruptly, annoyed. To calm herself, she took a deep swallow of her coffee. It was excellent, warming, rich with whipped cream. It relaxed her, made her feel lighthearted. Sighing, she set the cup down. "Well, I suppose that is how it looked to outsiders. But there were extenuating circumstances. My sister Georgiana is better known as Georgia Malone."

"The country and western singer?" He looked amazed. "You sure don't look anything alike."

Maddy visualized Georgia's mane of curly blond hair, her fiery green eyes, the strutty way she moved. "I know," she said with a sigh. "The mouse and the tiger."

He studied her over the top of his mug for a moment, then said, "Oh, I don't know, I wouldn't call Georgia Malone mousy."

Maddy laughed aloud. She liked this man's sense of humor, she really did. "Georgia was never cut out to be a wife and mother," she explained. "Even as a kid, all she thought about was becoming a successful singer. But then when she was eighteen, fame wasn't coming fast enough, and she got scared and married Brennan Malone, of all people." She drank some more of her Irish coffee and felt it warm her all the way down.

"Why 'of all people'?" Nate asked.

"A research biologist? Who lives for his work? Can't tear himself away from it? Loves, adores, worships his work? Married to a woman who thrives on attention, needs attention, can't live without attention?"

"Boredom set in, I take it."

"Fast." She drained the rest of the coffee and set down the mug. "One of the problems, you see," she said slowly, "was that Georgia was an extraordinarily beautiful child, the kind that makes you catch your breath just to look at her. Genes are funny things, I guess. Georgia inherited her ambitious nature from our father, her voice from our maternal grandmother, and got our mother's striking beauty thrown in for good measure. I look like my father, everything brown, but fame and fortune don't interest me, and I can't sing a note. Either I'm a maverick or just unlucky."

She sighed. "Anyway, Georgia's voice was always exceptional, even without training. With training, it became sensational. Mom and Dad didn't quite know what to do with this prodigy, so they spoiled her, gave her anything she wanted. She never learned about delayed gratification. We moved a lot because of Dad's work, and Georgia was the focus of attention everyplace we lived. What child can handle that? She developed a need, a hunger, for applause and attention. She never learned how to get along without either."

"What about you? What kind of child were you?"

She smiled wryly. "Much as I am now, I guess. Serious. Solemn. A worrier. Someone had to worry. Mostly I worried about Georgia. Our parents were always busy, and Georgia needed an audience. She wasn't always choosy about where she found it, so I was constantly looking out for her. I guess I was born with a latchkey around my neck. I was the responsible one, the one my parents relied on."

She shook her head. She was talking too much. Maybe it was the whiskey. What was she thinking of, guzzling down the Irish coffee so fast, talking a blue streak, criticizing her family?

"Don't get me wrong," she added hastily. "I loved Georgia. I still do. I just wish she hadn't married Brennan. He wasn't ever *there* enough to keep her happy. For the first time in her life she felt lonely, unloved. At first she thought a baby would cure her depression. When it didn't, she had another baby. And then when Hannah was four and Adam three, Brennan asked her to sing at a benefit for the hospital that helps support his laboratory. There was a talent scout in the audience.

Within a month, Georgia was gone. The rest, as they say, is history. She found an agent who put her in touch with a genius of a teacher.... Her voice keeps getting better and better, she's in demand for concerts all over the world—she's touring Europe right now, going on to Japan in a couple of months. Her latest album is top of the charts this week."

"*Lovin' Wild*? I've heard it. She's a talented lady. She has the ability to move the listener with the *sound* of her voice and not just the words of the song. I have to confess though that I'm not a country and western fan."

"Nor am I," Maddy admitted with a wry grin. She was still talking too much, she chided herself. But it *helped* to talk...she felt much more relaxed than usual. Her jaw wasn't hurting at all. Nate Ludlow listened, she thought, he really listened, without treading on her sentences the way most people did, only waiting to say their own piece. A rare man, an attractive man, and one who was making an unfamiliar warmth mushroom inside her every time he looked at her.

"Well," Nate murmured after a brief silence. "I can't say I'm ever surprised to hear of a marriage breaking up. Marriage is an unnatural state, after all. Two people promising to love each other until death do them part is asking an awful lot of a temporary emotion." He leaned forward confidentially. "I have this theory that relationships are at their best in the first six to seven months. After that it's downhill all the way. Given that, it seems to make sense to keep relationships temporary. People would be much happier if they'd just accept the fact that passionate love doesn't last forever."

She laughed. "If everybody accepted your theory, there wouldn't be any marriages."

"So everybody would get along a lot better. Bosses would be kinder to employees, because they wouldn't be having a hard time at home. Employees would work longer hours without complaining, no reason to rush home and fix meals for someone else. Next thing you know you'd have world peace."

The man was impossible, but definitely entertaining. "No children in this utopia of yours?"

"None at all for a while. Solves the population problem. And the economic one. Nobody taking time out for childbirth, less mouths to feed, increased productivity. Later on, we could work out something to keep the world alive."

He leaned back, frowning. "Must have been rough on you, Georgia leaving like that. Did she just walk out, or did she *ask* you to take care of the children?"

"She asked. It would just be for a few months, she said. She just wanted to have her chance. Of course I agreed. What else could I do?" Maddy looked earnestly at Nate. "I'm not complaining, believe me. I helped make Georgia the way she is. I padded her way, made it too easy for her. It didn't occur to me that she'd expect the same treatment from everyone after she'd grown up."

Her slow, wonderful smile lighted her face. "When I hear her sing, however," she added with a sigh, "I forgive her everything. How can I ask her to give up her career when she gives such tremendous pleasure to everyone who hears her? It might have helped if she'd married a stronger man, instead of a sweet, uncomplaining man like Brennan."

Nate didn't like the sound of Brennan at all. "How long has it been?" he asked.

"Four years. Georgia comes back once in a while to see the children, but she doesn't stay long. She and Brennan are divorced now." She sighed. "Usually she brings piles of presents and spoils the kids rotten. Buying their affection. It takes me a couple of weeks to straighten them out again after she leaves."

"Four years," Nate echoed. "You were just a kid yourself."

"Twenty-two."

"And you got stuck with two kids. Tough luck."

She sat up very straight and tall. Two bright spots of color appeared on her cheeks. "I'm not *stuck*. I've loved those kids since they were born. There is nothing more rewarding than raising children."

A waitress stopped at their table, and Nate ordered a plain coffee for himself, then glanced at Madeleine. "Please," she said. "I'm afraid the whiskey's gone right to my head," she added to Nate. "I must be boring you."

He shook his head, then frowned. "Doesn't your brother-in-law help with the children?"

"Sure he does, financially. I mean he pays for everything. So does Georgia. She sends money regularly."

"But?"

"Well, Brennan's very busy. He directs the immunology research at Lowther Institute, and spends all his time searching for causes and possible cures for children's diseases. He gets totally engrossed in his work." She laughed. "Sometimes he forgets to come home. If too many days pass, I have to call someone to make sure he's eating."

There was a fond note in her voice that Nate didn't appreciate. "He should at least take care of the children some of the time," he said disapprovingly. "They are his kids, after all."

"He does help sometimes, but how can I ask for more? The work he's doing may save thousands of children's lives. I can't take him away from that."

"So you've sacrificed yourself."

"I don't look upon it as a sacrifice, Nate."

"I'm sure you don't. You remind me of Emma."

"Emma?"

"My office manager. She's a patsy for everyone who comes along. Everyone in the world takes advantage of her generosity and loyalty."

"Nobody's taking advantage of me," she said flatly. "I made my own choices, Dr. Ludlow."

Dr. Ludlow. He was losing points here. He frowned at her. "Don't you or Brennan have any parents?"

Maddy laughed. "As I told you, my father's an engineer. He's in Saudi Arabia. Mom, too. Unfortunately, they blame Brennan for the breakup—they feel he neglected Georgia, which he did, I suppose, but not intentionally. It's just the way he is."

Again the fond note. Nate frowned.

"As for Brennan's folks," Maddy went on, "for years and years they were both real estate brokers, absolute workaholics. They finally retired about six years ago, sold everything they owned, bought a huge motor home, tied a little orange Porsche behind it and went off to explore the North American continent. Their last postcard was postmarked from Moose Jaw, Saskatchewan." She laughed again, more wryly. "Grandparents aren't what they used to be, Nate. They've all become modern-day nomads, packing up their tents and moving on when the mood seizes them."

He drank his coffee in silence for a few moments. What this attractive, but far too serious young woman needed, he thought, was a chance to learn how to play. Question was, did he want to be the one to teach her? He watched her as she looked around the crowded bar. Her cheeks were flushed from the heat of so many bodies in one place, or maybe from the Irish whiskey in her coffee, or just the coffee itself. The color was wonderfully becoming to her, making her look freshly scrubbed and wholesome and altogether appetizing. How on earth could she think of herself as a mouse? Obviously she needed to have her self-image upgraded. And he was just the man to do that.

"You ready for *Abraham Lincoln* yet?" he asked softly.

She shook her head, then to his dismay, she stood up, showing every intention of leaving. "I have to get back to the children, Nate."

He couldn't detect a single note of regret in her voice. Those children definitely came first with her. Did he want to play second fiddle to someone else's children? He didn't think so. All the same, he did like Madeleine Scott an awful lot.

"What happens if Georgia comes back for good?" he asked as he walked her to the parking lot where she'd left her car. He liked walking beside her. Most women he knew teetered along in high heels, and he'd always thought he liked that, but Maddy wore sneakers; there was something very companionable about a woman who could match him, stride for stride. He kept wanting to reach out and take her hand and hold it in his own.

"Georgia won't ever come back to stay," Maddy said firmly, then frowned. "What do you mean, what would happen?"

Nate maneuvered his bike around a group of tourists, who were happily eating ice-cream cones in spite of the cold weather. "Supposing she did come back," he said when he returned to Maddy's side. "Supposing she comes back in four or five years, Brennan decides he's still madly in love with her and she decides she's madly in love with him. Where does that leave you? You'll be thirty years old, all your juices dried up, an old maid."

"Thanks a lot," she said curtly.

"You're avoiding the question."

She shook her head. "Georgia will never settle down, Nate, not now she's tasted the excitement of success. However," she added as he started to interrupt, "if by some miracle she did come back for good and wanted her children, or if, by another miracle, Brennan lifted his head from his beakers and test tubes long enough to find another wife, then I would surrender the children at once, keeping visitation rights, of course."

Maddy looked at him earnestly. "The children don't belong to me, Nate, they are just on loan. But as long as I have them, they will have all of me. I will never try to get out of that commitment."

She was telling him that she and the children were a package deal. She always made that clear to any interested male, right from the start. She had ended several promising relationships that way, but always figured that if it was going to end, it was better to wind things up before there was a chance of either person getting upset.

Nate seemed impressed by her honesty. "Okay," he said. "I understand."

He understood all right, she thought as she watched him ride away into the evening traffic on his mountain bike. His long, strong jean-clad legs pumped easily, his head and back wonderfully erect, the dark curly hair ruffled by the wind. He hadn't said anything about calling her. So she had probably squelched any hope of anything developing between them, which wasn't at all surprising—she'd known right at the start that he was a lightweight, too deliberately charming to have much substance. *Marriage is an unnatural state. Love is a temporary emotion.* What statements for a grown man to make!

The effects of the whiskey had certainly worn off, she decided as she unlocked her car. Just as well—sitting around in cafés, drinking Irish coffee and talking her fool head off, wasn't her usual behavior and wasn't going to be. All the same it had felt good to relax, to talk to an interested listener.

She sat in the 280 for a moment with her head bowed. Sometimes she dreamed in weak moments of finding true love, romantic love, lasting love. Twice in the past she had thought herself in love and had been attracted to several men, but whatever feelings had been present had never been strong enough to surmount the obstacles that had come up.

What she needed, what she longed for, was a man who would come into her life, sweep her off her feet and carry her away into the sunset, while music swelled to a resounding climax in true movie tradition. Preferably the theme from *Dr. Zhivago*—complete with balalaikas.

Trouble was, this wonderfully romantic man would also have to be some kind of superman who loved children as much as she did, specifically a man who could love Hannah and Adam. They were such great kids, so stoical, so understanding of their absent mother and their absentminded father. It would be so wonderful to have a companion, an escort—face it, a lover—who could not only tolerate her particular set of circumstances, but even enjoy having such an extended family.

Straightening, she put the key into the ignition and smiled tightly. Nate Ludlow, charming and entertaining and outrageous as he was, was not, definitely not that man.

CHAPTER FOUR

IT WAS IRRITATING, the way Madeleine Scott stayed in his mind. Nate tried to distract himself during the next few weeks with plenty of sporting activity, but she kept walking into his mind—as a solemn-eyed child with a key on a string around her neck, or as the enchanting woman he'd sat with in the Buena Vista, made voluble by unaccustomed whiskey, her face relaxed and rosy-cheeked.

He couldn't even date—nobody interested him, not even the beauteous Teddie, who had finally come back from Hawaii and called to say Paul Duval wasn't as divine as he'd appeared, and if he liked, she wouldn't mind going back to the "status quo" with him. It wasn't sour grapes that had made him put Teddie off with lame excuses. He just didn't want to be with anyone if he couldn't be with Madeleine Scott.

Reminding himself of those two children and of his vow to keep all relationships light and carefree, he would forcibly evict Maddy Scott from his thoughts, but again and again on Wednesdays at three twenty-five he'd be at his office window, watching her stride so elegantly across the parking lot. He felt good when he saw her, he acknowledged. He felt strong and virile and purposeful. He felt as he had told her he felt—me male, you female. He *wanted* Madeleine Scott.

And then one Wednesday toward the middle of March she didn't come. "Do you suppose Casey finally cured her TMJ dysfunction?" he asked Emma.

"Ask her out again," Emma advised. "Anything's better than moping around at the window all the time."

She was right. But he had to devise a strategy. Madeleine Scott would require slow and cautious wooing. Her dark eyes reminded Nate of those of a doe, wary and watchful—one fast move and she would head for the forest, never to be seen again.

Obviously the situation required careful planning. He needed to come up with somewhere to take her where the children wouldn't be likely to come along, too.

"IT'S A MALE PERSON," Hannah said, handing the telephone receiver to Maddy. There was no inflection at all in her usually expressive voice.

"Today is Thursday," the voice on the phone said. A month since she'd seen him or spoken to him and he didn't even give his name. He didn't need to, of course. The distinctively warm sound of his voice went straight through her ear to her blood, sending it shooting through her veins. "I remembered you said one of your days off was Thursday." He hesitated. "The sun is shining."

"I'd noticed. I'm cleaning windows."

"I'm sorry to interrupt your fun, but by another of those fateful coincidences that have marked our relationship, I usually take Thursday afternoon off. How about some tennis?"

"I can't. I'm sorry."

There was a short silence. Then he asked, "Would you prefer golf?" Evidently it hadn't occurred to him that the rejection was of him rather than the activity.

"I'm busy, Nate. I'm always busy. I don't have time for—"

"I remember—outside activities. You know what the problem is, don't you?" he added.

"Why don't you tell me your interpretation?"

"You're looking at me from a long-term view. Telling yourself I don't suit because I'm not crazy about children. Now if you just think of me as short-term, someone to have fun with for a while, you'll probably change your mind about seeing me."

"Will I now? Well, as it happens, I don't have a baby-sitter."

"You couldn't call Kat Caley?"

Of course she could. Kat would be happy to have another day's pay.

"You didn't come to see Casey yesterday," Nate said, when she didn't reply immediately.

Did he have her under surveillance? "Dr. Dixon referred me to Dr. Jason Ross," she said slowly. "He's a chiropractor, too."

"Yes, I know him." He sounded mildly annoyed. Should she tell him Dr. Dixon had suggested Dr. Nate Ludlow first, and she'd told him she'd prefer another chiropractor? No, he'd want to know why, and what could she say? That she was afraid to be around him, because he tempted her to be carefree and irresponsible like himself, and she couldn't possibly be that way?

Maddy wished Hannah would go off to play with Adam, instead of standing there, staring at her with her round blue eyes while she talked to Nate.

"Does this silence mean you are thinking it over?" Nate asked.

"I'm sorry. I really can't. I have chores to do."

"You really are the most exasperating woman. Other women want to get out of chores."

"Maddening Maddy, that's me."

"How about tomorrow? I could be through by four."

"I'll probably work later than that." Should she tell him she had Sunday off this week? No, of course not. "We have a lot of schoolchildren coming through on tours this time of the year, and I'm short on volunteer help," she said. "We've lost quite a few volunteers lately."

"Lions get 'em, did they?"

She laughed. This man always made her laugh. But she mustn't. Laughter could weaken resolve. "General attrition," she said seriously. "People move away, take up other interests, get tired of working at the zoo."

"Maybe I should volunteer. What would I have to do to get started?"

He wasn't serious, of course, but if she answered him seriously, it might throw Hannah off the track. The child was still standing there, and listening, eyes narrowed now. "You'd have to attend weekly orientation classes for fourteen weeks," she explained. "You would have to learn basic biology, animal handling and the zoo's philosophy and goals. Then you'd need to decide which program you wanted to get involved in—zoomobile, children's zoo programs, guided tours or whatever. The training course is pretty intense and requires a good deal of study at home. Volunteers also make extra trips to the zoo to do tag-along tours and animal behavioral watches, and they have to commit to a certain number of hours of work every month." She paused for breath, then added wryly, "Add all that to your regular job, and you wouldn't have much time left for golf and tennis and lady-killing."

He sighed. "I guess all this volubility means it's no go, huh?"

So much for subterfuge. "I'm sorry, Nate."

She really was sorry. She must have looked it, too. Hannah gazed at her as she hung up the telephone receiver. "Are you sad, Maddy?" she asked.

Maddy managed a smile, then affectionately twitched the little girl's blond braid. Hannah leaned against her, returning the affection. "I'm fine, honey," Maddy lied. She glanced out the window at the sunshine and the clear blue sky and was suddenly acutely aware of a yearning sensation that was becoming familiar and was very close to pain. Sighing, she picked up her can of glass cleaner and a wad of paper towels.

FRIDAY WAS a busy day. To the relief of Maddy's conscience, three large groups of schoolchildren did come in, one after the other, and she was kept busy in the barnyard, making sure nobody poked fingers into the animals' mouths to see if they'd bite—which several of them would—quieting the noisier kids so they didn't startle the animals, answering innumerable questions about the miniature horses, the silky chickens, the sheep and goats and Holstein calves.

After that she talked for a while with an eighty-year-old lady who visited the nature trail every Friday, complete with ivory-handled cane and scarlet backpack, then delivered a minilecture on the fundamental concepts of wildlife conservation to a smart-alecky sixth-grader, who insisted that all the animals in the zoo should be allowed to run free. After she pointed out that most animals in zoos live longer than they would in the wild, and that an animal knows no abstract idea of freedom but only the urge to survive, the boy seemed apologetic and convinced. However, Maddy alerted zoo security when he left, just in case he decided to try to put his beliefs into practice.

Her next visitor was a young Australian man with a roguish smile and wonderfully brilliant blue eyes. He talked for a couple of minutes to Crackerjack the parrot, who was perched in his favorite place on Maddy's left shoulder, then confided he had a problem. Somehow he had managed to spill a bottle of suntan lotion into his camera case and wanted her assistance in cleaning up the resulting mess. He had recently graduated from college, he told her, while they were sitting on a bench by the pond, working companionably together after she'd found a box of tissues. Crackerjack, of course, insisted on supervising the messy task, managing to get a considerable amount of lotion on his feathers. The Australian was traveling all over the U.S. and Canada before going to Europe, he told Maddy. He thought he might start work on his father's farm in three years or so.

"It sounds wonderful," Maddy said wistfully.

"Wanna come along?" he asked with a flirtatious grin.

"She can't. She's too busy," Nate Ludlow said behind him.

Crackerjack said, "Hey, babe," in a cross-sounding voice, and Maddy was so startled by Nate's sudden appearance that she almost dropped the telephoto lens she was wiping.

The young Australian made a fast rescue, then scowled up at the friendly, craggy face that had appeared above his left shoulder. "A friend o' yours?" he asked Maddy.

"That's debatable," Maddy murmured. "What on earth are you doing here?" she asked Nate. She must have sounded as irritable as she felt. The young Australian, having repacked his gear, stood up with a muttered "G'day" and hurried off toward the large red building that housed the insect zoo.

"Learning about the zoo, of course," Nate said, flourishing the zoo's brochure and taking the place on the bench that the young man had vacated. "I haven't visited the zoo in years, and it occurred to me that I might be missing a great deal." His earnest, apparently innocent gaze held her mesmerized, while at the same time seriously affecting her ability to breathe. "I'm also indulging the noble side of my character," he continued solemnly. "I've decided you take life much too seriously, Madeleine Scott, and you need to learn to play. I've elected myself as teacher. I've also brought you coffee."

She hadn't even noticed that he was carrying a Styrofoam cup in his left hand. She took it from him and sipped the coffee gratefully, hoping it would settle her suddenly nervous stomach. "I know how to play," she said defensively, reflecting immediately that she seemed fated to make suggestive remarks when this man was around.

"Play, play," Crackerjack echoed. "Let's play, babe. Let's do lunch. Go for it."

"I wasn't asking you," Nate said to the parrot.

"My work is play," Maddy said lamely, gesturing around her, realizing as she did so that she must look a mess. Most people weren't aware that a large part of a zookeeper's duties involved cleaning up after animals. By the end of a day, Maddy always felt like the little boy in the *Peanuts* comic strip who trailed a miniature dust storm around with him. Her hair was straggling around her face, and she reached up to retie the narrow ribbon that usually held it in place while she worked, only to find that Crackerjack must have tugged it loose hours ago. The parrot was now nibbling affectionately at her left earlobe. She seemed fated to be caught at a disadvantage by this man.

"Let me put it this way," Nate said. "When did you last have a date?"

"Last week," she said without a moment's hesitation. No need to tell him she'd gone to a zoo lecture with the elephant keeper, her good friend Tom Farraday, who had yet to notice she was female.

"And before that?"

"The previous week." Same friend, different lecture.

"You allow yourself only one evening a week for socializing?"

Would he consider a weekly lunch with her three closest women friends a date? Probably not. "It's enough," she said.

"Is it?" Those expressive eyebrows of his had a way of slanting upward that spoke volumes. "Then how come you grind your teeth at night?"

Hazel eyes were very interesting, she decided. You could never be sure what color they would be when you next looked at them. It was rather unsettling.

Nate was wearing sneakers, blue-jean cutoffs and an oversize gray sweatshirt with the sleeves pushed up. He looked comfortable and casual and very, very masculine. Sitting here in the sunshine with this attractive man was really quite pleasant. Whom was she kidding? she chided herself. "Pleasant," didn't come anywhere near to describing the sensations that were rattling around inside her. Nate Ludlow had apparently tapped some deep well of hunger that she hadn't even known was there—a hunger to play and have fun, a hunger to be held close in a man's—*this* man's arms. He didn't believe a relationship could last past seven months, she reminded herself. Ah yes, but they would be a great seven months.

Deciding to ignore his question, she sat up straight and looked around her domain. At the moment there seemed to be a lull in the activity. It would be closing time soon, of course. One attendant was already cleaning up the chicken brooder, another the birthday party court, which had been kept busy most of the day. Only one mother and child were in the general area, and the mother was keeping a tight hold on the toddler's hand.

Nate Ludlow had extraordinarily strong-looking legs, Maddy thought distractedly. They were covered with silky-looking dark hair that was as inviting to the touch as the unruly dark curls on his head.

"I guess I'd better tread water for a while," he said at last, pushing a hand through the curls in question. "I'm going to lead up to a proposition here and I don't want to do it too abruptly. So let's converse first, okay?"

"Okay, babe," Crackerjack agreed.

"What kind of proposition?" Maddy asked suspiciously.

"Patience," he counseled. "I'll get to it. I'm starting off obliquely so you won't see me coming. Tell me about your friend here," he suggested, gesturing at Crackerjack. "Was he born in the wild?"

"Unfortunately, yes."

"Why unfortunately?"

"He was smuggled into the country. If people would only realize what wild parrots go through when they are captured, they might not be so willing to acquire them. If they are born and raised to be pets, it's okay, but when they are captured in their natural habitat, only one out of five survive being caught in a net, jammed into a tight cage in order to be transported, or worse, wrapped tightly in newspaper. Crackerjack did survive, but then his owner got tired of the mess he made and dropped him off at the zoo. He was half dead when we got him." She broke off abruptly. "Sorry, I didn't mean to get up on a soapbox."

"That's okay. I admire your passion."

There was that word again. Their eyes met. Maddy swallowed. "Crackerjack took a fancy to me when we acquired him," she said lamely.

"I can see that," Nate said, eyeing the gaudy bird, who was now leaning against Maddy's head, combing her hair with his beak. "I can also understand it," he added.

Maddy suddenly noticed that the toddler was getting a little too close to Brenda the goat. Mother's attention had wandered to the mallards and geese on the pond, and Brenda was of uncertain temperament by the end of a busy day. Excusing herself, Maddy hurried over to the child and distracted him with one of the silky chickens. "See how her fluffy feathers grow all the way down her legs and over her feet," she murmured.

"Quack-quack," the little boy said, successfully distracted. Maddy and the child's mother both laughed.

"I'm going to have to start closing up," Maddy said briskly, handing over Crackerjack to an attendant and returning to the bench.

"You're throwing me out?"

"The zoo's closing."

"But I didn't get to see the elephants."

"If you hurry you can make it."

"I can't hurry. You haven't heard my proposition yet."

Maddy sighed. "You're very persistent, aren't you?"

"Did I ever tell you it took me four years at Washington State University and four years at chiropractic college to get qualified for the work I do? And that I worked my way through both with night jobs and a little help from the bank? Then it took me three years to pay off the loans. That's eleven years of hard labor, Maddy, but I made it. I have a successful, thriving practice. Yes, I'm persistent. I don't give up on anything."

"All right. Let's have the proposition," she said resignedly.

He grinned. "I thought I'd offer to teach you how to sailboard."

Her mind conjured up an image of colorful sails billowing in a stiff breeze, boards racing across waves, strong young bodies clinging to booms. It must feel wonderful to glide over the water like that, she thought. So free!

"You wouldn't just be playing, you'd be getting good exercise *and* an education," Nate added, watching her face.

How well he'd read her to know that she hated to waste time, always needed a goal.

"You could look upon it as a challenge."

Was that how he looked at her?

Maddy had never been so actively pursued. She had no idea what Nate's motivation was—a need to conquer, perhaps. Probably few women, if any, turned

Nate Ludlow down. Whatever the reason, it was all very flattering; he was obviously going to keep on showing up in her life until she agreed to see him. Perhaps if she accepted his offer of a lesson, he'd leave her alone. Date him to get rid of him? *Weak, Maddy, very weak,* she told herself.

All the same, she really would love to learn how to sailboard. Later, perhaps, she could even teach the children how it was done. A pretty amazing bit of rationalizing there, she thought, even as she said, "I might manage to get Brennan to stay with the children on Sunday afternoon. I do happen to have the day off."

She was rewarded with a wide smile that succeeded in ambushing her breath somewhere in her chest. "Persistence really does pay, you see," he murmured.

Pulling a local map from a pocket of his shorts, he pointed out a place, his sun-warmed, sweatshirt-clad arm brushing hers, apparently by accident. "I've done a little research and found a small lagoon in Foster City, sheltered, not too deep. Good place for a beginner." He was all business now. Maybe he did just want to give her a sailboarding lesson. *Be serious, Maddy,* she chided herself.

She had thought Nate would leave once he'd achieved his purpose, but he stayed around while she washed up and locked up, looking perfectly at ease, hands in the back pockets of his cutoffs, dark hair tangling in the breeze as he chatted with the other attendants, obviously setting more than one heart aflutter. Conchita, a young and very pretty Mexican woman, was especially taken with him and sent an envious glance Maddy's way, when she left with him.

To tease him, Maddy offered to take him along to visit the elephants. She always went to say good-night to Tangerine, anyway. Tangerine was a young Ceylonese elephant, just past babyhood, very lovable and sweet with long orange bangs down to her eyes.

One of the keepers was oiling one of the adult elephants, to keep her skin from drying out. Big Tom Farraday was just finishing trimming Tangerine's toenails, and called out a warm greeting to Maddy. She saw Nate glance at him thoughtfully, probably assessing the competition. She could have told him Tom was nothing but a buddy, but that might encourage him to think she was setting his mind at rest because she was interested in him. Was she interested in him? *Be honest, Maddy,* she scolded herself, *you've gone beyond interest here.*

Tangerine stomped over as usual to receive the sweet potato Maddy had brought her, then patted Maddy's face with the moist tip of her trunk. She eyed Nate with apparent interest and sniffed at him a couple of times, but decided he hadn't brought any treats along and trundled over to her pile of hay.

"How tidy she is," Nate murmured. "She folds the hay into such neat little stacks before she tucks it into her mouth." He grinned at Maddy, putting an arm around her shoulders as they turned away. "It's just as I thought, you see. Zoos are very interesting places. I may have to visit quite often."

The weight of his arm was light, the gesture casual, but Maddy's already nervous stomach was suddenly in turmoil. She couldn't believe how much his touch affected her. She probably shouldn't have agreed to see him again, she thought as he accompanied her to the parking lot. Hadn't she decided that she didn't want to get involved with a man who couldn't wholeheartedly accept children? Certainly she didn't need complications in her life, and Nate Ludlow showed every sign of becoming one.

She was overreacting again, she told herself firmly. Surely she had room in her life for a friend. This was only going to be a sailboarding lesson, after all, not a candlelit dinner for two. There wasn't anything intimate about a sailboarding lesson.

SHE COULDN'T have been more wrong.

Sunday was another beautiful day, cloudless and sunny, with a breeze that was just brisk enough to create small wavelets in the lagoon water. The park was small but beautifully maintained. Contemporary condos ringed most of the lagoon, shining white in the sunshine. There was a coolness to the air, and the sleek wet suit Nate had brought along for her didn't feel uncomfortably warm. How had he happened to have a suit of the right size on hand? she wondered. Did he only date tall woman?

"You appear to be in good shape," he said solemnly after she'd pulled on the suit, looking her over in a clinical way that she certainly couldn't object to.

He was as beautifully put together in his own trim-fitting wet suit as he'd looked in regular clothes. Very strong and muscular, athletic, far too attractive for her peace of mind—or body. But he approached the lesson in a businesslike manner, talking her carefully through the various parts of the board and sail, explaining the maneuvers she would need to master—how to stand on the board, how to raise the rig ready for sailing, how to turn the board and steer it. Then he demonstrated, first on the grass and then in the water.

She held her breath at the beauty of man and sail and board as he caught the breeze, skimmed away from the shore for a short distance, swung the rig around and sailed back. "That's all I want you to do at first," he told her. "We'll worry about fancy stuff at a later date."

The actual physical part of the lesson started out innocently enough with the board back on the grass, the skeg removed. She walked back and forth on the board, getting the feel and the balance of it, learning to keep her weight centered. There were few people in the park, some sunbathers, some toddlers playing on the grass, and two other sailboarders on the water, obviously not far removed from the beginner stage themselves.

After a while, Nate taught her how to haul up the sail and demonstrated the various angles from which the wind would pull it. Then he showed her where to put her hands, front hand holding the mast, pulling it toward her forward shoulder so that it was perpendicular to the board. "Soon as you get hold of the boom with your back hand, the wind is going to pull at the sail," he told her. "You have to bring your back hand in toward you. Sheeting in."

Maddy tried hard to concentrate on everything he was telling her, but it was tough to take in. With endless patience, he explained the maneuvers again and again. At one point he stood very close behind her, putting her hands in the proper places, guiding her body into various positions. That made the lessons clearer, but concentration even more difficult.

"Don't grind your teeth, Maddy. This is supposed to be fun," he murmured when she tensed up. He didn't make a single move that was suggestive, however; it was her own traitorous body that was causing such havoc with her thinking processes. Even through the wet suit his hands were warm, his breath stirred her hair and caressed the back of her neck.

"Beginners have a tendency for the board to go up into the wind too much," he said into her left ear. "To make the board go downwind, bring the mast and sail forward toward the nose of the board. Then to move back into the wind, bring mast and sail toward the tail of the board. Got it?"

She nodded, though she wasn't at all sure she was telling the truth.

"When you fall off, try not to pull the sail with you," he said as they carried the gear to the water's edge.

"*When* I fall off?"

He grinned at her. "*When* you fall," he repeated. "Also, when you haul the rig out of the water, it's going to be heavy, okay? The sail and the mast sleeve are full of water, and with the wind holding the sail down, it seems to weigh a ton. Don't try to get it up with one gigantic pull. Do it by degrees. Take your time, and make sure you use your legs and not your back. Bend your knees, keep your back straight."

"Is that the teacher talking or the chiropractor?" she asked.

He grinned again, his wonderfully expressive face crinkling. "Both." His eyebrows lifted. "You ready to go for it?"

Maddy took a deep breath. "No."

He took her seriously. "You want to go over it all again? I want you to feel confident."

"I was joking. I'm ready."

"Okay then. Remember, keep the board at right angles to the wind and your back to the wind."

She thought she'd never get the damn sail up. Every time she was about to succeed, she fell off the board. She began to feel incredibly stupid, but Nate was there each time, holding on to the tail of the board, ready

with a word of encouragement or advice. "Everybody
falls," he kept telling her. "I fell every thirty seconds
when I started out. Try again."

After half an hour of abject failure, Maddy was almost ready to give up. But Nate wouldn't let her. And
then, suddenly, miraculously, the rig was up and in
proper position; she let out a yelp of surprise that
turned into a shout of absolute glee. Nate was cheering
too, and it all felt as wonderful as she'd thought it
would—air rushing past her, exhilarating her, her wet
hair flying around her face. She was skimming the
smooth water. It was like skiing, better than skiing, she
was part of the water, an extension of it, feeling incredibly buoyant and free and young. She felt that she could
let go of every care and every inhibition if she wanted
to. She could jump waves and pirouette and spin and
even turn upside down, the way she'd seen sailboarders
do it on videos. She felt—invincible.

Dimly she realized that Nate was shouting, warning
her not to go too far. But how the hell was she supposed to turn around? She couldn't remember. Yes, she
could. She could hear Nate saying, *Whichever way you
tilt the sail, the board turns the opposite way.*

All very well in theory, but she didn't do it anywhere
near as smoothly as Nate had done. Once more she fell
off the board, then she absolutely couldn't get the sail
up and had to paddle ignominiously to shore.

Nate met her in the water, smiling. "You were great,"
he told her, sweeping her into his arms in a bear hug.
"You were really cruising. I knew you could do it."

It was just a friendly hug, at least at first, then he
suddenly dipped his head and looked at her in a bemused sort of way. Before she could pull away from
him, he had kissed her very lightly on the lips, and the

hug had somehow changed into an embrace. His hand gently smoothed the wet hair that had come loose from the barrette she'd used to fasten it back, then his thumb found her lips and stroked them once from one side to the other, as though to erase the kiss, or perhaps impress it indelibly. His expression as he looked at her was very transparent. Nate Ludlow wanted her. There was no doubt about that.

Maddy seemed incapable of movement. Her heart was pounding, either from her minitriumph over the sailboard or because she was anticipating another kiss— one that didn't come. After another quick hug, Nate released her and laughed. "Back to work," he ordered. "You did well, but not well enough. No use getting out there if you can't get back."

"Slave driver," she complained breathlessly, and wasn't sure if she was glad or sorry that he hadn't prolonged the moment of intimacy.

By the time they left the lagoon, she could feel every muscle she possessed, but she also felt incredibly lighthearted. She had done it; she had actually succeeded in sailboarding a fair distance. More importantly, she had learned how to come back to where she'd started.

"You did good, kid," Nate told her as he drove her home. "Next lesson, we'll concentrate on tacking and jibing." He grinned at her, obviously delighted with her progress, looking so windblown and healthy and allaround devastating that her heart started pounding again. "Maybe you'll even get to make a beach start next time," he added.

Next time. Yes, it felt good to know there would be a next time. "Thank you for a terrific afternoon," she said wholeheartedly as he drew up at her front gate.

He looked startled. "That sounds terribly final."

It seemed he'd expected her to invite him in. "I promised Brennan he could go to work this evening," she confessed. "I have to feed the children and get them to bed...."

"Okay," he said resignedly. "Another time then, I guess."

She *could* invite him in to dinner, of course, but Brennan wouldn't be there, and then the children would go to bed. She wasn't sure if she was ready to be alone with Nate Ludlow. After that kiss...

"Would you like to come to dinner tomorrow evening?" she asked.

He gazed at her very sternly. "You strike me as a woman who always does her duty—writes thank-you notes, sends flowers to hostesses, visits people in hospital—is that right?" he asked.

Feeling mystified, she nodded. "Well, yes, I guess so."

"So this is a duty invitation? Thank you for the lesson?"

She hesitated. "Partly."

"Partly." He sighed. "Okay, as long as you're going to be honest about it, I'll be honest, too. I'd love to come to dinner tomorrow."

"The children will be here, of course."

"Of course." Was it her imagination, or did his smile seem forced now? Should she tell him Brennan would be there? At least she hoped he'd be there. She'd make *sure* he was there.

"We eat a little early because of the children, so we're pretty casual about it. You won't mind the kitchen table?"

"I like kitchen tables," he assured her.

He insisted on seeing her to the door. Hannah and Adam appeared so quickly that she knew they must have seen Nate drive up. "Did you have fun?" Adam asked. "Your face is real brown."

"Glowing," Nate added, looking at her admiringly. "Sparkling even."

"I had a great time," Maddy admitted. "Dr. Ludlow is a terrific teacher."

Hannah sniffed, but didn't say anything.

"I guess I'd better go then," Nate said awkwardly. He really did seem uncomfortable around the children. All the same, he kissed her very gently on the lips, just as though two pairs of round blue eyes were not watching closely.

"I enjoyed today very much," he said softly. "What time shall I come tomorrow?"

Maddy could feel Hannah's disapproving gaze on her face. She glanced at her. The little girl was scowling. Maddy sighed. "Six o'clock?" she suggested to Nate.

"I'll be here," he said, then touched her cheek lightly, grinned vaguely at the children and left.

"He likes you, doesn't he?" Hannah said accusingly as soon as Maddy closed the door behind Nate.

"Yes, I think he does," Maddy said.

"You like him, too?" Adam asked.

"He's a nice man," she hedged.

"You invited him to dinner tomorrow." There was still an accusing note in Hannah's voice.

"I did."

"We're not going to bed early."

Maddy laughed. Putting her hands on the children's shoulders, she walked with them into the living room, where Brennan was sitting with his nose firmly buried in a scientific magazine.

"I'm not sending you to bed early," she said. "We'll all have dinner together."

"Daddy, too?" Hannah asked.

"Daddy, too," Maddy agreed.

"You hear that, Daddy?" Hannah asked.

Brennan looked up over his spectacles, his expression vague. "Dinner," he echoed.

"Dinner *tomorrow*. You have to be here," Hannah said emphatically. "Maddy's bringing a man over."

Brennan regarded Maddy with interest. "Anyone I know?"

Maddy was determined to be casual. "Someone I met, a doctor, a chiropractor," she explained. "I went sailboarding with him today, remember? Dr. Nate Ludlow?"

"Oh yes, sure." Brennan was mumbling, which probably meant he didn't remember at all. Quite possibly he hadn't even noticed that Maddy had been gone half the day.

Maddy sighed softly and started toward the kitchen to fix dinner, hoping she'd get it on the table before Brennan realized he was free to go. He needed some good square meals; he was getting much too thin.

As she opened the refrigerator, she heard Hannah say loudly, "You will be here for dinner tomorrow, won't you, Daddy?"

She didn't hear Brennan's answering mumble, but it was obvious that Hannah didn't intend Maddy and Nate to spend any time alone—which was probably just as well, she thought.

"WE HAVE TO HAVE a discussion," Hannah said.

Adam made a face. He'd just got his stacks of books and race car tracks arranged in his bedroom so that he could run the English race car his mother had sent him for his last birthday. He never liked Hannah's 'scussions, anyway. Usually she wanted him to do something he didn't want to do, or else would get into trouble for doing. "What about?" he asked resignedly.

"Maddy and Dr. Ludlow."

"I like Dr. Ludlow," he said, then looked at Hannah's face and realized it was probably the wrong thing to say. "You don't like him?"

"Don't you know what it means?" Hannah demanded.

Adam thought very hard, screwing up his face. "Nope," he said.

Hannah sighed. "Maddy likes Dr. Ludlow. Didn't you see the way she looked?"

"She looked happy," Adam said.

"That's what I mean. She likes him. And she invited him to dinner. When did she ever do that before?"

"She didn't know him before."

"I mean, when did she ever invite a man to dinner before?"

"I don't remember."

"Because she didn't do it before," Hannah said patiently. "Which means Dr. Ludlow is special. She *really* likes him."

"I get it," Adam said, though he didn't at all. He studied his track lineup once more. Maybe he should put one more book under the hill part.... "That's good," he added, feeling something more was expected of him.

"It's not good at all," Hannah said, making a sound of exasperation. "Listen to me, Adam Malone," she insisted. "We don't have Mommy around much, right?"

"Right." There was a time he'd cried himself to sleep all the time because he missed Mom, but he was much older now and was used to it.

"And Daddy isn't around much either, right?"

"Right."

"So who does that leave us with?"

"Maddy?" he guessed.

"Exactly," Hannah said, rolling her eyes. "And what happens if Dr. Ludlow decides he likes Maddy enough to marry her?"

"I like weddings," Adam said, finally tearing himself away from his racetracks. "We went to Daddy's friends' wedding, remember—Julia and John. There was a really neat cake with a man and a lady on top of it."

"And where would Dr. Ludlow live if he and Maddy got married?"

Adam stared at his sister's face, suddenly conscious of a cloud on the horizon. "Here?" he asked. "We've got lots of room here."

"He has a house of his own, Adam, a condo at the marina. I heard Maddy tell Daddy that. He'd want Maddy to live in his condo with him. And he sure wouldn't want us around."

"Why not?" Adam was beginning to feel alarmed.

"Don't be such an airhead, Adam. Men don't want kids that don't belong to them. We don't even belong to Maddy, not really, but she's all we've got and we have to keep her."

"How do we do that?" Adam asked.

Hannah didn't seem to hear him. Now that she'd got him all worried, she wasn't even paying any attention to him. She was gazing at the maze of race car tracks that wound across Adam's bedroom, but as if she wasn't really seeing them, either. After a while she seemed to remember he was there. She had a funny, tight little smile on her face. Adam wasn't sure he liked that smile.

"I'm working on a plan," Hannah said slowly.

CHAPTER FIVE

ON MONDAY, Nate found a parking spot across the street from Maddy's house at exactly 6:00 p.m., noticing as he turned off the ignition that her silver-gray 280Z was on the apron in front of the garage and Hannah and Adam were washing it. He watched them as he took off his jacket and tie, opened his shirt collar and rolled up his sleeves. Maddy had said casual, but he'd had a very busy day and had no choice but to come directly from the clinic, so this was as casual as he could get.

He grinned wryly, noting that Adam was doing all the scrubbing and Hannah was standing back directing, occasionally rinsing off with a turbojet attachment to a garden hose. Their jeans and shirts were getting as wet as the car. They were doing a good job, all the same. Maybe he should offer to pay them to do his Audi?

He was determined to make points with the Malone children tonight. Obviously the way to Maddy was through those two. He'd even thought of bringing them presents, but then he'd remembered Maddy's criticism of Georgia for doing just that. Probably paying them for a car wash would be construed as buying their affection, too. He'd just have to rely on charm.

He had brought flowers for Maddy, however, and he picked the wrapped bouquet out of the passenger seat before getting out of the car. He'd decided against roses. Maddy would probably think roses were too meaningful to accept. Instead, he'd accepted the advice of the sexy young florist near his clinic and brought Shasta daisies with baby's breath mixed in. A man who brought daisies couldn't possibly have seduction on his mind, he and the florist had agreed.

"Hi, guys," he called as he struggled with the gate latch. "Looks like you're doing a terrific—"

He didn't get to finish his sentence. Afterward he wasn't quite sure what had happened; he only remembered Adam waving the thick soapy sponge he was using and Hannah jerking around, as if he'd startled her. The hose, of course, was still in her hand.

The high-powered jet of water hit him squarely in the chest, drenching him instantly. Apparently shocked, Hannah froze, and he had to leap to one side to escape the spray. "Turn it off!" he yelled, and she finally let go of the trigger.

"You're all wet," Adam observed.

He looked down at himself and groaned. His shirt and pants were clinging to him, his shoes were flooded, his socks sodden. The daisies had also been caught in the blast—what petals were left were hanging limp, the paper wrapping saturated.

"I'm sorry, Dr. Ludlow," Hannah said in a choked voice. For a split second he thought she might be laughing, but when he looked sharply at her, her face was solemn.

"What on earth happened to you?" Maddy was standing on the doorstep, staring at him, looking crisp and clean and very pretty in a yellow linen jumpsuit.

"What the hell do you think happened?" Nate yelled back, still in a state of shock.

Maddy looked startled, for which he could hardly blame her, then her gaze went from Nate to Hannah, still gripping the hose. A second later, she was flying down the path to the gate. Opening it, she gestured Nate in, at the same time shouting furiously at Hannah, "Why did you do that?"

The little girl's face crumpled, as though she were going to cry, and Nate felt a pang of sympathy for her.

"It was an accident, Maddy," he said, though he wasn't quite sure about that. There had been a distinctly satisfied expression on Hannah's face as she stared at him. "I called to the kids and startled them, and Hannah turned around, forgetting the hose was in her hand." He laughed weakly. "This relationship seems doomed to dampness. Haven't you noticed? Rainy days, sailboarding, garden hoses. What difference does it make?"

Maddy looked at him with narrowed eyes, then turned her head again to regard Hannah. "Okay," she said evenly. "I'm going to take Dr. Ludlow inside. Rinse the rest of that soap off the car, then come in and change before dinner. We'll talk about this later."

"It really was an accident, Maddy," Nate said. "My fault if anyone's, for startling them."

He caught the flash of Hannah's eyes as she turned away. Gratitude, or contempt that he could be so naive?

"You look like a daffodil," he said as he squished alongside Maddy to the front door. The comment reminded him of the daisies and he presented them to her with a flourish. "These are for you," he said solemnly.

She looked at the bedraggled flowers, then at him. He saw the brief struggle for control flit across her face, then she was laughing and so was he. Then they were holding on to each other, and he decided he might as well seize the moment to kiss her. He liked kissing

Maddy Scott. Her lips were like velvet; he liked touching them very delicately with just the tip of his tongue. He began to understand how a bee must feel, flitting over a flower in search of honey.

Maddy was stiffening in his arms, probably conscious of the children watching or the neighbors. He let her go at once. "I've made you damp," he apologized.

"I'll dry." She looked at him. "I'm not sure you will, though."

"I could go home, but the way traffic is, it would take forever."

She frowned. "I'll find you something of Brennan's. He's almost your height, skinnier though."

He loved it when she frowned like that, her silken eyebrows coming closer together over the bridge of her straight nose, her beautiful brown eyes looking so concerned, her mouth pursing. Her long straight hair was obviously just washed. It smelled like the lavender his mother used to pick from the garden and hang to dry. He remembered how she'd brushed her hair after the sailboarding lesson, with her head down between her knees. Then she'd flipped back her head and pushed at the top of her hair, and it had fallen perfectly into place.

Their brief embrace had stirred his blood just as thoroughly as the last time they'd hugged. She'd felt so good in his arms, as though she belonged there. Her minty-sweet breath had mingled with his. And for one whole minute she had returned the pressure of his body against hers. She was sexually attracted to him, he was sure of that. Now if he could just get her somewhere where he could hold her in his arms for a longer period of time—like all night, for example . . .

He sighed as he leaned over to pull off his shoes before entering the house. He pulled off his socks, too, then wrung them out and swiped at his damp feet with them. "Did I ever mention that I'm not too fond of slapstick comedy?" he asked.

"Go on into the children's bathroom," Maddy suggested, sounding suspiciously close to laughter again. "I'll get you something to wear."

"Don't forget to put the flowers into water," he called after her, wanting her to laugh. She did. He loved the sound of her laughter almost as much as he loved her slow smile, he decided.

FIFTEEN MINUTES LATER Maddy surveyed him as he emerged from the bathroom. Brennan's blue Lacoste shirt was as tight on him as she'd feared. It clung lovingly to every one of Nate's muscles, especially the biceps, reminding her of how they'd felt under her hands—like iron. The jeans were a disaster. She wasn't sure he'd be able to sit down. They fitted him like a second skin. He was wearing the knitted shirt on the outside; probably he couldn't even fasten the zipper— Brennan was even skinnier than she'd thought.

"Just don't make me laugh tonight," Nate warned. "I'll disgrace myself if you do."

"Maybe I should have brought a dressing gown instead."

He shook his head. "I feel dumb enough like this."

He'd toweled his hair dry and combed it with his fingers, she noticed. It curled over his forehead in a way that made her want to smooth it back. His feet were bare; she hadn't thought about shoes. He had elegant toes, she thought irrelevantly.

"Elevens," he said, reading her mind.

Brennan's were tens. She shook her head. "Sorry about that."

Taking his suit pants from him, she hung them carefully on a hanger over the shower rail, hoping they wouldn't be ruined. She'd already put his socks and shirt into the dryer, and suddenly remembered vividly the glimpse she'd had of his muscular shoulders and tanned, hair-matted chest as he'd handed them out to her. She'd wanted to reach past the door and touch the dark curling hair that disappeared so mysteriously below his belt. Down, girl, she scolded herself, as she led him toward the living room. "Come and meet Brennan," she said, watching his face.

He hadn't really rolled his eyes, she decided. Naturally he had been surprised.

Brennan rose when they entered the room and came toward Nate with his right hand outstretched. He looked a little startled when he saw Nate's bare feet, but didn't comment. Probably he didn't recognize his own clothing, though he was wearing a similar outfit. He loved Lacoste shirts, because he didn't have to worry about matching up buttons. He was wearing shoes, however.

"My feet got a little damp," Nate explained as the two men shook hands.

"It's raining?" Brennan queried.

"Sporadically," Nate said. Evidently he didn't intend telling on the children. He was studying Brennan with great interest and looking rather taken aback.

"Don't get too comfortable, Brennan," Maddy warned her brother-in-law as he seated himself. "You promised to carve the chicken."

Brennan stood up again at once. "You're in for a treat," he told Nate. "Maddy's roast chicken is wonderful. She rubs all kinds of herbs on it and stuffs it with sage and onion. She's a marvelous cook."

"You're lucky to have her," Nate commented, with a sideways glance at Maddy.

"Don't I know it," Brennan said. He put an arm around Maddy's shoulders with a rare show of affection and beamed at her like a proud husband. "She saved my life. I couldn't have managed without her. My gratitude knows no bounds."

Nate was looking depressed, Maddy thought. "The chicken," she reminded Brennan. "We can talk at the table." She glanced at Nate. "We'll only be a few minutes."

"Fine," he said heartily. He always got hearty when he felt awkward. He had a right to feel that way, he told himself after Maddy and Brennan left. Not only had he been given an unexpected and unwelcome shower bath, but he had certainly not expected Brennan Malone to be present for dinner. Maddy had given him the impression that Brennan was never home. He had thought the children would go to bed at a reasonable hour, say eight o'clock, and he'd finally have Maddy Scott to himself. Besides all that, he had imagined Brennan Malone as a kind of mad scientist with wild hair like Einstein. Instead he was an undeniably good-looking man in a studious, bespectacled, round-shouldered sort of way, as innocently blue-eyed as his children. He seemed fond of Maddy.

Nate looked suspiciously around the beautifully furnished blue and white room. It was a comfortable-looking room, clean and tidy, but obviously lived in, with a stack of magazines on the coffee table, and a few toys scattered around. A small pile of clothing lay beside a rocking chair, topped by a sewing box and evidently waiting to be mended. A family room. What

kind of living arrangement did these people have, anyway?

"Hi," Adam said warily from the doorway. "Are
you all dry now?"

Hannah followed him in. Her hair was freshly
braided, and both children had changed into clean
flannel shirts and jeans. They had a scrubbed look that
was attractive in a wholesome way. There was no need
at all for Nate to feel as nervous as he did.

"Maybe we should have put you in the dryer like we
did Pookie," Hannah said, her round blue eyes innocent.

"I'm okay. Maddy loaned me some of your father's
clothes."

"They're too tight."

"I've noticed."

She and Adam settled themselves opposite Nate on
one of the matching sofas that bracketed the empty
fireplace. For a full minute they stared at him in silence, while Nate racked his brain for something to say.

"I met your father," he said at last.

"We don't call him Father, we call him Daddy,"
Hannah said.

So much for that conversational gambit. He could
hear Maddy and Brennan talking in the kitchen amid
the rattle of pots. Then Maddy laughed and Nate
shifted uneasily on the soft sofa.

"Daddy's very handsome, isn't he?" Hannah said.

"He's clever, too," Adam said. "Everyone says so."

Hannah nodded. "Maddy's pretty, don't you
think?"

"Very," Nate agreed heartily.

"They're going to get married, you know."

Stunned, Nate stared at her. "Daddy and Maddy," she explained when he said nothing.

Adam giggled. "Sounds like a poem, Daddy and Maddy."

Hannah quelled him with a stern glance.

"They're as good as married already," Adam added brightly.

And what did that mean? Nate wondered. He hadn't been around children much lately, but at one time he had been intimately acquainted with the way their minds worked. And children, he knew, quite often sensed secrets that were hidden from others. Hannah hadn't chastised Adam this time, she'd looked at him approvingly. With a sudden, startling clarity, Nate remembered Maddy's bedroom on the day her floor had leaked. Her bed had been pushed to the wall, and some stuff had been piled on it, but it was a queen-size bed, no doubt about that. He felt a red-hot streak of jealousy shoot through him, but then assured himself that Maddy wasn't the type who could sleep with one man and go out with another.

Could he be certain of that, though? "You don't even know me," she had said to him once.

He was relieved when Maddy came into the room and smiled at him, and even more relieved when she sent the children off to set the kitchen table. "Feeling okay?" she asked, settling down beside him with a glance at the blue jeans that were cutting off his circulation.

"Fine," he said, though that wasn't strictly true. Adam's remark was still rankling. "What exactly is your relationship with Brennan?" he blurted out.

She looked surprised. "He's my brother-in-law. I thought I told you that."

"Yes, you did." He allowed the silence to build and saw comprehension dawn on her even features, then change to a stillness edged with storm clouds.

"Are you suggesting our relationship might be more intimate?" she asked sharply.

"Well, I did wonder...one roof and all...and the children—"

Now she was on her feet and glaring down at him, her face suffused with color. "Nate Ludlow, I thought better of you," she snapped. "How dare you assume that just because Brennan and I live in the same house, we are...sleeping together! You know where my bedroom is, you've seen it. The children's bedrooms are next to mine. And Brennan's is upstairs. He has his own suite up there. I've known Brennan since I was sixteen years old. I've never even thought of him as anything but my sister's husband, or the big brother I never had. There's never been a hint of anything...untoward between us."

"I'm sorry," Nate said.

But Maddy was just warming up. "I'm a very honest person, Nate. Honesty is important to me. I would have thought anyone with an ounce of sensitivity would have deduced that about me. How could you even think I'd invite you here if I was, if Brennan and I were—?"

"Would you mind very much if I didn't join you for dinner?" Brennan inquired from the doorway.

Maddy's face had flushed an even brighter pink as soon as her brother-in-law began to speak. Now she turned her glare on him; Nate was happy to be out of the spotlight. "Of course I mind," she said. "You promised me you'd be here."

Had she *made* Brennan promise? Nate wondered. Why so insistent? Was she determined never to be alone with *him*?

"You promised the children," she went on rather lamely, as though she'd realized her words were open to misinterpretation.

Brennan looked sheepish. "Well, okay then, if you think I should. It's just that I've suddenly got one of those awful headaches again."

"Brennan," Maddy said reproachfully, clearly sure he was making excuses.

Obviously Brennan had heard their miniquarrel, Nate thought. In her anger, Maddy's voice had risen considerably. "You get headaches often?" Nate asked.

Brennan sighed and nodded, massaging the back of his neck with one hand. "Occupational hazard, I guess, Nate. My optometrist says the prescription for my spectacles is okay, so it must be eyestrain."

Not necessarily, Nate reflected, glancing at Brennan's rounded shoulders and hazarding a guess. "Where do they start?" he asked, getting to his feet and moving closer to Brennan.

"Base of my skull, radiating to my forehead," Brennan answered, gesturing.

"You'd say they are chronic?"

Brennan nodded. "I keep the aspirin companies going all by myself."

Nate was willing to bet that it was Brennan's posture that was at fault. "I might be able to help," he said, fishing his billfold out of the back pocket of his borrowed jeans and extracting a business card. "I've had considerable success with headache patients. If you'd be interested in coming into the clinic to talk about it, give my office manager a call. Her name's Emma. She's in

Sacramento right now, visiting her mother, but she'll be back some time tomorrow. Tell her I suggested a consultation and full chiropractic examination."

He handed the card to Brennan, who glanced at it and nodded. "Emma," he repeated vaguely. "Nice name, Emma."

"Of course you don't have to eat with us if you feel unwell," Maddy said, having watched this exchange closely. "I'll have Hannah bring you up a tray. And maybe you *should* go to see Nate. He gave me an exercise for my jaw, and it's helped me a lot."

This was the first Nate had heard of that. He glanced at Maddy and saw that she looked embarrassed. "Dr. Ross is helping me too, of course," she said.

"Of course," he murmured, elated to think she was using the exercise he'd shown her.

"Do you think Brennan really does have a headache?" she asked as soon as Brennan had left.

He nodded. "Closer up, his pupils looked constricted."

She sighed. "I thought he'd heard what I was saying and concluded we were quarreling. Brennan tends to avoid quarrels."

"Weren't we quarreling?" Nate asked. He wanted to put his arms around her, but this didn't seem a good time. Her tone was still fairly stiff.

She looked at him. Her mouth was set in an uncompromising line; she obviously hadn't forgiven him yet. "I'm sorry, Maddy," he murmured. "I shouldn't have said what I did. It was just that..." No, he wasn't going to tell her what the children had said; that would be cowardly.

"You had no right to jump to such conclusions," Maddy said stiffly. "Ours is an unconventional arrangement, I know, but it's the only workable one. The children need a mother and a father in their lives."

"I understand," Nate said softly. He believed her totally, of course. If Brennan hadn't looked at her so fondly, and if the children hadn't put doubts into his mind, he would never have brought up the subject. He felt ashamed of himself, which was unusual for him. "I'm sorry," he said again.

For a moment her mouth showed signs of softening. It seemed to him that if he took one small step forward and carefully put his arms around her, she might just melt completely. She might even smile at him. The thought was an encouraging one, but before he could put the plan into action, a figure appeared in the doorway.

"The rice is burning," Hannah said, with clearly deplorable timing, but great satisfaction.

This isn't going to work, Nate thought.

THE MEAL wasn't going well, Maddy decided. If only Nate hadn't made those insinuating remarks; if only Brennan hadn't developed that convenient headache. She still wasn't sure it was a real headache, no matter what Nate said.

She *had* been able to save the rice. It had only singed a little on the bottom, and she'd managed to disguise the burnt taste with a healthy dollop of soy sauce. The chicken was just right, tender and juicy, and the spinach salad was fine. Nate was eating with every sign of enjoyment. The only real problem was the atmosphere. Normally the children would be chattering away about the day's happenings—usually she had to keep reminding them to eat. But tonight they were eating silently, with admirable manners, their eyes fixed on Nate as though he were an exhibit at the zoo.

Hannah wasn't usually too good with strangers, of course, but Adam was. And neither of them had ever before stared with quite so much concentration at a visitor. She had a feeling that they were up to something, something they had planned. Children did tend to make you paranoid, though. Probably they were just suffering pangs of guilt over drenching poor Nate like that, and were trying to look bright and interested so that she'd forget to give them the third degree she'd promised them. Fat chance. She still intended to question them very closely about that little incident with the hose.

Nate looked uncomfortable. He had tried to converse with the children, asking them about school and what kind of sports they liked. Both children had answered tersely, though with admirable politeness. Adam had even called him sir, which had made him wince. Now he was shifting on his chair every once in a while, as though Brennan's blue jeans were constricting him in all the wrong places; he was obviously aware of the children's odd behavior. She had a good mind to kick them both under the table, but was afraid she might connect with Nate's long legs instead. Maybe that wouldn't be such a bad idea. She was still furious with him for implying that she and Brennan were lovers.

In the meantime, the silence was becoming very uncomfortable.

"I wish you'd explain chiropractic to me, Nate," she said desperately. "I was surprised when you suggested it as a cure for Brennan's headaches. I'm afraid I don't really know how it works."

He looked relieved to have something to talk about, and even managed a slight grin. "You sure you want to know? I tend to get fired up. Hannah and Adam might get bored." He smiled tightly at the children, who stared unwinkingly back at him.

"That won't hurt them a bit," Maddy said with a meaningful glance at each of them. Hannah stared back innocently. Adam looked worried.

"Okay then, here goes," Nate said with a false-sounding cheeriness. "It's possible that Brennan's postural faults are creating stress on his spine and muscles, causing irritation to the greater occipital nerves. We need to reinstate the proper cervical range of motion by removing vertebral fixations and nerve irritation and restoring functional integrity."

He was leaning forward now, gesturing as he talked, and a note of excitement had come into his voice that reminded her of Brennan discussing his work. Obviously Nate Ludlow took his job just as seriously as Brennan did. She remembered him giving time to the old people at the nursing home. She remembered that she'd thought him a lightweight when she'd first met him, and felt guilty about misjudging him.

"The chiropractic adjustment is very powerful," Nate was saying; she realized she'd missed a chunk of conversation. "It provides stimulation to the nervous system, which allows the body to achieve a homeostatic state." He paused. "You're not following me, are you?"

"I was doing okay until you got to homeostatic," Maddy said with a smile.

"Sorry. Balanced. The idea is to get the body into proper balance, alignment, to give the joints optimum motion. This allows the muscles, which guide the movement of the joints, to go through a full range of motion, allowing the nervous system to function properly, which in turn provides the body with the ability to heal itself."

"That's what Brennan's working on," she told him, then shook her head. "I didn't mean chiropractic, I meant the body's ability to heal itself. He's working on the immune system."

"I'd like to have talked with him about his work," Nate said.

They both glanced automatically at the ceiling, then Maddy saw Nate look at her inquiringly. Did he expect her to say, "Next time you're here you can talk to Brennan?" Was she going to ask him back again? What was the point? They were both so stilted and uneasy. What had happened to the easy conversation they had shared before? The children. She groaned inwardly. It had not been a good idea to mix Nate and the children.

She was relieved when the meal ended and certainly didn't blame Nate at all for refusing coffee. "I should probably be getting along pretty soon," he said. "I'll help you with the dishes first, of course. But I do have some chores, well, some reading to do."

Now he was making excuses. What had she expected—that Nate Ludlow would enjoy a happy family evening? But this evening had hardly been that. She could not blame him for wanting to escape.

"You don't have to do the dishes, Nate. You're a guest. Hannah and Adam will take care of cleaning up."

Both children groaned. Nate looked at them sympathetically. "Sorry guys, I tried," he said lightly, then stood up as they again stared at him unblinkingly. "I guess I'll go get my clothes," he said awkwardly.

There was a moment's silence after Nate left the room, then Hannah and Adam looked at each other and started to push back their chairs. "No, you don't," Maddy said grimly. "You both sit right down again and tell me what really happened this evening."

The two children exchanged guilty glances, which confirmed Maddy's suspicions. "You turned that hose on Nate deliberately, didn't you?" she said to Hannah.

"Me?" Hannah asked, wide-eyed.

"You."

Hannah tried to meet Maddy's gaze directly but failed, then hung her head. "Yes," she admitted.

"Why?"

Adam piped up. "We didn't want him to have a good time."

"That much was obvious. All that staring. I'm disappointed in you both. I know you don't know him well, but Dr. Ludlow's a very nice man, believe me. He certainly hasn't done you any harm. Why on earth were you so mean to him?"

There was a long silence. Hannah finally raised her head and looked at her defiantly. Maddy thought for a minute that the little girl was going to refuse to answer, but then Hannah said in a miserable-sounding voice, "He likes you, Maddy."

"Well, I know that," Maddy said without trying to conceal her exasperation. "But that doesn't mean—" She broke off. That wasn't defiance in Hannah's eyes; that was desperation. Suddenly she was inside Hannah's eight-year-old mind, understanding her thought processes completely. To Hannah, and probably to a lesser degree to Adam, Nate was an adversary, a threat to the status quo. They were afraid of the competition for Maddy's affection. Possibly there was also the thought that if they made him look ridiculous, or made him lose his temper, Maddy wouldn't like him anymore. Only Nate hadn't lost his temper—he had taken the whole incident extremely well—and he certainly hadn't looked ridiculous. He should have looked ridiculous in Brennan's too-tight clothes, but instead he had looked magnificent.

All the same, the children had to learn that they couldn't treat people that way. They had to make amends. She studied their sad little faces, longing to take them into her arms. It was so hard for her to be stern with them. But she had to teach them that every action had its consequence. They had a far from ordered life. Before Georgia left, their schedule had been arranged around hers and they had been allowed to stay up until all hours. And then their mother had deserted them without warning. When Maddy had first started taking care of them, they had rebelled against her attempts to give them a disciplined, orderly life. Even after they had settled into a proper schedule, they had cried every time their daddy left the house, afraid he wouldn't come back. They had clung to Maddy every time she came home from work, far more excited than the situation called for, obviously relieved to see she had come back at all. Only recently had they started to seem more secure, as though they finally believed they were safe. Whatever happened, she must not jeopardize that.

"When you and Daddy were cutting up the chicken, we told Dr. Ludlow you were going to marry Daddy," Adam confessed, obviously wanting all sins to be taken into account before punishment was meted out.

For a minute she couldn't speak. "You told him what?"

"We figured he'd go away if he thought you were going to marry Daddy," Hannah said miserably.

No wonder Nate had questioned her about Brennan. And she had delivered a lecture about honesty. "Don't you ever tell anyone that again," she said sharply. "It's not true. You know it's not true."

Hannah and Adam exchanged a glance, but said nothing. Then Adam asked plaintively, "Don't you love us anymore, Maddy?"

"I'm always going to love you," Maddy said softly, wanting to show that even though she was angry, she understood that they were troubled.

"Always and forever?"

"Always and forever."

"But Dr. Ludlow does like you," Hannah repeated.

Adam stood up and came to lean against Maddy. "Do you like him?" he asked.

"Yes, I do, very much, and I want you to like him, too." She took a deep breath. "When he comes back in here, I want you to tell him what you did and why."

"No, Maddy," they chorused, but Maddy held firm.

"I don't see why you need to see him, anyway," Hannah said mutinously. "You always said *we* were your best friends."

Maddy sighed. "You are my best friends. But you must understand, both of you, that adult people, women, have needs that can't always be met by children."

"What kind of needs?" Hannah asked.

Good question. She could hardly say a woman needed an emotional life, a sex life, needed to feel a man's arms around her sometimes. Nor could she say that she often felt lonely for just such a man. Or that since she met Nate Ludlow, her dreams had become in-

creasingly interesting, featuring herself and Nate in each
other's arms, making love to each other with equal fer-
vor, uninterrupted by outside distractions, unencumbered by the demands of work and children and
responsibility. How easy it was to be together, really
together in dreams, yet how frustrating—so often she
woke up in the night grinding her teeth, awash with
sexual desire.

I'm only twenty-six years old, she wanted to blurt
out. *I'm not a nun in a convent. I love you both so
much it hurts when I see you hurting, but I need, I
need* . . .

"Sometimes women like to go out with men—to
dinner, dancing, the theater," she managed at last.

"We could go dancing," Adam said staunchly. "I
like to dance."

Maddy sighed, then noticed that Nate was standing
in the kitchen doorway gazing at her. The children had
their backs to the door and hadn't seen him yet. Their
eyes met and she wondered how much he had heard.
Judging by the glint in those devilish eyes of his, he
might even have heard the parts she hadn't spoken
aloud. A wave of heat rushed through her, but she
wasn't sure if it was caused by embarrassment or re-
membrance of those graphically sexual dreams.

Nate looked more like himself, even though his pants
were still a little damp and the shine was gone from his
shoes. "Come on in," Maddy said. "Hannah has
something she wants to tell you."

Hannah looked at her pleadingly as Nate came in and
sat down, but Maddy met her gaze without wavering.
Finally the little girl stood up, lifted her chin and said
very rapidly, "We got you wet on purpose, Dr. Ludlow, but we won't do that again and it's not true that

Maddy's going to marry Daddy and Maddy says we have to say we're sorry.''

"We're sorry," Adam echoed.

"Hannah," Maddy scolded. "That was hardly an apology. Try again."

Nate put his hand on Maddy's shoulder as Hannah's lower lip began to protrude ominously. He looked as though he was having a hard time suppressing a grin. "Hannah doesn't have to apologize," he said in a careful voice. "I quite understand."

Conscious of the weight of his hand and of the fact both children were looking at it, Maddy glanced at him hopefully. "You do?"

Nate nodded, then looked directly at Hannah. "You just thought it would be a fun idea to get me all wet. It's no big deal. I'm washable."

He didn't understand. Was it worth trying to explain that Hannah was different from other children, that she'd had to grow up in a hurry, that she had sensed Maddy's growing attraction to Nate and had wanted to put a stop to it? Maybe not. She felt disappointed in him as she accompanied him to the front door, and when he asked to see her again, she came very close to saying no immediately.

"Why on earth would you want to see me again after tonight?" she asked.

He looked thoughtful and didn't answer right away. Then he said, "I have...certain *feelings* for you, Maddy. I told you that right from the start. But it's more than that. I *admire* you. I admire your commitment to the children. And to Brennan."

Just as she began to hope he might really mean that, he grinned and added, "Then again, maybe it's the thrill of the chase."

This was a game to him, she thought. He was good at sports, probably competitive. He liked to win.

"Or perhaps you're a secret masochist," she suggested dryly.

He laughed. "Come on now, it wasn't that bad. I get wet sailboarding. I'm used to it. Next time I'll wear my wet suit."

He was treating the children's enmity as a joke. What would she have preferred? That he'd get flaming mad and shout at everybody concerned? All the same, Hannah's despair wasn't a joke, not to Hannah and not to Maddy. It was very real.

Next time, he had said. It was her move. "I'm going to be busy all week," she said carefully. "We're taking a petting zoo to the Special Olympics."

"Next Sunday then?" he asked, persistent as always.

He looked so winning, standing there with that confident grin on his face, as though he just couldn't possibly imagine any woman saying no to him. And she had to admit that he had been a good sport about the awful way the children had treated him, and about the awful way she had treated him, when all he'd really wanted was to find out where she stood with Brennan. How could she just tell him to his face that she thought it would be best not to see him again? "Why don't you call me about Wednesday or Thursday?" she suggested, compromising.

He knew she was putting him off; she could see it in his eyes. For a second he looked crushed but almost immediately his mouth hardened and his jaw lifted. She thought he was going to tell her off, but instead he said, "You can't just dismiss what we have going for us, Maddy," then reached for her and pulled her close.

Before she could recover from her surprise at his quick action, his hands moved quickly, strongly, down her back to her buttocks, then his mouth covered hers hungrily, kissing her in a far less gentle way than he had before, though there was nothing rough about his mouth, only firmness and impatience.

It was a demanding kiss, one that said he was losing patience with her delaying tactics, one that said he'd had a frustrating evening and wanted to get some good out of it. It was a kiss that made it quite clear that Madeleine Scott was eventually going to have to make a decision about Nate Ludlow.

All of this went through her mind, but it didn't distract her from what was happening to her body. Real life was duplicating the dreams that had kept her wakeful. The word passion had come between them a couple of times since they had met, and tonight Maddy's body was catching fire with it—her real body, not the blurred figure of her fantasies. To her dismay, she imagined that in the distance she could hear music—romantic music, movie music, sunset music, the notes building as the unseen orchestra prepared to soar to a crescendo. It was the theme from *Dr. Zhivago*—balalaikas and all—no doubt about it.

CHAPTER SIX

NATE SLUMPED into his office chair and gazed morosely out of the window at the sunlight glinting on office windows across the street. After a Rotary breakfast meeting, he'd come in early to catch up on some reading, but the *American Chiropractor* still lay unopened on his desk. It had occurred to him this morning that in spite of the passion that had leaped between Maddy and himself the previous night, he hadn't made any real progress toward getting this relationship off the ground.

Call me on Wednesday or Thursday, she'd said. So that she could think up an excuse not to see him? After the kiss he'd told himself that of course she would agree to see him again, but his confidence seemed to have deserted him this morning, even though he'd worked out an offer he hoped she couldn't refuse. He wanted so very much to see her again. Alone. His hormones had never been as active as when he was around Madeleine Scott. Her mouth tasted so wonderful, her body against his lighted firecrackers in all his senses, the feel of her satiny brown hair under his hand set his pulses throbbing—and more than his pulses.

He shifted uncomfortably in his seat. Patience had always been one of his virtues, but it was really being tested in this yet-to-be-consummated relationship. Why was he so anxious to hang in there? He answered his own question almost before it was formulated—this wasn't just a matter of a challenge, nor was it all hormones. This was something more, something he didn't even have a name for.

He had told Maddy the truth—he *liked* her, he admired her devotion to her work; he even admired her loyalty to those two children and to Brennan. He also admired her determination to be a good surrogate mother, a good zookeeper, even a good sailboarder. He could still see her biting her lower lip as she struggled to haul up the sail—the curve of her body...no, better not think about the curve of her body. He groaned aloud. If only fate hadn't dealt him the joker to end all jokers. Two jokers—named Hannah and Adam.

"Are you still moping?" Emma asked from the doorway.

He swiveled around to greet her, happy to see she was back from her trip. "How was Sacramento?" he asked, avoiding the question. "Mom okay?"

Her face devoid of expression, Emma plunked the appointment book in front of him, then slumped onto the opposite chair, leaned her elbows on the desk and propped her chin in her hands. "She's as energetic as ever. Wore me out."

Nate had met Emma's mother only once. She was a small birdlike woman who fluttered around endlessly, talked nonstop and had definite opinions on all topics. Yorkshire-born and -bred, she had married a GI during World War II and moved to Sacramento. She had never become the least bit Americanized, in speech or habit. *You can take the woman out of Yorkshire,* Nate mused, *but you can't take Yorkshire out of the woman.*

He studied Emma's face. "You look tired. Drawn. Haggard around the eyes."

"Thanks a lot. That makes me feel much better."

"Want to talk about it?"

She sighed. "I ate too much, Nate. I hate it when I eat too much. But what could I do faced with roast beef and Yorkshire pudding, shepherd's pie, minced beef and dumplings, not to mention scones and three different kinds of cake?"

"Awesome."

She nodded. "Especially with Mom hovering over my shoulder chanting, 'Eat, eat, eat!' Unfortunately, cooking up a storm is the only way she's ever known to show love." Emma sighed. "I think I'll take the day off and run five miles."

"Feel free." He gave her a sympathetic smile. "You only see her every three months or so. It'll wear off."

"Try telling that to my hips."

She wasn't just tired, she was depressed, Nate decided, just as he was. What had happened to the two cheerful souls who used to inhabit this office? "Food wasn't the only problem, I take it," he said, to draw her out.

Emma slumped a little lower in her chair, not looking at him. "Mom thinks I ought to get married. To Gary."

Nate forcibly suppressed his immediate sense of distaste. "Why Gary?"

"She thinks I'm running out of options."

"Has she met Gary?"

Emma shook her head. "She doesn't need to. He meets all the requirements. He has a job."

"Has he asked you to marry him?"

"Not yet. But I think he's going to."

"But surely you won't say yes? You told me Gary depressed you—all that talk about the old days and calling you pumpkin."

She winced. "We had a talk about that. He's trying to improve. Mom says I'm too choosy, anyway. Sometimes you have to settle for less, she says." She stood up. "I'd better call home and make sure Muggsie's okay. I came straight here from Mom's."

"You didn't take Muggsie along?"

"She gets carsick. And Mom doesn't like dogs, anyway." She hesitated. "Gary took care of her."

"At the Fairmont?"

"No. He spent the weekend at my place. That way he could work on the burglar alarm system some more. He's staying through today until I get home from work, maybe through tonight. We're having dinner."

"Obviously the relationship has progressed," Nate commented.

Emma shook her head and started toward the door. "Not in the way you mean," she said flatly. At the door she paused to look at him thoughtfully. "You don't seem too chipper yourself," she said. "How did Madeleine's sailboarding lesson go?"

"Terrific," he said gloomily. "Maddy even invited me to dinner last night."

"And?"

"Disaster."

Briefly he brought her up-to-date on his thwarted romance with Maddy Scott. When he got to the drenching Hannah had inflicted upon him, a teasing glint appeared in Emma's brown eyes. "Hannah and Adam sound adorable," she said when he was done.

"Adorable is not the first word that came to my mind," he said.

She laughed, looking much happier than when she'd come into the office. She really was a pretty woman, Nate thought. Her white uniform was very becoming and she'd left her freshly washed hair loose to swing around her face, instead of tucking it behind her ears. Emma was a great person. She deserved better than Gary Conrad.

"So what are you going to do now?" she asked.

He shrugged. "Call Maddy tomorrow. Hope she can find time to come out with me on Sunday." Suddenly he grinned, remembering the campaign he'd worked out. "I'm planning a theater outing, followed by a seduction supper at my place. I figure all I have to do is spend some time alone with her, and she'll be putty in my hands."

"That won't solve the problem of the children." Emma shook her head. "Seems to me you need to work at getting Georgia and what's-his-name together again."

"Brennan."

"Would a runaway wife come back to him?" she asked. "What's he like?"

Nate pondered her question for a while then said, "Scholarly. Gregory Peck in *To Kill a Mockingbird*."

"You and your movies." Emma laughed. "Well, anyway, if you could get Georgia and Brennan back together, you'd have an unencumbered Maddy to bend to your will."

An unencumbered Maddy sounded wonderfully exciting to Nate. He sighed. "According to Maddy, there's no hope of a reconciliation. That reminds me, though. Brennan may call for an appointment—he has chronic headaches." Reaching for the appointment book, he turned it around and flipped a page. "Looks as if Jamie already made an appointment for him tomorrow." He frowned. "Dammit, she's only given him fifteen minutes. See if you can squeeze a half hour out for him, okay? I want to do a full examination."

Emma nodded. "You want me to tell him his head-aches will go away if he gets his wife back?"

"I can't in all honesty say that would be true. But any little hints you can give him toward finding a mother for his kids would be appreciated."

She grinned. "I'll see what I can do."

"Emma," he called as she turned to leave.

She looked back at him over her shoulder.

"Don't be in too big a hurry to decide on marriage," he said. "You have a pretty good life."

"I'm lonely, Nate," she said simply.

Lonely. The word seemed to echo in the stillness of the office. Nate looked compulsively out at the parking lot again. If he squinted, he could just about imagine Madeleine Scott walking toward the building, her long brown hair lifting behind her.

Lonely. It wasn't a word he'd ever considered seriously before.

IT WAS ALMOST SEVEN O'CLOCK before Emma got away from the office. Jamie might be a terrific chiropractic assistant, but bookkeeping wasn't her forte. In only a couple of days she had managed to mess up Emma's carefully kept records.

At seven-fifteen Emma climbed the steps to her apartment, clutching her suitcase in one hand, the panic button Gary had given her in the other, listening intently. Sure enough, when she reached the top of the steps, Muggsie started to bark. But there was no immediate response from the siren. Emma had no need to use the panic button. Probably Gary hadn't switched the alarm on, she thought, but a second later he flung open the door and beamed down at her, looking very handsome and macho in a navy sweatshirt and faded blue jeans. "Looks as if we've got it licked, Em," he called out happily.

Em was better than pumpkin, she supposed, though it did make her feel like Auntie Em in *The Wizard of Oz.* Dowdy and middle-aged. *You're too sensitive for your own good,* her Mom had told her. Emma sighed.

Gary aimed a kiss in the direction of her lips, but Muggsie was putting on her usual, "My God, I thought you'd gone forever," performance, jumping up and down and squealing with joy, and the kiss grazed Emma's hair instead.

"Did you remember to give Muggsie her hormone pills?" Emma asked, then groaned when Gary looked sheepish.

There were three stains on the carpet—one in the living room, one in the hall, one in the bedroom. No effort had been made to clean them up, so it took Emma almost half an hour with PDQ to erase all traces of Muggsie's accidents. Then she fed the dog a piece of wiener with a pill concealed in it, straightened and went on an inspection tour.

The kitchen sink was full of dirty dishes and newspapers littered the living room, along with a couple of pairs of shoes and several socks. The remains of popcorn sat in one of her precious cobalt bowls with several hamburger wrappers, and half a dozen coffee cups with sludgy-looking interiors stood around, not to mention three or four beer bottles.

Sighing, she picked up her suitcase and took it into the bedroom, Gary trailing behind her. He had obviously slept in her bed, even though she'd prepared the guest room for him. The bed was unmade. Beyond it, in the corner, where she hadn't noticed them when she cleaned the rug, were three large suitcases.

"Where did *they* come from?" she asked, pointing. When he arrived, Gary had been carrying only an overnight bag.

"I brought them over from the Fairmont," he said, in what was evidently supposed to be a casual voice.

Emma opened her own suitcase on the bed and started lifting out her neatly folded blouses, skirts and underwear. There was a sinking sensation in her stomach. "You moved out of the Fairmont?"

"I had to." He came to sit next to her suitcase and put his arms around her waist, pulling her in to him so that his face was lightly pressed against her breasts. He didn't look as if he'd shaved in a few days. Shades of Don Johnson on *Miami Vice*. She held herself stiffly.

"What happened?" she asked.

He gave her the mischievous, little-boy smile she remembered from their school days. "Nothing *happened*," he murmured. "I just ran short of money temporarily."

She pulled herself free and stepped back, so that she could see his face clearly. "Are you telling me you're broke?" she demanded.

His laugh wasn't at all convincing. "My gosh, no, Em. I have several deals pending. Why, just next week I have three appointments alone."

"What happened to the twenty-five hundred dollars I paid you for the security system?"

He shrugged. "I paid the Fairmont what I already owed them, of course."

"You didn't pay the company? What happens if I want my money back?"

"I'll catch up with the company. The system's working fine now, Em, honestly. Why would you want your money back? Listen, the siren didn't go off when

Muggsie barked, did it? It didn't go off the whole weekend, and I left it on all the time."

"Even while you did the dishes?" she asked pointedly.

He had the grace to flush a little. "I was pretty busy," he said defensively.

"So I see. Reading newspapers, drinking beer, eating hamburgers. A regular workaholic, that's you."

"I made a lot of phone calls. That's how I set up my appointments."

"Long-distance phone calls?"

"Well, one or two, I guess, to L.A. I read about this company, see—in the paper—they suffered a major loss in a burglary on Friday."

She shook her head. "Where are you going to live if you're broke, Gary?"

He glanced at her with that same engaging smile. "I'm not broke," he insisted. "It's just that my cash flow isn't liquid right now." He hesitated. "I was sort of hoping I could stay with you a few more days, just till I get some orders. We could sort of try things out, I thought, see how we get along."

Try what things out? she wondered.

"The orders will be pouring in, believe me," he said hopefully.

If the deliberately engaging smile had stayed in place, she might have been able to tell him to get lost, as Nate had once advised, but as he talked, the grin had slipped, and she caught a glimpse of desperation in his eyes.

"For old times' sake, Em," he murmured.

Even though she recognized that he was manipulating her, even though she knew she was falling into the same trap she'd occupied with Lawrence and Chance and numerous other men, how could she resist the appeal in those spaniel-puppy eyes? It was all so clear to her now—the successful appearance had been carefully contrived. All the previous jobs he'd dismissed so cavalierly as stepping-stones on the road to prosperity had probably been abject failures, just as this one seemed doomed to become. Gary was no more a success today than he'd been in school, when she'd helped him with his homework, to the detriment of her own. Unfortunately, realizing this made her feel more sympathetic rather than less. How could she possibly turn out a destitute friend.

"For a week then, no more," she told him, trying to sound firm. "And I'm not cooking. You've obviously been existing on junk food. Salads and fruit from now on. And you do the dishes. Every day. And we sleep in separate beds, you in the guest room, me in here."

"Aw, come on now, Em."

"Take it or leave it."

He stood up at once, nodding and smiling, and took her into his arms, obviously hoping to change her mind about the beds. As he kissed her, she tried not to analyze her response, but the facts were inescapable. She *wanted* to respond to him—after all, he was handsome, he was her own age, he probably would eventually succeed—the burglar alarm was a good one, now that its bugs had been straightened out. And she didn't actually mind being kissed by him, even quite enjoyed the sensation of a strong male body pressed against her own. She had to acknowledge that he was pretty good, one might even say *practiced* at kissing—but her overall conclusion was that sexually, Gary Conrad left her totally cold.

You have to settle for less sometimes, her mom had said. Was that really true? she wondered, with a feeling close to despair.

SHE WASN'T GOING TO TELL Nate that Gary had moved in with her, she decided as she drove to work the next day. It wasn't just that Nate would give her a hard time—that was a given—but he'd also worry about her, and he had enough problems going on in his own life right now.

She laughed shortly as she slid the car into its parking slot. Seldom in the whole history of their business and personal relationship had she considered the possibility of Nate Ludlow having problems of any kind. With the sole possible exception of a woman named Leonie, who had suffered from some kind of obsessive complex where Nate was concerned. Normally Nate was the eternal carefree bachelor. He hadn't even come close to marriage in the years she'd known him. As soon as women started taking him seriously, he shied away fast. Ditto if any complications raised their ugly heads. Madeleine Scott must really be something. She sure seemed to be getting to him. Emma had never seen him so gloomy, even on Leonie's worst days. It was interesting to see that certain women could effect change in even a happy-go-lucky type like Nate.

It would also be interesting to see what Maddy Scott's brother-in-law was like, Emma thought, remembering he was scheduled for today. Brennan Malone. Georgia Malone's husband. The incredibly sexy, incredibly talented Georgia Malone.

NATE HAD MENTIONED Gregory Peck, but given Nate's devotion to old movies, Emma had allowed room for exaggeration. It hadn't entered her mind that Brennan Malone would be absolutely drop-dead gorgeous. He was brown-haired, lean and tall, though slightly stooped, which only added to his scholarly appearance. The eyes behind his tortoiseshell-rimmed glasses looked strained, but they were blue as a summer sky and unmistakably kind.

"I'm afraid we're running a few minutes late," Emma apologized, coming out of her cubbyhole to meet him in the waiting room, clipboard in hand. "Maybe we can fill out the necessary forms while you're waiting."

"I'm not sure I can see the questions," he said apologetically, putting one hand to his forehead. "I'm having a pretty bad headache right now."

"I'll help you," she offered at once.

Oh, she did like his shy smile. There was more to it than just pleasant agreement. A smile like that might almost make a woman feel that a man thought she was attractive.

Taking a seat next to him on one of the office sofas, trying not to notice that she was suddenly short of breath, she carefully filled out the form. Age thirty-six. Height six feet. Weight one hundred sixty-five pounds. Maybe not sky-blue eyes. Cornflower blue? Larkspur blue? Delphinium blue? He was too thin, a separate part of her mind noted. God, she was getting to be like her mother, wanting to fatten everybody up.

Previous illnesses—none since childhood.

Occupation. Director of immunology at the Lowther Institute. "I work on children's diseases," he explained.

"That's wonderful," Emma breathed, hoping she didn't sound too gushy. She *felt* gushy, though she had always despised gushiness.

"What exactly do you do?" she found herself asking, then felt stupid when he glanced in a startled way at her clipboard. "We don't need the information for your chart, of course," she explained, "but the more we know of your work habits, the better we can judge the cause of your headaches."

Nate would just love to hear her, she thought derisively. She could hear him asking, "Who's the doctor around here, anyway?"

"I'm afraid my work habits are disastrous," he said with a wry smile. "I'm the original absentminded professor, who gets so involved in his work, he forgets to eat or sleep or go home to visit his family. Maddy's constantly nagging me about that." He hesitated. "Maddy's my—"

"—Sister-in-law," Emma supplied, when he seemed at a loss for a description.

He gave her a shy but grateful smile that raised her blood pressure several notches. "Maddy takes care of my children, Hannah and Adam," he said.

Emma nodded. "Dr. Ludlow explained your... situation to me."

He laughed. "I think Dr. Ludlow is *very* interested in my sister-in-law," he said unexpectedly. "I have a reputation for not noticing things that are right under my nose, but the...what do the kids call them—the vibes?—were very strong."

"Do you mind?"

"Why should I mind? Maddy is a lovely young woman and certainly a free agent." He shook his head and sighed. "I'm not being truthful. I do mind. Quite frankly, I'm concerned about losing Maddy. I don't know what I'd do without her. She makes my selfish indulgence in my work entirely possible."

"You need to know a couple of things," Emma said. "One—Nate's relationships never last. Don't get me wrong. He's never unkind. Usually his women stick around as friends, but he doesn't get into any long-term stuff. And two—according to Nate, Maddy would never desert the children. So I don't think you need to worry, Dr. Malone."

"Call me Brennan, please," he said softly. "And you are Emma, I believe?"

She liked the way he said her name, investing it with an almost tender warmth. But how did he know—?

"Nate mentioned your name," he explained. "I associated it at once with *Madame Bovary*, one of my favorite novels. Emma Bovary was such an incurable romantic. Are *you* an incurable romantic, Emma?"

She swallowed. "I like to think of myself as a realist, but I believe deep down I'm really very romantic." Was she really flirting with a patient? Strictly against policy, of course. But somehow policy didn't seem too relevant at that moment. She didn't even want to remember that Emma Bovary's romanticism had ended in her own destruction. "I loved *Madame Bovary* myself," she said.

Brennan smiled ruefully. "It's been so long since I had time to read novels." He frowned. She liked the play of expression across his even features—nothing was hidden; his face reflected exactly what he was thinking. "I do worry, though, Emma, that Maddy is sacrificing her own life for the benefit of Hannah and Adam."

"Nate says she loves them."

"That's certainly true. And they adore her." Another frown, then a singularly sweet smile. "I've been remiss, Emma. You asked about my work, and I digressed into personal matters. How nice of you to be so patient. Are you still interested?"

"Very," Emma said firmly.

He shook his head. "It's difficult to put into lay terms without oversimplification, but a woman of your abilities must certainly have picked up on some of our inescapable medical jargon."

He hesitated again, looking at her directly, but as if he wasn't really seeing her. His thoughts had gone to his work, she supposed.

"In a healthy person," he began, "as I'm sure you know, the immune system reacts very efficiently to combat invading infection. Unfortunately, the immune system can also turn against the body, causing such diseases as rheumatic fever, rheumatoid arthritis, and even some forms of diabetes, along with many other disorders."

Emma nodded, fascinated not only by the information he was giving her but by the intensity that had invaded his voice and facial expression.

"For a long time," he continued, "I was working on rheumatic fever, in which the immune system, after grappling with the original streptococcal infection of the throat, goes into overkill and attacks the joints, heart and central nervous system. I wanted to know what caused the immune system to go awry. The question I set up was—could there be a similarity between the strep organism and our heart, muscle and joint tissues? In other words, did the antibodies manufactured by the body to fight the streptococcus confuse the body's membranes with the invader?"

As he went on, Emma listened happily to the vibrant sound of his voice. He was likening the immune system to an army, a home guard that sent out soldiers on reconnaissance, watching for foreign substances or intruding cells.

After a while Emma realized vaguely that Nate had appeared in the waiting room. He was standing back in the shadows, looking from her to Brennan Malone and smiling. How long had he been standing there? How much had he heard? He must be ready for Brennan now. She'd rescheduled Brennan for the last appointment of the day and Nate would be anxious to get away. She had no idea how much time had passed, while she sat so enthralled next to this vitally interesting man.

"After some success with this line of thinking, I worked on children's diabetes for a time," Brennan went on earnestly.

From the corner of her eye Emma saw Nate grin again, then disappear in the direction of his office.

"Now, with the results of my earlier experiments, I'm no longer engaged in trying to repair autoimmune disease. I'm trying, with the help of my lab crew of course, to perfect a negative vaccine that will prevent autoimmune diseases from wreaking their havoc at all, something that will stop the production of those antibodies that we do not want, but still allow normal production of other antibodies."

"Something that will help the body heal itself?"

"Exactly." He beamed at her, causing chaos in her upper respiratory system. God, he was such an attractive man, such a brilliant man. It had been so exciting to be caught up even briefly in the drama of his life. She could listen to him for hours, but unfortunately Nate was waiting. "I'll take you in now, Dr. Malone," she said reluctantly.

"Brennan," he repeated as they both stood up. "I've enjoyed talking to you, Emma. You are a wonderful listener. I'm afraid I've talked too much. I didn't give you a chance to say anything in return."

"I was fascinated," she said truthfully.

He grinned as she showed him into a treatment room. "I do believe my headache is gone, Emma," he said. "Perhaps I don't need Nate, after all."

"Oh, yes, you do," Nate said cheerfully from the doorway. "If Emma starts curing my patients before I get my hands on them, I'm going to lose my terrific reputation." He laughed. "I must say you two were going great guns out there. I was afraid to interrupt, in case Emma chewed me out." He quirked his eyebrows at Emma with such obvious curiosity that she could feel heat rising into her cheeks.

Ignoring Nate, she extended her hand to Brennan. "I enjoyed our talk very much," she said carefully.

"Could we continue it over dinner?" he asked, taking her breath away completely this time. "The electricity has gone berserk in my lab, and I can't work for a couple of days." He smiled ruefully. "The repairmen don't have my sense of urgency, I'm afraid."

He was still holding her hand. Nate was delightedly gazing from Emma to Brennan and back again. Emma knew what he was thinking.

About to say, *Of course I'd love to go out to dinner,* without any thoughts of playing "hard to get"—one, because she never had been a game player, and two, because she had never met a man she wanted so much to be with—she suddenly had an image of Gary's anxiously pleading spaniel-puppy eyes. Gary. He was living in her apartment, expecting her home for dinner. How could she turn her back on him?

She felt desperate, trapped. "I can't, I'm afraid," she said slowly. The hardest words she'd ever had to speak—torn from her against her will. Yet somehow they came out sounding flat, perhaps even cold.

Brennan blinked in surprise and looked disappointed, but smiled and released her hand. "Another time, perhaps," he said in a polite voice that convinced her there would never be another time.

And then Nate was showing Brennan into the X-ray room, looking back over his shoulder at Emma in a puzzled way, and she was suddenly feeling thoroughly confused and somehow bereft.

"What was all that about?" Nate asked an hour and a half later. Emma had heard Brennan taking his leave at least twenty minutes ago, but she had hidden out in her cubicle with some paperwork, unwilling to face Brennan in case her confusion showed on her face.

"All what?" she asked.

Nate slid one hip onto the corner of the desk and lifted her chin, so that she had to look up at him.

"Don't play the innocent with me, Emma Fieldstone. You were out there in the waiting room, looking at Brennan Malone as if he were the second coming, and then all of a sudden you're Miss Frigid, saying 'I can't.' What gives?"

She sighed. "Gary."

"You mean you have to be true to one man and all that?"

"Not exactly. It's just that Gary...needs me. And he's well, sort of living with me."

Nate groaned and ran a hand through his hair. "Tell Papa," he ordered, and she did, beginning with the mess she'd found on her return from Sacramento and ending with her discovery that Gary was totally broke. "How can I go out with someone like Brennan, when I have Gary living with me?" she concluded.

Nate made a sound of exasperation. "Are you in love with Gary?" he asked.

She shook her head. "I thought in the beginning that I wanted to be, but I just couldn't, he just doesn't . . ."

"Turn you on?"

She nodded miserably.

"And Brennan does?"

"For heaven's sake, Nate, I hardly know the man." As Nate continued to gaze at her, she hesitated, then nodded. "Okay. Yes, I do like Brennan Malone. He's a fine man, absolutely brilliant, he's working on the immune system and might even be able to . . ."

"Don't change the subject. Does he make your hormones gallop?"

"Nate!"

"Aha!" He leaned over and kissed her soundly on her burning cheek. "That's settled then. He turns you on. Now what do we do about Gary?" He pondered for a moment, narrowing his eyes and screwing up his face in a comical manner that made Emma laugh.

"Okay, here's what we do," he said. "You bring friend Gary in here tomorrow—no, tomorrow's Thursday and we're off—bring him in on Friday. Tell him I want a demonstration of his security system."

"Nate, you don't have to—"

"Don't interrupt, woman. I need a better system. Dr. Langley, the optometrist downstairs, got broken into a week ago. He had the same Mickey Mouse system we have right here. The thief broke the code before the alarm could go off. So I'll take a look at Gary's stuff, but believe me I won't buy it if I don't approve of it."

He slid off the desk and started for the door, then turned. "Also, on my way in this morning, I noticed a For Rent sign in the window of an apartment in that complex on the corner, next to the florist's shop. Should be pretty reasonable. Tell Gary to check it out. And call up Brennan and tell him you've changed your mind about dinner."

"I can't do that," Emma protested. "I promised Gary I'd be home."

"Okay then, call Brennan and tell him you're free tomorrow. He said he was off, remember?"

"But Nate..."

"Do it," he said, then came back to the desk and reached for the telephone. "On second thought, I'll do it. I want to call Maddy, anyway. I've been putting it off, in case she gave me the brush-off forever, but time is running out. Who knows, she might even be... Maddy?"

There was such delight in his voice that Emma studied his face very thoughtfully as he continued speaking. "You're still working tomorrow?" Disappointment washed over his face. "Yes, of course I understand— the Special Olympics, I remember. But how about Sunday? I know you are busy, but..."

Emma was surprised to see how tightly he was gripping the receiver. This young woman really mattered to him. "Well, it's just that I managed to get tickets for *Beach Blanket Babylon*, the revue that's been running forever. Yes, at the Club Fugazi. You have? Me, too. The tickets are for the matinee, I'm afraid, but I thought maybe afterward we could have dinner somewhere. Yes. Hey, that's great. I'll pick you up at two o'clock, then.''

He smiled brilliantly at Emma, his whole face lighted with pleasure and mischief, eyes shining more green than brown, as they did when he was truly happy.

Emma was so enthralled by this obviously smitten Nate that she almost forgot the other reason for his call until he said, "Brennan. Yes. Tell him Emma wants to talk to him. Emma Fieldstone, my office manager. He has, has he?" He cupped the receiver and winked at Emma. "He's been raving about you, how intelligent you are."

Emma's heart began to pound. When Nate handed her the receiver, her mouth was suddenly so dry that she could barely formulate words. "Emma?" Brennan said, sounding startled. "How nice of you to call. Please tell Nate I feel exceptionally well. The treatment really helped. I'll definitely call for another appointment as soon as I know my schedule. And I will do the exercises and use the cervical pillow."

"That's good, Brennan. I—I just called because I...well, I got to thinking. I wondered if..." She stopped, drew in a deep breath and tried again. This time she managed not to stammer. "I'm sorry I couldn't make dinner, but I am free tomorrow. I wondered if—"

"Splendid," Brennan said at once. "I've just been talking to the children, and we've decided to go kite flying tomorrow. Would you like to join us?"

"Kite flying?"

"I have an administration meeting in the morning, and of course the children will be in school, so we thought about four o'clock. May I pick you up? Afterward we thought we'd go to Fisherman's Wharf for dinner. Hannah and Adam are crazy about fish and chips."

"Oh. Yes. Sure. It sounds..."

"I have a pencil. I'm not too good on directions, I'm afraid, but Hannah is, as long as I write things down correctly."

She gave him careful directions to her apartment, then hung up and sat back in her chair, feeling stunned. "We're going kite flying," she told Nate. "Brennan and Hannah and Adam and I."

Nate groaned. "The impossible two out of the way and Maddy's working. It's not fair. God doesn't like me." He patted Emma's shoulder. "Sorry to be so selfish. It just seems ironic." He sighed. "Oh well, so it goes."

Emma turned to look up at him. "You don't suppose Brennan's just looking for a substitute for Maddy, do you?" she asked slowly. "I mean he is worried about losing Maddy, and going on past history, it's obvious I look like a patsy. Is he just wanting me for a baby-sitter?"

Nate shook his head. "I thought Maddy had a lousy self-image. Yours is even worse. Listen, Emma dear, you are a charming, caring woman. A lovely person. Brennan couldn't possibly fail to see that. He did ask you to dinner alone at first, remember?"

"That's true." Emma looked up at him with a wry smile. "All my life I've wanted to be a sex kitten, and all my life people have been saying I'm a lovely person. Kiss of death."

"It's not such a bad description, Emma."

"I know." She sighed, then glanced at him again, feeling mischievous. "One other thing, Nate," she said. "Don't be in too much of a hurry to follow my former suggestion. I'm suddenly not so sure it would be a good idea for Brennan and Georgia to get back together." She shook her head, her smile fading. "He's such a special sort of man, Nate. It seems too good to be true that he'd ask me out. I'm a little afraid...."

"Don't be. Live dangerously. Enjoy." He started for the door again, then turned and grinned at her. "One minor suggestion for tomorrow, Emma, as long as Hannah and Adam are going to be with you."

"What?" she asked.

"Wear something waterproof," he advised.

THEY WERE BEAUTIFUL CHILDREN, Emma thought—so cute in their blue jeans and matching blue T-shirts, with silky blond hair and large blue eyes that regarded her with an interest that was at first suspicious and then merely curious.

Though she had never had a problem getting along with children, she had been afraid after listening to Nate's stories that Hannah and Adam would be difficult. But evidently they did not regard her as a threat, which might be construed as either a compliment or an insult. In any case, after a few strained minutes in the car on the way to the park, they acted like any other eight- and seven-year-old recently freed from the classroom, chasing each other across the grass, somersaulting and doing handstands and generally showing off for Emma, while their father assembled the kite he'd bought earlier in the day.

The kite appeared to be giving Brennan a lot of trouble, and as it was unlike any Emma had ever seen, she was unable to offer suggestions, so she just watched him instead. It was a novelty to be out with a man who was not trying to pressure her into doing something she didn't want to do.

She had agonized over what to wear for the outing, knowing she'd have to wear pants, which were never her most flattering garment. Finally she had gone shopping in Macy's and come up with a pair of pleated jeans that made her waist and hips look relatively shapely. With a loose-fitting khaki cotton top and her beige Reeboks she felt she looked athletic and trim, born to fly a kite.

"Is there anything I can do?" she asked as Brennan swore under his breath.

"I can't figure out these handles," he said with a rueful grin.

Handles? She took a closer look at the kite. It was awfully big, she thought. And she didn't remember ever seeing a kite that had two strings attached to it. "I think you've got the handles backward," she said, eyeing the finger grips.

"So I have." He shot her a grateful glance that melted her right down into her Reeboks. In the sunlight, his eyes were *periwinkle* blue, she decided, definitely periwinkle, like the tablecloth she'd bought to go over the round nightstand in her bedroom. Her mind built a lightning fantasy of Brennan in her bedroom, standing beside the table with the cloth that matched his eyes, reaching for her....

"Can't you do it, Daddy?" Hannah asked impatiently.

"I'm getting there, honey," he said.

"What kind of kite is this?" Emma asked, eyeing the huge delta wing that Brennan was setting carefully on the ground.

Brennan stepped away from the kite, straightening out the strings, one eye on the instruction book he was holding in one hand.

"A Hawaiian stunt kite," he muttered. "The man in the store told me it was the latest craze. Expensive as hell."

"Let me do it, Daddy," Adam begged.

"In a minute," Brennan said, still walking backward. "I just have to figure out this part...."

"Nate talks about Hawaiian stunt kites," Emma said slowly, remembering. "He has one."

"You know Nate?" Hannah asked. "Nate Ludlow? Dr. Ludlow?"

Maybe she could do some public relations work for Nate here. "I sure do," she said warmly. "I work for him. He's a chiropractor, you know, a very good chiropractor. He's a wonderful man, kind and generous and funny. He makes me laugh all the time. He's one of my best friends."

Perhaps she was laying it on a bit thick. She glanced over at Brennan, who was still fiddling with the kite handles. "I'm trying to remember what Nate uses his Hawaiian stunt kite for," she murmured to Hannah. "There's something special he does with it." Suddenly alarmed, she yelled, "Brennan, I've just remembered Nate uses his kite to sand-ski. It's for experts only."

She was too late. Brennan had finally figured out how to get the kite off the ground. The wind caught it immediately and drove it up and forward. Before Emma could catch up with Brennan, he was being dragged across the grass, yelling, "Oh, my God, it's taking off with me!"

"Dig in your heels!" Emma yelled back, and he made a valiant effort to do so, but the kite was pulling his arms straight out from his body. He couldn't seem to stop.

Hannah and Adam were clapping and yelling with delight. "Help me grab hold of him!" Emma shouted at them, and they all ran to anchor Brennan's legs before he could be lifted off his feet. "Bring the kite straight up above you!" Emma called, suddenly remembering a movie she'd seen on television.

Brennan did so, the pressure slackened immediately and he was able to pull the kite down to the ground. He and the children and Emma collapsed into a thankful heap, all laughing hysterically.

"I do believe you saved my life, Emma," Brennan said when he caught his breath.

"We did too, Daddy!" Adam shouted happily.

"Yes, you did. My goodness, I thought I was going into orbit. I couldn't seem to let go." Brennan took off his glasses and wiped them with a pocket handkerchief, replaced them, then grinned at Emma. "I guess I bought the wrong kite, huh?"

"I would say so," she managed to gasp between bursts of laughter. She wasn't sure if her breathless state was due to laughing so much, running so much, or being so close to Brennan, who was now sitting next to her with an arm around her shoulders.

"You looked like Mary Poppins, Daddy," Hannah crowed.

"Peter Pan," Adam suggested.

Emma couldn't imagine what problem Nate could possibly have had with these delightful children.

"You suppose we should trade in this kite on another one?" she suggested.

"One *we* can fly," Hannah said firmly. "You sure are an airhead, Daddy. You should have taken me with you to buy the kite. That one isn't suitable at all."

"You were in school," Brennan protested. "And the man said . . ."

"Wouldn't you think the man could tell Daddy isn't athletic?" Hannah asked Emma, with a grin of complicity that delighted Emma's soul.

The man in the kite shop was at first reluctant to comply with the request. "You said you wanted something macho," he said reproachfully to Brennan.

Brennan blushed, which endeared him forever to Emma, a frequent victim of embarrassment. "I wanted to impress you," he admitted with a shy grin.

"You impressed me the moment I met you," she said warmly.

The new kite was much smaller, but made satisfyingly swooshing noises, and Hannah and Adam had a great time flying it. Afterward they ate fish and chips with English malt vinegar at the wharf, and as they drove home, Emma felt happier than she had in a long time.

The children were asleep in the back seat, leaning against each other, their faces flushed, their silky blond eyelashes spread like miniature fans.

"Hannah and Adam liked you, Emma, I could tell," Brennan said softly as he stopped outside her apartment building. "Adam likes everyone, of course, but Hannah is usually difficult with new people."

"So I've heard," Emma murmured.

"Nate?" He laughed. "Maddy told me about that. Poor Nate, I doubt he's crazy about my children. But Hannah responded to you immediately. That's quite rare." He looked earnestly at Emma. "It's your warmth, I suppose. You have this incredible aura that—" He broke off, looking embarrassed again. "It was nice, seeing the children so happy. I don't spend enough time with them, I'm afraid. Since Georgia left..."

"It must be difficult for you without your wife," Emma said sympathetically. "Nate told me what happened."

This time he looked at her *very* earnestly. "People tend to blame Georgia, you know, but most of it was my fault. I hadn't taken Georgia's ambition into account, you see. I hadn't realized that her compulsion to pursue a singing career was as strong as mine for my work. I dismissed her singing as a hobby. I was the complete chauvinist, I'm afraid, concerned only with my work, my comfort...and all the time Georgia was churning away inside. It's not surprising that she left me. It's surprising that she stayed around as long as she did."

"But the children—"

"Georgia just literally had no idea how to be a mother," he said slowly. "She does love the children, there's no doubt about that, just as the children love her, but her compulsion to sing is greater than her maternal instincts."

What about *his* love for Georgia? Emma wondered. Would he make all these excuses for her if he didn't still love her?

He shook his head. "I can't imagine why I've bored you with all this. I'm not usually so loquacious. I think you must be an unusually good listener."

His smile did all kinds of damage to her equilibrium. "I had a very nice time, Emma," he said.

"Me, too."

For a moment she thought he was going to kiss her. There was the slightest movement of his head toward her, then he checked himself, pushed up his glasses on his nose and smiled shyly instead. "May I see you again? I have an awful lot of stuff to do in the lab this week, but maybe next weekend? No, that's Easter. Maddy has plans for the children. I'm supposed to do something or other with them. It may be the week after."

"Anytime is fine," she said wholeheartedly.

"I like to go sometimes to Shakespeare in the park. It gets me outdoors. Would you like that?"

"I'd love it." She'd have said the same to beer at Napper Tandy's or sushi at Kinokawa.

"I'll call you, then."

"Great."

It didn't occur to her that he might call when she was out.

CHAPTER SEVEN

NATE STEPPED BACK from the table and decided he was well satisfied with his arrangements. The table itself, an octagonal sheet of glass that seemed to float on a marble pedestal, fitted perfectly into the bay window, surrounded by the banquette of softest dove-gray leather. He'd used burgundy place mats, gray enameled flatware, white china rimmed with silver, plain but elegant crystal that would catch the light from the candles. The fondue pot was in place, along with the cooking forks, the beef was marinating in the refrigerator, the wine cooling and the romaine crisping, ready for him to impressively toss the Caesar salad at the table.

Mrs. Oliphant, his weekly lady, had cleaned the condo until it shone. His king-size bed was made up with fresh linens, a lone lamp burning dimly beside it.

For a moment he toyed with the idea of pulling down the pleated shades on the bay window for intimacy, but decided that the view of the Golden Gate Bridge, especially later when it was lighted, would be infinitely more romantic.

Yes, the stage was set. All he needed was Madeleine Scott to complete the picture.

In the shower, soaping vigorously, aware of a feeling of delighted anticipation, he tried to figure out why he had decided to feed Maddy with his own two hands. It had always been his custom to take dates out to dinner in town. Afterward, if everything went well, he would escort the young woman to her home, hoping to be invited in. Not that seduction was always the outcome. Some of his friends, he knew, would be surprised at how seldom Nate Ludlow pursued romance to a sexual conclusion. He enjoyed women, loved women, but he was not a promiscuous man. However, by following his cautious scenario, he was always in control of his comings and goings, always in control of the course of the relationship.

During several of his longer-lasting relationships, he had learned that it was wiser to keep his home sacrosanct. Particularly after Leonie, the woman who had carried jealousy to an extreme of possessiveness. The memories of the times Leonie had let herself into the condo and waited in the dark, brooding, for him to come home were still vivid and appalling, as were the accusations and insults she had slung at him with such venom.

Drying himself with one of his favorite huge terry towels, he wondered again how he had failed to see Leonie's psychotic nature from the beginning.

He shook his head. He was not, repeat not, going to think about past mistakes today. Today was for Madeleine, his mystery lady. As for tonight—ah, *tonight* he and the enchanting Madeleine were finally going to be alone.

MADDY GLANCED at the mantel clock for the hundredth time in the last hour. One-fifty, and Kat had still not arrived. It wasn't like her to be late—she had never let Maddy down before. Once more she went into the hall and dialed Kat's number. No answer. She'd already tried every other baby-sitter she'd ever used,

without success. She had even called her three closest
friends, though normally she hated to impose on them.
Two of them were out and the third was "entertaining" at home, with no desire to be chaperoned by Hannah and Adam.

Nate would be here in less than ten minutes, and she
had no idea what she was going to do. Her jaw was beginning to hurt. She made a conscious effort to relax.

"You look pretty, Maddy," Adam said as she walked
back into the living room and looked at the clock again.
He and Hannah were sitting side by side on one of the
sofas that bracketed the fireplace, reading quietly, obviously aware that Maddy's nerves were stretched to the
breaking point and they'd better not misbehave.

"Is that a new dress?" Hannah asked.

Maddy nodded. She rarely bought dresses—working
at the zoo certainly didn't call for them, and at home
she usually wore blue jeans or sweats. She had intended wearing the yellow jumpsuit that Nate had said
made her look like a daffodil, but then last evening,
when she had taken the children out for *gelato* at the
Cannery, she had seen this pale turquoise cotton with
the fashionable flounce around the hips in the window
of a small boutique, and had made the mistake of trying
it on. The salesgirl had been lavish with compliments,
and even Maddy had to admit that the style was feminine and flattering, and that the color against her
tanned skin made her eyes shine and her hair glow like
brown satin.

She wanted to look good for Nate Ludlow. That in
itself was surprising, as she usually dressed for comfort
and to please herself. She had no patience with women
who felt they had to make themselves over, in order to
attract a man. Nevertheless, while looking at her trans-

formed self in the boutique's dressing-room mirror, she had visualized the approval in Nate Ludlow's eyes and hadn't hesitated, even when she learned the price. She had even taken her precious pearl necklace and earrings, which her parents had brought her from Japan, from their little brocade envelope, knowing they would enhance her appearance even further.

And now she wasn't sure she would be going out at all.

A few minutes later the doorbell rang. Hoping it would be Kat, but sure it would be Nate, she ran to open the door.

He looked wonderful. What a gorgeous man he was. Whether he was in cutoffs and sweatshirt, a wet suit, Brennan's too-small clothing, or dressed as he was now in a beige silk sport coat and brown pants, with an off-white shirt, he looked magnificent.

The approval in his eyes was even more evident than she'd imagined. "The Club Fugazi will never be the same again," he murmured, then kissed her gently on the lips. He smelled wonderfully clean. She liked the fact that he never seemed to use any kind of cologne or after-shave. Whatever kind of soap he used was enough—fresh as a spring breeze, with just a tang of lemon underneath.

"Are we all set?" he asked.

Maddy took a deep breath. "I have a problem, I'm afraid. Kat didn't show up."

She saw the implications of that register in his eyes. "Brennan?" he said hopefully.

"He's working on a new method of growing specific antibodies in the laboratory, in tissue culture. It could be a very important breakthrough."

"Okay. No Brennan. We certainly can't ask him to leave that. There's no one else, I take it." He was beginning to look grim.

"I'm afraid not. I've tried everyone I can think of." She suddenly realized that they were still standing in the doorway. "I'm sorry, Nate. You can at least come in."

"At least? The theater is definitely out, then?"

Maddy felt every bit as disappointed as he looked. As she led the way into the living room, she explained again that Kat just hadn't turned up, and she hadn't been able to reach her.

"This isn't just an excuse is it, Maddy?" he asked abruptly. "You didn't decide at the last moment you'd rather not—?"

"I really want to see that show," she interrupted indignantly. "I wanted to see you. I had no idea Kat wouldn't turn up. She's never done such a thing before. Perhaps you could find someone else to use my ticket," she added lamely.

"Hello, Dr. Ludlow," Hannah said politely.

"Hannah. Adam." Nate smiled at both children, but there was a definite edge to the smile. "I don't want to take someone else," he said firmly to Madeleine. "We'll just have to see what we can do." He thought for a moment, then said, "My first inclination is to beat my head several times against the wall over there, but failing that, I do have an idea that might rescue the day. May I use your telephone?"

Maddy nodded toward the hall, hoping he didn't intend bringing in some strange baby-sitter. She wasn't about to leave Hannah and Adam with someone they didn't know. It wasn't their fault Kat hadn't shown up.

"All set," Nate said a couple of minutes later, coming back into the living room. "The friend who got the tickets for me originally has arranged for two more for the children. They'll be waiting at the club for us."

"We get to go with you?" Adam exclaimed, jumping up.

Hannah looked pleased, too. "We have to change," she said to Adam. "We can't go in jeans. Come on."

The afternoon was suddenly transformed. Maddy smiled gratefully at Nate. "You're sure you don't mind? This is so nice of you. The children have wanted to see the show, too. They love going to the theater. What a nice thing for you to do."

"I'm a nice person," Nate said softly, coming closer. "I'm also dry. We both are. Perhaps we should take advantage of the fact."

Without consciously moving forward, Maddy was suddenly in his arms, being kissed most thoroughly and arousingly. He really was good at this, she thought. There was no sudden thrust of tongue, no painful grinding of teeth against teeth, which some men seemed to think constituted a show of desire, just this soft brushing movement of his lips against hers, a delicate teasing that brought heat rising from low in her body to tighten her flesh with wanting.

Even as she thought this, the pressure of his mouth increased in a subtle way and she felt the first touch of his tongue, gentle but persistent. It seemed the most natural thing in the world to let her lips part, and almost at once the whole tenor of the kiss changed. The pain in her jaw had completely disappeared. Her mouth was moving just as hungrily as was his, her breath was mingling with his, her own tongue seeking, searching, matching his for haste.

Her arms were around him, her hands somehow under his jacket, feeling the strength and heat of his body through the cotton shirt, feeling the ridged muscles of his back, the curve of his waist, while his hands moved over her with infinite gentleness, stroking her back, moving up under her arms to cup her breasts, his hands hard and strong through the thin cotton of her dress. She felt her nipples respond instantly to his touch, aching as though they had waited hungrily for this moment, becoming hard immediately, as hard as that other part of him that was pressing urgently against her as she tightened her arms and pulled him close.

The clattering of feet in the hall sent them jerking apart, both breathing heavily, staring at each other with surprise that was indisputably edged with delight. His eyes were green as a cat's, brimming with mischief, his smile crooked and amused. "Well, now, Maddy," he said with deep satisfaction in the second before the children exploded into the room.

"Your face is all red, Maddy," Hannah said suspiciously, coming to a halt.

"I had a sneezing fit," Maddy lied with an apologetic glance at Nate.

"Definitely a fit of some kind," he murmured, his gaze meeting hers with such wicked innocence that she found it difficult to breathe.

THE REVUE WAS WONDERFUL. Maddy had heard stories about *Beach Blanket Babylon* for years. Overflowing with zany comedy, it had been running for fourteen years through several incarnations—Beach Blanket Babylon Goes Bananas, Goes to the Stars, Goes to the Prom and now, Beach Blanket Babylon Goes around the World—featuring a host of famous and infamous international characters from the past and present, most of them wearing spectacularly towering headpieces.

The children were entranced. So were Maddy and Nate as the fast, flashy revue delivered hilarious songs and dances. The story was a slight one, dealing with a young woman named Dorothy searching throughout England, France, Italy and the Orient for love with a view to marriage, but the thin plot didn't seem to matter at all.

During the intermission, Maddy was startled to see a young woman approach Nate at their front-row table. She was about Maddy's height, but there all resemblance ended. She was a dynamically beautiful brunette with glossy dark waves curving around her exquisitely made-up face, wearing a high fashion suit of heavy white silk with an outrageously short skirt and long loose jacket. "Nate, darling," she murmured in a husky voice that literally oozed sex.

Nate stood up, obviously feeling awkward, almost knocking over the small table. "Teddie!" he exclaimed. "I didn't know you were going to be here."

"I'm not. I just got off work half an hour ago, and I'm having a late lunch with a friend at the Ristorante Griffone. Halfway through I decided I couldn't stand it any longer. I had to pop in here and see this situation for myself." She glanced at Maddy and the children with a smile of utmost goodwill, edged with just a little malice. "It's really true, a domesticated Nate Ludlow. Wonders will never cease."

She held out her right hand to Maddy and shook hands with a firm, steady grip. "I'm Teddie Darcy. I was so astonished when Nate asked for tickets for two children that I couldn't resist checking up on him. I hope you'll excuse me." She smiled sweetly at Hannah and Adam. "Are you enjoying the show?"

They both nodded vigorously without speaking, evidently rendered speechless by the gracious beauty who was smiling down at them. Maddy felt stunned. Who was this woman to call Nate darling in such an intimate tone of voice? Had she owned the wet suit Nate had loaned her?

None of your business, Maddy Scott, she chided herself, but all the same she was conscious of a white-hot shaft of jealousy that stayed with her long after Teddie had swayed languorously away. The image of Teddie patting Nate's cheek and murmuring, "Call me, darling, I've missed you," also showed no signs of fading.

"I didn't think to thank your friend for getting the tickets," she whispered to Nate during one of the quieter periods of the revue.

"I'll thank her for you," he said.

She darted a glance at him, startled by the grim sound of his voice. He was annoyed that Teddie had come, she realized. Why? Because he didn't want Maddy to know he was acquainted with other women?

"A close friend?" she found herself asking.

"Not anymore," he said lightly.

She had never experienced jealousy before. It made her look at Nate in a new light. Somehow he had managed to become important to her. Was that good, or was she being stupid, laying herself open to hurt, making herself vulnerable?

"Was it Teddie's wet suit you borrowed for me?" she asked.

He laughed explosively, covering his mouth with one hand to smother the sound. "No way you'd ever get Teddie involved in outdoor activities," he said when he recovered his breath. "She's the original hothouse flower."

"Then where *did* you get the wet suit?" she asked, hating herself for asking, but needing to know.

He didn't answer for a moment, then said with obvious reluctance, "I bought it for you."

"You bought it!"

"Shh," someone hissed behind them, and Maddy sat back in her seat, feeling mortified. For a while she stared at the stage unseeingly. She just couldn't believe Nate had gone to all that trouble and expense just for her—was he really telling the truth?

She suddenly realized that one of the young actors was singing quite close to her. As a matter of fact, he was singing *directly* to her. She stared up at him in amazement, as he held her gaze and crooned a love song. Was this part of the act? If so, it was an embarrassment. People in the club were craning their necks, trying to see who was getting all the attention. Maddy began to feel more and more embarrassed, especially when the song ended and the young man, though he moved upstage and did a little dance with the leading lady, still managed to keep glancing her way.

"I think you've made a conquest," Nate whispered.

Maddy looked quickly at the children, but they were gazing at the stage in such awe and such delight that it was obvious they hadn't noticed the young man's attentions. She felt rather than saw Nate follow her gaze. "Rapt, would you say?" he murmured.

She nodded and they exchanged glances that were almost those of a proud father and mother. From time to time after that she caught Nate watching the children's upturned faces, looking very thoughtful. Their attention didn't waver for a second, not until the last number that featured the lead singer in a hat bearing a model of the island of Manhattan. Both Hannah and Adam burst into spontaneous applause as the lights in the skyscrapers came on, their faces shining with absolute rapture.

"Children are so...impressionable," Nate said as they left their seats and joined the crush in the aisle. "I'd forgotten how new everything is to them. All the old clichés and trite situations that make adults feel so jaded seem fresh and original to them. You really enjoyed it a lot, didn't you?" he said to Hannah and Adam.

"Oh, yes," Hannah breathed. "And did you see, Maddy? The boy with the blond hair kept looking at me when he sang. I'm going to date a boy like him one day."

"Not till you're sixteen," Maddy warned.

Nate laughed softly. "He was after Hannah all the time? And there I was, raging with jealousy."

Surprised, Maddy exclaimed, "You, too?" before she realized she was giving herself away.

Nate glanced at her swiftly as they came to a halt in the logjam near the exit. "Teddie?" he asked with obvious disbelief. "You were jealous of Teddie?"

"She's so...stunning," she said apologetically.

He shook his head. "Don't you worry about Teddie," he said.

"I've always wanted to look like that," she murmured. "So amazingly beautiful, the kind of woman who turns men's heads."

He grinned wryly. "You're talking *envy* now. You don't need to be envious of any woman, Maddy Scott. You turn my head for sure, especially when you smile the way you do."

She smiled at him.

"Yeah, like that," he said.

She was feeling remarkably happy, she realized. The show had exceeded expectation, the children had behaved well, and she was already forgetting Teddie. "I was jealous, Nate," she confessed. "But only for a minute. Jealousy is such a childish emotion, and I'm just not the type to eat my heart out over anyone's old... *friends.* I'm too sensible for that, I hope."

He grinned. "Thank God for that, Maddy. I have to admit I've been feeling pangs myself, however, not only today when that precocious infant was singing at you, but even about Brennan. And I despise jealousy." He suddenly sounded quite fierce and evidently realized it. He shrugged apologetically and said, "I was involved a few years ago with a woman named Leonie, who made the other woman in *Fatal Attraction*—the one played by Glenn Close—look like an understanding sweetheart."

Maddy had seen the movie, had thought it stretched belief, but had been convinced and repelled by the possessiveness that motivated the woman's pursuit of Michael Douglas. "Did you love her?" she asked softly.

He looked bleak. "For a while, until she changed character on me. Served me right, I guess, I forgot my own rule. We went out for nearly ten months, far too long." He gazed at her. "You aren't going to change character on me are you, Maddy?"

It was the first time she had sensed that he could be insecure. The troubled expression in his eyes was very endearing. She shook her head. "I'll probably go right on being maddening Madeleine," she said with a laugh.

And then the people in the doorway were finally able to move, and they managed to make their way down the steps to the sidewalk outside. Hannah and Adam held on to Maddy's hands. "Thank you so much, Nate," Maddy said. "That was a great experience."

He looked alarmed. "Oh, no, you don't," he protested. "You're not running out on me now. I've got dinner all ready to go at my condo." He glanced down at Hannah and Adam's upturned faces. "Could we try Kat again, do you suppose?"

Maddy nodded, but when she called Kat, there was still no answer.

"I may have a nervous breakdown," Nate said.

"You can drop us off at home," Hannah said stiffly. "I can fix hot dogs for Adam and me. We'll be fine by ourselves."

It was Adam's turn to look alarmed, but his expression changed to one of relief when Nate said, "No way, Hannah. Not until you're sixteen."

Hannah shot him a mutinous look, but Adam laughed and Maddy thought, well, at least *he's* coming to appreciate Nate's humor. All the same, as she waited for Nate to bring the car around, she began to worry about taking the children to Nate's condo. But not as worried as she might have been, had she been going there alone, she conceded, as Nate drove up his Audi in front of them, and she and the children climbed aboard.

NATE HAD OBVIOUSLY GONE to a great deal of trouble planning the meal and setting the table. Even while Maddy was exclaiming over the view of Golden Gate Bridge, she was imagining how romantic it would have been to cook fondued meat alone with Nate at this pretty table, in this window, with this view. Nate's disappointment was almost palpable. So was hers. But there was certainly nothing to be done.

"I could cut up some vegetables and add the meat and make a stew," Nate suggested when she looked doubtfully at the fondue pot. "Somehow the idea of Hannah and Adam dipping chunks of beef into boiling oil doesn't exactly thrill me."

She nodded. "That would probably be best," she agreed.

At Nate's invitation, she looked around the condo while he went to work. It was a lovely place, three-storied, with a garage and utility rooms on the ground floor, living room, kitchen, two bathrooms, master bedroom and study on the main floor, two guest rooms and another bathroom above. Very luxurious, all burgundy and gray, with the softest leather upholstery imaginable—masculine, but no less attractive for all that. The dim light in the master bedroom didn't escape her attention, and one look at the king-size bed, so invitingly piled with pillows, made her realize that Nate had planned the evening very carefully. Poor Nate. He was beginning to learn that when you had children to care for, even the best-laid plans quite frequently went up in smoke.

The children were happily playing Go Fish in Nate's study. Nate was still puttering in the kitchen. Maddy allowed herself a few moments of looking at that king-size bed and imagining what it would be like to be in it with Nate Ludlow.

She'd had two lovers in her life—one the man she'd thought she was going to marry when she was twenty years old. She had thought then that lovemaking was fairly pleasant, but a very awkward, uncomfortable business altogether. She hadn't changed her opinion during the months of her engagement to Brad, and had been surprised whenever her sister Georgia raved about how wonderful sex was. Sex was all right, Maddy had thought, once the initial pain was over. It wasn't something she'd ever refuse to do with the man she loved, but it wasn't something she'd volunteer to do, either.

The engagement had ended without recrimination on either side, when she and Brad had found themselves wanting to go out with a crowd of friends all the time, rather than spending time alone as an engaged couple surely should. Every Friday and Saturday night they had gone out to eat and dance with four other couples, married couples older than themselves, often dancing with each other only once during the course of an evening. Eventually they had confessed to each other that they were bored with this constant social round, but didn't particularly want to go back to being a twosome. They'd continued for a while, then Maddy's fiancé had found someone he did want to be alone with all the time—one of the wives in their group. In the resulting furor, Maddy had been the only one who wasn't horrified and shocked. Her primary feeling had been one of relief.

Her second lover had come along shortly before Georgia took off to pursue her career. He had professed himself in love with Maddy, and she had felt she was coming to love him. Sex with Jonathan had been more than pleasant. He had been more considerate than Brad, and had made sure Maddy had time to savor some of the delights of lovemaking. But just as she was beginning to think Georgia might have been right about sex after all, she had inherited the children, and Jonathan had decamped very rapidly. Until now she hadn't met anyone else who even remotely interested her sexually.

I wish Kat hadn't let me down, she reflected, and immediately felt guilty, because the thought implied that she didn't want to be burdened by the children, and that was far from the truth. No, she should be honest with herself. Of course there were times when she didn't want the children around; even a married mother with kids wanted time to herself sometimes, it was only natural, only human, and tonight Maddy Scott felt very human indeed.

The stew was delicious, fragrant with herbs, accompanied by crusty French rolls and a Caesar salad that Nate tossed in a manic imitation of a French chef, making the children laugh.

As they ate, the children chatted about *Beach Blanket Babylon*, and the atmosphere was light and happy and relaxed. Afterward, Hannah and Adam went back to Nate's study to watch their all-time favorite movie, *The Wizard of Oz,* which Nate happened to have in his video collection, and Maddy and Nate finally watched D. W. Griffith's *Abraham Lincoln* on the living-room television set. Starring Walter Huston, Una Merkel and Kay Hammond, the biographical drama seemed definitely outdated in terms of technique, but very interesting, all the same.

Sitting with her on the soft leather sofa, Nate held Maddy's hand throughout the entire ninety-seven minutes. She was amazed at how much feeling could come through a hand. It was as though their palms shared the same system of arteries and veins, as though the same blood flowed through from one to the other. By the time the movie drew to a close, she was filled with a nameless wanting that she was afraid to analyze.

Just as the movie ended, Adam came into the room, looking unmistakably guilty. His round face was usually so transparent that it was impossible for him to cover up any wrongdoing. "What have you been up to?" Maddy demanded as Nate switched on the lights.

"Watching the movie," he said innocently. "I don't like the part in the forest where the trees come to life, Maddy. I wish they'd take out that part. I don't like the monkeys, either. I do like the Wicked Witch of the West, though. She's such a *nasty* old witch."

He was talking more than usual, always a bad sign. "Adam?" Maddy inquired.

"You mean in the kitchen?" he asked. "We weren't doing anything."

"You were in the kitchen?"

Nate had already left the room. Maddy jumped up, grabbed Adam's hand and dragged him with her. Nate was taking cans out of a lower cabinet, lining them up on the tiled counter. In the trash bin Maddy could see, as Nate had evidently seen, a pile of labels twisted together. Every can that Nate was lining up had had its label removed.

"Hannah!" Maddy shouted.

Hannah appeared in the doorway, rubbing her eyes. "Was this your idea?" Maddy asked.

Hannah had never been a devious child. When she was caught out, she always confessed quickly. Tonight was no exception. She nodded, then looked defiantly from Nate to Maddy.

"Why?" Maddy demanded.

Hannah shrugged.

"Just for fun, Maddy," Adam said. "We thought it would be fun after, trying to guess what was in each can."

Maddy quelled him with a look. "We're going home," she said sternly. "First you apologize again to

Dr. Ludlow, then we're going home. There we will decide what your punishment will be. You should be ashamed of yourselves. Dr. Ludlow gave you a lovely afternoon at the theater, cooked you a great dinner and this is how you repay him. *I'm* certainly ashamed of you. We are going to have to leave right away."

"I'm sorry, Dr. Ludlow," Adam said. "Would you like me to glue the labels back on? I think I can guess which ones go where."

"Don't be silly, Adam," Hannah said with great disdain. "You wouldn't have a clue where to start. Nobody would."

"I might," Adam said, sounding close to tears. "We shouldn't have done any of it, Hannah."

"I know, Adam."

There was a note of satisfaction in Hannah's voice that really disturbed Maddy. "You haven't apologized to Nate, Hannah," she pointed out.

"I'm sorry," Hannah said with a sharp glance at Nate, in which no apology was apparent.

About to remonstrate with the little girl, Maddy suddenly realized that Adam had said they shouldn't have done *any* of it. Which implied more than one mischief. That thought immediately gave birth to another, and she stared at Hannah in horror. "What do you know about Kat not coming over today?" she demanded.

One look at Hannah's suddenly pale face, and she knew she was right on target. "Hannah?"

Hannah's head hung low.

"What did you do? Did you call her?"

Hannah nodded, her lone braid bobbing. The back of her neck looked vulnerable, small-boned and delicate as a baby's. Little Girl Lost, fighting to keep her world intact. Fighting to keep out all intruders. All the same ... Maddy hardened her heart. "Tell me, Hannah."

"I told Kat that Daddy had the day off and would take care of us himself," Hannah said to the gray-carpeted floor. "She said that was great. Rocko had asked her to go with him on his motorcycle to some kind of fair in Oakland. It was going to be a blast, she said."

Nate hadn't said a word so far, Maddy realized. He must be very angry. Then she looked at him and saw he was fighting laughter. She darted a furious glance at him. He must not laugh, or Hannah and Adam would think they could get away with anything.

He made a determined effort and straightened his face. "Don't take it to heart, Maddy. We all had a good time at the show, and as far as the labels are concerned, I can open a can a day and eat whatever's in it. It'll be an adventure. Please don't leave. Every time you get mad at Hannah and Adam, either I leave or you leave. We're letting their mischief come between us."

"I'm sorry, Nate," she said as evenly as she could manage. "I had a lovely day, but I'm going to have to take the children home. I'm really furious with them and I do apologize for their barbaric behavior, but there's more to this than mischief. I need to have a long talk with them." She hesitated, wondering if she should explain to him what was at stake here, but decided he probably wouldn't understand. "I really am sorry I have to go," she added softly.

"Me, too," he said, sounding exasperated.

Looking beyond him, she saw at the end of the hall the open door to the bedroom, the dim light glowing in there, the edge of the king-size bed. Sighing, she turned away, herding the now very subdued children ahead of her to the front door.

"I'll call you," Nate said behind her. She was so choked with disappointment and frustration that she couldn't speak.

NATE CHANGED out of his suit into a pair of tan shorts before starting to clean up the dishes. It took him the best part of an hour to get everything put away and the movies rewound, which gave him plenty of time to think. He found himself remembering his own adventure with canned food. Shortly after his mother had remarried, he had placed two cans of tomatoes in the oven. Some time after his mother had turned the oven on to Preheat, the cans exploded, the oven door blasted open and tomatoes flew in all directions. He had been in the doghouse for days. His stepfather had had to repaint the entire kitchen.

At the time he hadn't been able to explain to his mother why he'd done such a stupid thing, but he had figured out years later that he was simply looking for attention. Since the advent of his stepfather, the wonderfully close, loving relationship he and his mother had enjoyed after his father's death had suffered a tremendous change. His two little stepsisters had demanded all her attention, which was natural enough since they were barely out of diapers. Not only that; his stepfather had seemed to think he could replace his father. There had been no resemblance. His father had been an indulgent, easygoing buddy—Joe was a disciplinarian who expected a boy to keep his room clean, his homework caught up, the lawn mowed. At the time he hadn't appreciated the good habits he was learning, but had simply rebelled.

Dropping the place mats into the laundry bin in the utility room, he suddenly stood very still as light fi-

nally dawned. Hannah and Adam were doing exactly
the same thing—looking for attention. Yet he hadn't
really *interfered* in their lives. So there must be more to
it than that.

He could swear they'd enjoyed themselves this afternoon. Those rapt, upturned little faces had moved him
tremendously. Such unmistakable pleasure could not
possibly have been faked. So what had gone wrong?

Abruptly an image of Hannah's pinched little face
flashed into his mind. Maddy had insisted that Hannah confess, and the child had looked triumphant, yet
indisputably frightened. Not frightened of Maddy—he
couldn't imagine Maddy's punishment ever being of the
physical kind. They weren't frightened of him, either.
No, those two little kids were afraid he was going to take
Maddy away from them, just as he had been afraid his
mother was lost to him when Joe arrived on the scene.
In a way, his mother *had* been lost to him; he'd had to
learn to share her, and it had taken him months to learn
how to do that.

The doorbell interrupted his musing, and he ran up
the stairs two at a time, hoping. . . .

She was standing on the front porch, still wearing the
turquoise cotton dress, although a chill evening breeze
was wafting off the ocean, tossing her glossy hair and
making her shiver. Under the porch light her face was
very solemn. She was alone.

"I just had to come back to apologize in person,
Nate," she said all in one breath. "Kat still wasn't in,
but I managed to reach Brennan at the lab and he came
home. I'm so sorry. You must have been furious. And
anyway, I didn't even thank you for buying the wet suit.
I thought you'd borrowed it, what a lovely thing for you
to do. And after all that, the children had to behave so

badly. I just couldn't let it go overnight without at least trying to—'' She broke off, looking at him nervously.

"It's okay, Maddy," he said, ushering her into the living room, trying not to show how elated he felt to have an apologetic Maddy here—alone. "There's no need for any apologies, unless they come from me. I've been blind as a bat, I'm afraid. I didn't figure out what was going on until the moment before you arrived. I should have realized before. I know exactly how Hannah and Adam feel.''

She looked surprised. "You do?"

He nodded, waved her to a sofa, then sat down beside her. "When I was ten, my adored mother remarried," he explained. "I treated my stepfather in much the same way Hannah and Adam are treating me. I hated Joe for months for stealing my mother away from me. I'd had her to myself for three years, you see, since my father died. The children are terrified of losing you, of course. Considering their past history, that's hardly surprising. They've obviously reached the conclusion that the best way to keep you is to drive any interested male away. You knew that all along, I'm sure. It must have happened before."

She was silent for a full minute, looking at him in her usual direct way. Then she sighed. "No, Nate. Actually, it hasn't. I haven't really brought anyone around as I have you. I haven't dated much since Georgia left. All I had to do was mention the children and, well, few men want to get involved in a situation like mine."

There was something scary about her statement that she hadn't brought anyone else around. Something satisfying, too. Those men, whoever they had been, had missed a hell of a lot in not getting to know Maddy Scott.

"I'm so glad you understand what's going on with the children, Nate," she added warmly. "I didn't think you did."

"I'm slow on the uptake sometimes. Question is, where do we go from here?"

"I've been thinking, too. I just hate to see the children so threatened. Their welfare has to come first with me, Nate. I think perhaps it would be best if—"

"No," he said abruptly, startled by the bleakness he could sense waiting for him if he let her finish. "You can't let them manipulate you, Maddy. It wouldn't be good for them." He paused. "I'm also selfish enough to want what's good for us, too. We have something very special going between us. You may have noticed."

"I've noticed." She glanced downward, her eyelashes dropping demurely, then she smiled wanly. "Do you suppose you could put some clothes on, Nate? This is very distracting."

He'd totally forgotten he was only wearing a pair of shorts. He often ran around the condo this way. It was comfortable.

He grinned. "I'm not sure I mind you being distracted, Maddy. I intended for you to be distracted this evening." He touched her cheek and groaned. "I had such plans for you, Madeleine Scott."

"What exactly did you have in mind?" she asked, feeling suddenly mischievous.

"Exactly? Let me set the stage for you." He stood up and walked over to the elaborate stereo system that was housed in glass and walnut cabinets against the wall. Picking up a tape, he inserted it into the cassette player, then turned to smile at her. "Imagine I'm still fully dressed, okay?"

"I'll try."

"We've been to the theater, right? And we've lingered over our wonderful fondued beef, with the most delicious sauces to dip the meat in."

"The stew was good," she pointed out.

"But with fondue you can feed each other choice morsels, like the sultans of old and their concubines."

"Ah. This was a very well-orchestrated plan."

"Down to the last sugared grape."

"Which we have now consumed? And the music begins? What is it to be? Rudolph Valentino and his famous tango from the *Four Horsemen of the Apocalypse*, complete with burning eyes and heaving bosoms?"

He shook his head. "Not subtle enough." He turned on the tape player and held out a hand to her. "Come here, woman," he said.

She came to him and he took her into his arms in proper dance position. "Hang on a second," she said, and kicked off her shoes. "I'm afraid I might stab your feet with my heels," she explained.

"Thoughtful of you," he said and pulled her head close to his bare shoulder.

It was a moment more before she recognized the music. The theme from *Picnic*. William Holden and Kim Novak had danced to that tune, outside under the stars with several other people watching. In Maddy's opinion it had been one of the greatest love scenes in music history—two beautiful people looking into each other's eyes, moving slowly together, just as she and Nate were moving now, not really dancing, just letting their bodies touch lightly, part, then touch again. She was trembling, she realized.

His arm tightened around her. "Are you still distracted?" he asked.

"Madly." She laughed softly, her breath fluttering against his smooth bare skin, then coming back to her. "You are an impossible romantic, Nate Ludlow."

"No, I'm not. I'm a very possible romantic. Try me."

She sighed. It was time to be practical again. "I told Brennan I'd be back in an hour, Nate. He wants to return to the lab. And anyway, this thing with you and me . . . it scares me, Nate. I'm afraid I'll start resenting the children for not letting me—" She broke off. "I really do think that the best thing—"

"No," he interrupted again, kissing her urgently to stop the words from coming out. "What we have to do first is find out exactly what we have. Maybe we'll find out it's not enough to warrant all this upset. But somehow I doubt that." He hesitated, then decided it was time to take the plunge—all or nothing—one throw on the roulette wheel. "Is there any possibility you could get away for a whole weekend?" he asked evenly. "Next weekend, perhaps?"

She moved back out of his arms, her dark eyes fixed on his face. There was another silence, longer this time, broken only by the low murmur of the music. Was it a shocked silence? Had he been too blunt? He wasn't sure. Maddy was no fool. She had to know he was asking her to go to bed with him. He had seen her look into his bedroom earlier, and had seen the knowledge of what he'd planned flare in her face. He hadn't seen any distaste follow, and knew without any doubt that she was sexually responsive to him; he'd had proof enough of that. However, that didn't necessarily mean she was ready to go all the way.

"I usually work either Saturday or Sunday or both, Nate," she said, still watching his face. "Zoos don't close on weekends. And next weekend is Easter, one of our big ones. If I have any free time at all, I have to be with the children. I've promised them an egg hunt, and I'm going to bring Annie Rose home for a couple of days. You remember Annie Rose? The rabbit?''

''Vividly.'' He also remembered the touch of Maddy's hands on his as they'd held the rabbit. He had thought about that moment often. He took her hands in his now and looked at them. Slender hands, long tapering fingers, short unpolished nails. He'd never realized before how much he disliked the long painted talons so many women favored. He lifted her hands and kissed each palm slowly and delicately, making her tremble again. ''How about the weekend after Easter then?'' he asked. ''Don't you have any sick time due, vacation time, something? Anything?''

This time the silence was even longer. The music was still playing softly, but they were no longer moving to it.

''I'll work it out somehow,'' she said, taking him completely by surprise. He'd thought that she would at least argue for a while. He felt elated, but decided against taking her into his arms again. He didn't want to press his luck.

''How about Carmel?'' he suggested, making his voice as casual as he could. ''We could drive down Saturday morning, come back late Sunday. A friend of mine owns a cottage there. I'm pretty sure I could get it for a couple of days.'' *And one night,* he added to himself, his mind already jumping ahead to the delights of uninterrupted hours with Maddy.

''I love Carmel,'' she said with a nervous smile. ''I haven't been there in years.''

''It's a very romantic place,'' he murmured.

"I know." Silence again. "Are you sure this is something we should do, Nate?" She was looking at him very earnestly.

"If we're ever going to get to know each other, we have to do something."

"True." She laughed. "How did you do that? I came over to apologize and to tell you we shouldn't ever see each other again, you play the theme from *Picnic*, and I'm all of a sudden committed to a weekend in Carmel."

"You'd be surprised how persuasive I can be."

"No, I wouldn't," she said.

Her head was lowered now, looking down at their clasped hands. Her hands were as brown as his own. So were her arms, and her neckline, where it was exposed by her pretty turquoise dress. Nate entertained himself, excited himself, by wondering how far her tan extended. It was natural that she'd be tanned, of course; she worked mostly outdoors. But the safari jacket and pants covered most of her body, and he wasn't sure she had time to sunbathe.

"What are you thinking about?" Maddy asked rather nervously.

"I was wondering if you were fish-belly-white in the parts that don't show," he answered honestly.

She laughed. "I guess you'll have to wait and see," she said, then blushed endearingly.

He raised an eyebrow. "After that suggestive statement I suppose you're going to tell me you have to rush back to the children."

Shadowed in the lamplight, her eyes were so very dark, mysterious. Then her slow smile started, and her face was lighted from within. "I still have half an hour, Nate," she said softly, taking his breath away.

At once he pulled her close, meeting no resistance. Her arms went around him, her hands tangling in his hair. With her usual honesty, she realized she had known what would happen, the minute he opened the door, clad only in those brief tan shorts, his dark hair untidy as always, due no doubt to his habit of raking it with his hands in moments of frustration. He must have felt very frustrated when she left with the children. Standing there in the doorway, obviously pleased to see her, yet unsmiling, almost stern, he had looked so perfectly made, so magnificently male.

No. She had known before that, when she decided to come back in person to apologize, instead of telephoning. She had never for a minute fooled herself that she was coming only to apologize—she had known all along that she wanted him more than she had ever wanted any man in her entire life.

She became aware that the music had ended.

"Maddy," Nate said into her hair. There was a note in his voice that she wasn't sure about. He sounded almost . . . frustrated again. But she was here, ready to go with him to that king-size bed that she had looked at so longingly a few short hours before. She was here, alone, without the children, without anything between their warm bodies but a thin layer of cotton.

She drew back her head and looked at him questioningly.

"I don't believe I'm going to say what I'm going to say," he murmured. His facial expression wasn't exactly humorous, just a little more wry than usual. His arms were still around her, but he was holding her more loosely than before, as though he was about to let go.

"I'm astonished and grateful that you came back," he said softly. "I'm delighted beyond measure that you seem to want—'' He broke off, looking embarrassed. She had never even imagined it was possible for him to look embarrassed. "I don't even know how to say this."

"You're turning me down?" She was too amazed to be embarrassed herself. Almost immediately, her amazement began turning to anger. Was this some kind of game he was playing, a cat's game of pursuing the prey until he caught it, then playing with it, teasing it, perhaps even turning it loose? Had she offended his male ego by making the offer to stay? Was this revenge for his own earlier frustration? Was he so insecure, or was this all a plot to drive her stark raving mad with wanting?

He had been watching the expressions move across her face. She saw him shake his head in the moment before his mouth came down hard on hers, hard with wanting, hard and hot with passion. She answered the kiss with passion of her own, letting her mouth part to his, her body soften against his. But a small, wary part of her held back, waiting for an explanation.

"Maddy, Maddy," he murmured against her lips. "I've dreamed of this moment, waited for this moment, thought about this moment. I've wanted you for so long, wanted to touch you, every inch of you." He punctuated his comments with soft kisses on her eyes, her cheeks, her lips, her throat, then touched her face with gentle fingertips, tracing her cheekbones, her jawline. And still she waited.

"I want to make love to you," he said. "I want to make love to you slowly and gently at first and then more roughly and passionately. I want it to build between us, Maddy. I want to take off your clothes and look at you. Then I want to lay you down and cover your body with my own and hold you like that until I can't stand it any longer, and then I want to wait some more. I don't want to rush it between us this first time, Maddy. I want it to be slow, painfully slow, so slow that we'll both go crazy with wanting before we'll let ourselves change the speed of it."

His eyes were dark, no green showing now. She couldn't doubt the truth of what he was saying. "You've really thought about this, haven't you?" she said, wanting to lighten the atmosphere.

He laughed, then let out his breath on a long sigh and hugged her.

"You *are* turning me down, aren't you?" she said flatly.

"Temporarily. Until Carmel. Until we can take the time to do it right."

She sighed. "Well, I was the one who talked about delayed gratification, I suppose," she said with what felt like a very weak smile. She felt weak too, relieved that he wasn't actually rejecting her, but definitely weak.

"Until Carmel?" he said again.

She nodded. "Until Carmel."

Then he wanted her to stay awhile, wanted her to have coffee, tea, a drink, wine, anything. But looking at the magnificence of him she knew that if she stayed even five more minutes, she would have to touch him; then perhaps his resolve would weaken in spite of himself. And now that he had painted such a vivid picture of his plans for her, she didn't want anything to spoil their first time together; not haste, nor thoughts of Brennan waiting impatiently to go back to work. Thirteen days, she reflected, counting them in her mind. How on earth was she going to wait thirteen days?

"I must be out of my mind," Nate said as he saw her to the door at last. She reached up and kissed him lightly on the lips, then trailed a hand down his bare, hair-matted chest, setting him groaning. "I *know* I'm out of my mind."

"Until Carmel," she whispered.

"Carmel," he echoed. It was almost a commitment.

CHAPTER EIGHT

"WHO'S LOOKING AFTER Hannah and Adam?" Nate asked.

"Brennan," Maddy said, surprising him.

They were sitting in a small Italian restaurant in Carmel eating scampi marinara and salad, having dropped off their bags at Nate's friend's cottage. Nate had thought they might linger at the cottage awhile, but one look at Maddy's nervous expression, as she gazed around at his friend Sam's somewhat hedonistic decorating scheme, had convinced him it would be better to delay things a little longer. So instead they had walked the picturesque downtown area, where a lot of other happy holidaymakers spilled onto the streets with little regard to traffic, crossing streets with evocative names like Junipero, Dolores and Monte Verde, exploring the charming little shops that were scattered around in courts and alleyways, most of them highly individualistic, reflecting the Bohemian influence that had founded Carmel-by-the-Sea.

"The results of Brennan's latest project were very promising," Maddy added as she finished her last shrimp. "He wants to collate all the data and write them up, ready to present at some conference he's going to. He said he could do that at home." She smiled. "He's really excited, I guess. He was whistling while he shaved this morning."

"So was I," Nate confessed.

Maddy smiled her wonderful slow smile, then looked thoughtful. "He also said he might call Emma Fieldstone and invite her to go with him and the children to the Exploratorium. The children love to go there."

Poor Emma, Nate thought. It was beginning to look as if Brennan *was* using Emma to help out with Hannah and Adam. He decided not to worry about Emma this weekend. Last week he'd spent $2500 on Gary Conrad's security system and had almost been persuaded to buy another for his condo. A friend could do no more for the moment. "Emma's a lovely person," he said staunchly, trying not to feel like a traitor.

After lunch they walked to the mission, a mile from the center of town, making their way through the residential area—where there were apparently no house numbers or mailboxes, no curbs or sidewalks, but plenty of trees—and little white posts bearing the names of each street at every corner. They explored the old mission, then returned by way of the beach, where they strolled along the edge of the Pacific. The beach wasn't as crowded as Nate had often seen it, probably because of the chill in the air. He and Maddy had dressed with ocean breezes in mind, and were both comfortable in their loose sweatshirts and brief shorts. Her long bare legs were as brown as her face and hands, he noticed, and wondered again how far her tan extended.

He was all for returning to the cottage as soon as possible, but Maddy wanted to stroll some more, so it was late afternoon before they meandered along Scenic Road to the cottage.

Nate had made dinner reservations at a French restaurant that was a particular favorite of his. They changed for dinner, Maddy disappearing into one of the two bathrooms almost before Nate had removed the key from the cottage door's lock. She came out, looking freshly scrubbed and brushed and adorable in her turquoise cotton, smiled approval at Nate in his striped shirt and white pants—and chivied him to the door, before he had a chance to execute the plot he'd put together while she was getting ready, one that was to have started out with a long and satisfying kiss.

He hoped she wasn't going to want to stay out late. He couldn't stand the frustration much longer. Every cell in his body was standing up and clamoring for attention. If this day lasted much longer, he was going to explode. He wanted this slim, golden-brown creature in his arms, and he wanted her now.

They ate dinner in the restaurant's delightful walled courtyard that was festooned with spring flowers in boxes and tubs and hanging baskets. The residents of Carmel obviously cherished flowers as much as they did trees—there were always flowers everywhere, at all times of the year.

When the waiter brought their menus, Nate chose roast quail, because he had never eaten it before and the occasion seemed to call for something special. Maddy refused to join him, saying that she'd seen quail walking across streets with their babies following them. Nate wouldn't let this spoil his appetite and was content to ask in a pained voice when Maddy ordered a steak, "Don't you like cows?"

The meal was accompanied by a wonderful Monterey Bay wine, followed by coffee and a shared helping of crème brûlée that was sinfully delicious. "I feel as if I've landed in the middle of an Impressionist painting," Maddy said, looking around as they drank coffee.

"Monet's *Women in the Garden*," Nate said.

Her dark eyes glowed. "You know the Impressionists?"

"You'll be amazed how much we have in common," he assured her.

Once more they strolled along Scenic Road. Nate rejected Maddy's suggestion that it would be romantic to walk on the beach in the moonlight—the moon wasn't due to show up for a while yet, and he had been patient long enough. He didn't say any of this aloud; he just gave her a long-suffering look, she smiled her wonderful slow smile and let him steer her straight back to the cottage.

He shut the door quietly behind himself and locked it carefully, then turned to find that Maddy had closed the miniblinds and was again looking around nervously. "Who does this place belong to?" she asked. "I've an idea it was designed with only one goal in mind."

Nate laughed. "My friend is a movie star. You've probably heard of him. Sam Lester. He's my sailboarding buddy."

Maddy looked astonished. "I certainly have heard of him," she exclaimed. "All those romantic adventure movies. He's always prominently featured in the tabloids with a new female in tow."

"You can't believe everything you read," Nate chided. "What are you doing reading those kinds of papers, anyway?"

She grinned. "I read the headlines when I'm standing in line at the supermarket. Doesn't everybody?" She shook her head, looking around once more. "Now I've seen this place, I'm going to believe every story."

Sam had certainly furnished the cottage with comfort in mind. The living room featured pillow-piled divans rather than sofas and chairs, and all of the fabrics were sensually soft, all the lighting was dim. There was an excess of mirrors. There was even a bearskin rug in front of the fireplace.

"Are we going to talk about Sam all night?" Nate asked despondently.

Instead of answering, Maddy turned to him, her hands outstretched. He felt a deep sigh of contentment welling up and audibly let it go, hoping she would smile again, but she didn't. Her face was solemn, her eyes somber in the dim interior of the cottage.

He took her hands into his and gently kissed each one, then eased her into his arms, shuddering in pure delight as she fitted her body against his. The kiss started as slowly as Maddy's smile; Nate just barely brushed her lips with his. His hands cupped her face, turning it up to his as he teased her, delicately pressing her mouth, withdrawing the pressure, touching again. Her breathing grew uneven and her own mouth more urgent; her hands tightened on his upper arms, but still he restrained both her and himself, drawing out each kiss now and gradually exerting more pressure, but refusing to allow himself to be hurried. He had waited a long time to be alone with his mystery lady; as he had warned her thirteen long days ago, he fully intended to take his time.

After a while, still kissing her gently, he eased a hand around the back of her neck and slowly pulled down the zipper of her dress. Smiling against his lips, she responded by unbuckling his belt.

He took a deep breath and stepped back, unzipping his pants and letting them fall to the floor. Reaching down, feeling unbelievably awkward, hopping from one foot to the other, he pulled off his shoes and socks, then straightened and looked expectantly at her. As always, the smile started in her eyes, spilling over as she shrugged herself free of her dress. When the turquoise fabric puddled around her feet, she eased down her half slip and panty hose, then stepped gracefully out of her sandals.

He was almost afraid to reach for her. Standing there in only a pristine lace bra and brief panties she looked so perfectly formed, slender and tall, her long brown hair falling forward over her smooth tanned shoulders, her firm breasts rising and falling unevenly, her waist curving inward without a trace of excess flesh, her stomach flat and mysteriously shadowed.

At last, with a sigh, she stepped forward and reached for the buttons on his shirt. A moment later he was clad only in his Jockey shorts, and they were both looking each other over without embarrassment.

Maddy made a low growling sound under her breath that he took as a compliment. He growled back. It was very quiet in the cottage. All he could hear was the sound of their breathing, echoed and counterpointed by the muffled roar of the Pacific Ocean across the street.

"You're not fish-belly-white," he murmured.

She smiled mischievously. "We have a small upper deck at the back of the house. I take a book and a bikini up there when I want to relax."

"Lucky neighbors."

She shook her head. "It has a privacy screen around it."

She sounded as breathless as he felt.

A heartbeat, and she reached around to unfasten the clasp of her bra, letting it fall. With another graceful motion she slipped off her panties and stood before him.

He swallowed, then touched her throat where a pulse was beating rapidly, letting his fingers trail downward to trace the tan lines left by her bikini top. "My mystery lady's a mystery no longer," he murmured.

The tiny puzzled frown he loved to see drew her silken eyebrows together, and he felt a need to explain. "I've always called you my mystery lady. Since November I've watched you from my office window, whenever you came to visit Casey Dixon. Every Wednesday at three twenty-five, I'd see you striding across the parking lot in your safari jacket, with your hair lifting behind you, and I'd wonder about you—who you were, where you were going in such a hurry, why you always wore the same clothing, why you looked so worried."

"All that time?"

"All that time."

"But that's four months, Nate. We're getting awfully close to your time limit."

He shook his head, still happily tracing tan lines. "We didn't meet until January, then it was Valentine's Day before we really got acquainted, March 20 before we dated, if you can call a sailboard lesson a date."

"Then we start counting from March? Have you marked the date on your calendar?" she asked.

"I'm not quite that calculating, Maddy. Considering how seldom we see each other, it's hard to keep count, anyway." He grinned. "I didn't say I wasn't flexible, mystery lady."

Maddy smiled. "I'm no mystery, Nate. I think men invented this idea of the feminine mystique from the fact that a woman's body doesn't reveal how she's feeling about a man, whereas a man's body does."

She glanced mischievously and pointedly at his Jockey shorts, which were having a difficult time containing him, and gave a small husky laugh that delighted him with its innuendo.

"I'm not sure that's so," he said softly and waited for the tiny crease to appear again on her forehead. When it did, he reached out to touch first one erect nipple, then the other. "Dead giveaway," he said.

Her smile was luminous, mysterious, tantalizing beyond belief. Shedding his shorts in one swift movement that certainly didn't match the grace of hers, he lifted her into his arms and headed toward the bedroom. Her hand on his shoulder stopped him in the doorway. "You understand I'm very much against taking the skin off an animal for decorative purposes," she said slowly.

"But all the same you'd like to try out the bearskin rug?"

She grinned. "Exactly."

The fur felt like purest silk against Nate's naked body. "I want to feel every part of you against every part of me," he told her softly, and for a long time he was content to hold her in his arms while he kissed her again and again. "Definitely worth waiting for," he murmured. As he'd promised her, threatened her, he didn't let her move for the longest time. Then quite suddenly his patience snapped, and the kisses he trailed across her eyelids, over her cheeks, down to her mouth, the tanned hollow of her throat, the swell of her breasts, were rapid, hard and fevered.

Her response was immediate and just as heated. Matching him for passion, she kissed his shoulders and the mat of hair on his chest, following it down with the tip of her tongue beyond the line of his suntan, feeling the utmost excitement when he moaned low in his throat as she gently explored him with tongue and lips and fingers.

Maddy had no idea that sex could be so marvelous. She certainly hadn't known it could be playful. But Nate *talked* to her as he made love, teasing her, telling her in graphic terms what he wanted to do to her next, before doing it. She even found that she could talk to him, too; she could murmur all kinds of loving nonsense while she touched him and he her, and their bodies moved and stilled and wound and unwound in patterns that seemed totally natural and desirable.

She had always admired his hands, and now she reveled in the feel of their strength as they tirelessly stroked her body, lifted and turned her. His face was shadowed in the dim golden light, but his smile flashed often. As for his mouth, she just couldn't get enough of it, so firm, so hard, yet so gentle, filling her with a sweetness that seemed to spill over into her veins. Her hands wound in his hair as his mouth moved slowly down her body yet again; she loved the crisp, clean feel of it. And then his mouth was teasing a response from her that she was sure she wouldn't be able to contain, a response that built inside her until every part of her stilled in anticipation of the explosion that must surely come. Her own tension lifted her against his seeking mouth, arching her back, stretching her body from head to toe as though she were an arrow about to be launched into space. And then her climax came, shattering her with its impact, making her whole body shudder again and again and again.

Before she could even begin to wonder about the force that had impelled her explosive response, he was inside her, sliding in as gently as he did everything, filling her, thrusting while she clung to him. Incredibly the pressure within her was building again, so that she moved with him in a perfect rhythm that could have been set to music. Now he was over her, smiling down at her in the tenderest way imaginable, moving slowly, lifting her with himself, then rolling with her so that she was above him and setting the pace, while he cupped her breasts and murmured incoherently, and her hair brushed against his hands. A few seconds later they were lying side by side, smiling at each other, kissing lightly and continuing to move, then kissing more and more deeply as the pressure built and built—and finally, magnificently, released itself with a burst of internal energy.

"So that's what Georgia meant," Maddy murmured contentedly a long time later.

Nate's hand caressed her face as he looked at her questioningly. "My sister, Georgia. She used to tell me sex was great, but I never quite understood what all the fuss was about." She grinned at him mischievously. "You're not going to treat me as a one-night stand, are you, Nate? It wouldn't be fair of you to take off, when I've just got around to enjoying sex."

He laughed explosively. "I love it when you're so straightforward. It's a very endearing trait."

"Answer the question," she growled.

"This is not a one-night stand, Maddy," he said solemnly.

"I guess we found out what we came to find out, didn't we? You said we should find out what we had, before we got too upset about everything."

"What we have is pretty special," he murmured.

She raised herself on one elbow, her hair trailing across his shoulder, her breasts touching his chest, giving him the most incredible sensation. To his amazement, he felt interest developing again in a certain quarter.

"It seemed special to you, too?" she asked with great interest. "I don't have a whole lot of experience, you understand, Nate, so I don't have much to compare it with, but it did seem pretty... sensational."

"Spectacular," he said.

"I've only made love with two men before," she informed him.

He hated both of them. "How long did they last?" he asked mischievously.

She pondered the question, frowning. "Fifteen months for Brad—we were engaged—and about eight months for Jonathan."

"How long did the good part last?"

She frowned again, then punched him lightly in the upper arm. "Probably six to seven months, but that doesn't mean you're right."

"Doesn't it?" He kissed her again. Her lips were swollen from his kisses, and he was afraid they would be tender in the morning, but not afraid enough to desist from kissing her. As he pulled her against him, she raised her silken eyebrows, looking astonished as she felt him pressing against her.

"Again? Really?" she asked, but he didn't feel it necessary to answer.

MADDY AWAKENED SLOWLY, hearing first the muffled roar of the Pacific Ocean, then seabirds mewling, and finally the sounds of cars swishing along Scenic Road. Swishing? She raised her head from the pillow. Rain was running down the windows, splashing onto the outer sills.

She lay down again and looked at Nate. The planes and angles of his face weren't nearly as craggy in repose. Asleep he appeared much younger, more vulnerable. Such a gentle lover. And such an inexhaustible one. She'd lost count of the number of times they had made love during the long night. Such luxury to have so much uninterrupted time. And a whole day yet ahead.

As though he felt Maddy's gaze on him, Nate opened his eyes and smiled at her, apparently instantly awake. "Here's looking at you, kid," he said in a fair Bogart imitation.

"It's raining," she told him after she'd kissed him.

"Good," he responded immediately. "We'll have to stay in bed all day." His arms reached around her, enfolding her, pulling her over onto himself. "When did you carry me into bed?" he asked. "I've no memory of getting here. The last thing I remember was taking a shower and being too tired to stand up. Were you there?"

"I was," she murmured. "You made me soap your back, but said you didn't have the strength to soap mine. I think we crawled in here soon after that."

He laughed. "It was an exhausting night, wasn't it?" He grinned up at her, his arms tightening around her. "Odd though, I don't feel at all tired now."

"Nate, I'm starved," she protested.

"Well, there's no food in the place. I checked last night. I should have thought to bring in some fruit or something, but I had other things on my mind." He grinned at her, his hands making suggestive patterns across her buttocks. "Now, which is it to be, mystery lady, food or nectar?"

"Nectar," she said promptly and almost at once felt that same incredible sweetness filling her as his lips met hers.

They fell asleep again after making love, and Maddy awakened feeling famished. "I need food," she moaned.

"There's no poetry in your soul," he complained.

"You can't have poetry in your soul, if there's no food in the larder," she told him.

He leaned over to kiss her, then lifted his head and studied her face. "You look remarkably bright-eyed for someone who didn't get much sleep," he said.

"These are the eyes of a starving woman," she said.

He hugged her, and his wonderfully craggy face crinkled with pleasure. She touched it with her finger-tips and knew quite suddenly that this was the happiest moment of her life. Nothing would ever be the same again. She loved this face. She loved this man, every magnificent inch of him. She loved his good humor and his patience and his lovemaking; oh yes, his wonder-fully sensitive, passionate lovemaking. She loved him and wanted him, and she was going to love him and want him for the rest of her life. There was no room for doubt in her mind.

Abruptly she was terrified. Madeleine Scott was a practical woman, had always been a practical woman, and certainly wasn't going to be so foolish as to imag-ine that Nate Ludlow would ever be interested in a long-term commitment. He had been honest with her right from the beginning. He had told her that six to seven months were his limit. She had also known all along that with her responsibilities, she couldn't possibly get deeply involved. And still she had allowed herself to fall in love with him.

Quickly she closed her eyes, not wanting him to see any change that might be reflected there. "Okay, I'm going, I'm going," he moaned.

She opened her eyes as he rolled away from her to the edge of the bed and sat up, stretching and yawning. Letting her gaze follow the lines of his suntanned shoulder down to his slim waist and the hard curve of his buttocks, she felt the beginnings of complete despair. Yet she would do it again, she thought; even knowing what she knew now, she would have come away with him. She would not have missed the experience of loving Nate Ludlow for anything in the world. Her former experiences had been merely intellectual, she decided. This, with Nate, had been born and had developed in her emotions. For once she had followed the dictates of her body, and the results had been astonishingly wonderful. But looking at him, loving him now, the only thing she wanted to do was cry—and she must not cry.

As she fought for composure, he turned his head and smiled at her. "Food," he promised. "First a shower, then we'll sally forth. Okay?"

"Okay," she managed to say.

He said something else, but she couldn't hear what it was, because at that precise moment the loudest heavy metal music in the world suddenly blasted forth outside.

Nate charged toward the windows, lifted the blinds, opened the casement window and stuck out his head. "Hey!" he yelled. "Could you turn it down a bit, please?"

A second later he backed out of the window and slammed it shut, grumbling inaudibly. The decibel level hadn't noticeably decreased. "Some fool working on his car next door," he shouted. "Got his head under the hood and the radio going full blast, can't hear me." He shook his head. "The police'll get him if he doesn't let up—noise isn't allowed in Carmel. There's even an ordinance against live music." He glared back at the window as he headed toward the bathroom. "Idiot must have moved in recently," he said. "He sure wasn't around when Teddie and I were here." The bathroom door closed behind him. Seconds later she heard the shower water splashing into the tub.

Maddy lay completely still in the large comfortable bed for a full minute. *Maybe I misheard him,* she thought. No, she couldn't possibly have done so. He'd had to shout over the music. "When Teddie and I were here," he'd said quite clearly.

Abruptly the music stopped. Her ears seemed to ring for another minute, as though the music had left a reverberating echo behind it. Again she heard him say, "When Teddie and I were here."

Feeling an overwhelming distaste, she jumped out of the bed, as if she'd just discovered that the beauteous Teddie was still inhabiting it. How could Nate Ludlow bring her here to the same cottage he'd brought his friend Teddie, the voluptuous, stunning, gorgeous Teddie! He had made Maddy feel that she was the only woman in the world who mattered to him, and now she was wondering how many other women he had made love to in that seductively sumptuous bed. Perhaps he'd even lain with other women on the bearskin rug, teasing them gently, smiling at them, murmuring suggestively ribald comments to them to make them laugh, to make them respond as heatedly and as unrestrainedly as she had done.

Pulling open her overnight bag, she dragged out the light robe she'd brought along and hadn't yet worn and put it on, still staring with fascinated disgust at the tossed covers and rumpled pillows, as though she expected a snake to come slithering out of them.

She was being foolish, she told herself. What if she'd gone to bed with Nate in his condo? Would she have expected to be the only woman ever to have romped on that king-size mattress? Of course not. Nate was thirty-two years old, single. Why shouldn't he indulge his senses with any woman who was willing? Whom could he possibly hurt?

Me, she acknowledged. He had hurt her at the very moment when she was most vulnerable. She felt betrayed and disappointed. Anger simmered inside her and she welcomed it. Anger was cleansing. It would clean all thoughts of love out of her brain.

She jumped, startled, as the bathroom door suddenly burst open. Nate stood there, a towel wrapped around his hips, water dripping from his dark hair and tanned muscular body. His eyes seemed darker than usual, fathomless.

In a reflex action, she pulled the sash of her robe tighter around her middle. He watched her do it, his face somber. "It was only once, Maddy," he said huskily. "I brought her here only once, before I ever saw you walk across that parking lot. It was a mistake."

"Perhaps this was a mistake, too," she said slowly.

"No. I won't believe that. Please, Maddy, don't be upset. I didn't even realize what I'd said for several minutes. When I did, I could have cut my tongue out. I'd almost forgotten I brought her here."

"Almost?"

His mouth hardened. "Maddy, please."

She swallowed and shrugged, forcing down her anger and with it every other unwanted emotion. "It's okay, Nate. I was shocked for a minute, but I quite understand. Why shouldn't you have brought other women here? Your love life has nothing to do with me."

"It has everything to do with you now. And there weren't other women here, only Teddie, only once."

"It's okay, Nate," she said again, but it wasn't, and they both knew it.

After that the day went downhill.

After Maddy had showered and they had tidied the cottage, they drove through the rain in search of breakfast, but found that they were too late, most restaurants were already filled with the lunchtime crowd. They ended up in a fast-food place, where Maddy found a ladybug in the salad that accompanied her sandwich. The waiter was apologetic, and she assured him she didn't have much appetite, anyway. That was the truth—when she tried to bite into her sandwich, her jaw was aching so much that it almost locked. Nate saw that she was in pain and insisted she let him help her exercise the area, but she didn't want him to touch her, not yet, and made some excuse about being in the public eye. Nate knew she was making an excuse, she could tell. His eyes were clouded, worried, and he seemed incapable of figuring out how to make things better between them, how to make things the way they had been before.

And then the waiter spilled coffee on Nate's white chinos. It was just that kind of day, Maddy supposed. Nate wasn't burned at all; the coffee had been lukewarm, anyway. He didn't make a fuss, waving off the waiter when he offered to try to clean up the stain. "My pants are washable," he said lightly. "I'll take care of it later."

When the waiter moved away, assuring them both that they wouldn't be charged for their meal, Nate attempted a smile that came out looking distinctly wan. "Maybe Brennan turned Hannah and Adam loose," he said.

It was entirely the wrong thing to say. Maddy felt her jaw tighten even more.

"Good God," he exclaimed softly. "I've sure got foot-and-mouth disease today. I'm sorry, Maddy. I didn't mean anything. I was trying to lighten us both up."

"Sure," she said tightly.

It went like that for the rest of their time in Carmel. It was obviously impossible to recapture yesterday's mood. Finally they agreed to drive home earlier than they'd planned. Naturally traffic was heavy; after all, it was Sunday evening, and it seemed an age before San Francisco's skyline appeared ahead of them. They talked in a strained fashion about every subject under the sun, their tone stilted and cool. "May I call you, Maddy?" Nate asked when he drew up outside her door.

"Of course," she said politely. She had to keep her voice under tight control. She was afraid that she would burst into tears if she let herself relax one iota. How sad it seemed that after only one lovely day and night their relationship should lie in ruins at their feet. But that was how it seemed to her, unsalvageable.

"Are you sure you're not looking for an excuse to break off with me, Maddy?" he asked heavily, as she started to open the car door. "If we part like this, you won't have to worry about how to solve the problem of the children's antagonism toward me, will you?''

That wasn't the only problem, she thought, but didn't say so.

"At the moment I'm more concerned with your total lack of sensitivity," she said coldly. Before he could reply, she climbed out of the car, yanked her bag from the back seat and slammed the door behind her. As always, the latch on the gate stuck and she struggled with it helplessly, feeling tears starting up behind her eyelids, blinking hard to keep them from flowing.

"Maddy," Nate called from the car. "Do you need help?"

Furious, she shook her head, just as the latch finally gave. She didn't look back, and heard Nate drive away as she inserted her key into the front door lock.

Brennan was sitting in the living room, gazing into the empty fireplace, looking gloomy. The children were evidently in bed. "Did you go to the Exploratorium?" Maddy asked, forestalling any questions about her own weekend.

He nodded. "Hannah and Adam had a great time, especially with the lasers."

Usually Brennan was as much a child as Hannah and Adam when it came to the science museum. "*You* didn't?" she asked.

"I'd hoped Emma might come along."

"She couldn't make it?"

"I don't know. I didn't ask. I called her apartment and a man answered. Said his name was Gary Conrad and he was living with Emma. They were old friends, he said."

"Oh, Brennan, I'm sorry."

He sighed. "That's okay. I think I'll go into the lab, if you don't mind. Are you home to stay? Is Nate coming over?"

She shook her head. "He went home. I'll be staying home. You go ahead."

For a second she thought that Brennan was going to question her succinct statements, but he didn't. A few minutes later he was gone, and she was left to face the rest of the night alone.

CHAPTER NINE

IN THE SPRING and summer San Francisco's recurring fogs are sucked into the city by warmer temperatures beyond the coastal mountain ranges—unlike many of his friends, Nate liked the fog. He liked to watch it slide in under Golden Gate Bridge, where it made Alcatraz disappear in the blink of an eye, then waft on to swallow cars, pedestrians and entire blocks of buildings.

The fog didn't always blanket the entire city. Often only one neighborhood would be singled out. If people didn't like the weather in their part of town, they had only to visit friends in another area. Sometimes Nate would leave his condo, dressed for winter, and arrive at his clinic to find glorious, golden sunshine and people wearing shorts.

On Monday the fog was wet, widespread and wintry, which seemed fitting, considering Nate's gray mood. He didn't have time to indulge in depression, however. By midmorning, when the fog started to lift, it began to seem to Nate that half the population of San Francisco had taken to the outdoors over the weekend—with disastrous results. On top of his usual hectic Monday, he had several emergency calls from people who had been waterskiing, bicycling, jogging—all without warming up their muscles beforehand, of course.

It was seven before Emma was able to start closing up. She and Nate hadn't had time to exchange more than a couple of grunts all day, but she had noticed that Nate's patients weren't laughing when they came out of the treatment rooms, and that was unusual.

"You need a friend," she said, poking her head around his office door as he was putting on his suit jacket.

It was a statement, not a question. Nate nodded in answer. "So do I," Emma said. "How does another pot of chili sound?"

After he parked his car behind Emma's and followed her up her steps, Nate noticed two things. One, even though Muggsie barked her usual shrill welcome, the burglar alarm didn't go off. Two, Gary was no longer in residence.

He took one look at Emma's sad countenance and decided not to mention either fact.

The chili smelled as great as always. "I guess neither of us has to worry about offending anyone tonight," Emma said mournfully as she piled raw onions onto each portion. She glanced at Nate as he pulled his chair in to the table. "You want to go first?"

He sighed, then confessed what he'd done. "I think Maddy would have forgiven me for taking her where I took Teddie, but when I made the crack about Hannah and Adam, it was the last straw. Honestly though, Emma, I hadn't even remembered taking Teddie to the cottage until that moment. And then it just came out." He sighed again. "Saturday was so perfect. Maddy was...it was...well, it was perfect, that's the only word."

"At least you had a whole day," Emma said gloomily. "All I had was a couple of hours of kite flying and fish and chips." Her face lighted up momentarily. "I guess I didn't have a chance to tell you about that. It was such a lovely time. The children were great, no problem at all. And Brennan had bought this huge Hawaiian stunt kite that almost pulled him off his feet. We laughed so much...." Now it was her turn to sigh.

"You didn't go to the Exploratorium with Brennan and the children over the weekend?"

She looked first puzzled, then upset. "Was that where he planned to take me? Dammit, he *was* just looking for a baby-sitter, wasn't he?"

"What happened, Emma?" he asked.

Frowning, she tucked her hair behind her ears. "Brennan called me on Saturday," she said flatly. "Gary answered. I was out, doing some grocery shopping—what that man could eat in one day defies description. I came home to find that Brennan had telephoned. Gary had told him he was living with me. We were old friends, he said. Goodbye Brennan. He didn't even leave a message."

"You didn't call him back?"

"What could I tell him?"

"The truth."

She shook her head.

"I notice Gary isn't here," Nate murmured around a mouthful of scalding chili.

"I made him move out yesterday. The proverbial last straw. I couldn't believe how furious I was." She laughed dryly. "Nor could Gary. But he finally got the picture. He went over to look at the studio apartment you mentioned and found he could move in right away if he could come up with the first month's rent, a cleaning deposit and a security deposit. Which he couldn't, of course."

"You loaned him the money?"

"I'm looking upon it as a farewell gift. I certainly don't expect to get it back." She shook her head and pushed her plate away, having apparently lost her appetite. "I guess it was worth twelve hundred dollars to get Gary off my back. But God, I wish I'd thought to stay home, in case Brennan called."

"Call him, Emma. Tell him what happened."

"You really think I should?"

He nodded and she headed immediately for the phone. Maddy must have answered. Nate felt his heart turn over at the thought, but he had already decided that it was best to leave it up to her to call him this time. If she had any interest in forgiving him his stupid blunders, she would let him know.

Now Emma was talking to Brennan, or rather listening. He seemed to be going on at length, and Emma's face was getting longer and longer. She said very little until just before she hung up the phone, then she murmured, "Of course I understand, Brennan."

"What?" Nate asked.

She sat down, reached over to pat Muggsie, who had emerged from under the table with an enquiring look on her gray woolly face, then pulled her plate of chili toward her and began eating, as though she were starving to death. "Whoa, Emma," Nate said gently, placing one hand on her right arm.

She set down her fork and looked at him in despair, her lovely brown eyes bright with moisture. "It never goes right for me, Nate. Never. I might as well be fat. Who cares?"

"I care. So do you. Now, tell me what happened."

She sighed deeply. "It was okay at first," she said. "Brennan understood about Gary when I explained. He said he was glad I'd called, because he'd been really

disappointed when it looked as if I had other interests." Her smile was wan. "I was happy for all of
twenty seconds, because if Brennan was disappointed,
then for sure he had some feelings for me, wouldn't you
say?"

"Indisputably."

"But then I realized there was an awful lot of noise
going on at the other end. I asked what was happening, and he said that Georgia had arrived unexpectedly
this morning. She flew into San Francisco last night and
is staying at the Hyatt Regency. She came over to the
house to see the kids, kept them home from school all
day. Brennan said she told him she's back for good.
She's sick of rattling around the world."

"Well, well." Nate sat back, wondering how this
would affect his relationship with Maddy. If he still had
one. "So where does that leave you?" he asked sympathetically.

Emma shrugged, still looking despondent. "Out in
the street, I guess. Brennan said it's a little difficult at
the moment. The kids are all worked up about Georgia
being there, Maddy and Georgia are quarreling, and
he's going into the lab to get away from it all."

"Well, it doesn't sound as if he's pleased about
Georgia being home."

"He sounded *defeated*, Nate. And he certainly didn't
suggest seeing me."

"You should have invited him over for chili. Break
down any man's defenses, this chili."

She attempted a grin, but it didn't quite make it to her
eyes.

ON TUESDAY EVENING, Georgia Malone appeared on
network news, looking sexy but innocent in a satiny

Western shirt, a full denim skirt and cowboy boots, her mane of blond hair flying out in all directions. She was conducting the press conference at home in the bosom of her family. Hannah and Adam stood each side of her, Adam wearing something that looked like the original suit worn by Little Lord Fauntleroy in the movie of the same name, Hannah an incredibly ruffled dress made of white chiffon or some such fabric, with a huge white bow tied at the top of her braid. Brennan loomed behind, and Maddy sat uncomfortably alongside in her yellow jumpsuit.

"My wand'rin' days are over," Georgia confided in her throaty voice. Nate wondered where she'd acquired her country and western accent. Maddy certainly didn't have one. He supposed it must have rubbed off from the songs she sang. "I'm just content as can be to be home with my babies and my husband and my little sister."

"Your ex-husband?" a reporter queried.

"Well now, yes, there was the matter of that little old divorce, but we can still be close as can be, cain't we, honey?" A bright look up at Brennan from those fabulous green eyes elicited a strained, somewhat bewildered smile. Maddy was smiling just as tightly. Was she afraid she was going to lose the children? Hadn't she insisted that she was ready for that, if the day ever came?

Nate hoped Emma wasn't watching the newscast. Now another reporter was asking Georgia about some rumors connected with her agent, who had apparently accompanied her on her recent tour of England. "Not true, not true," she said with a beaming smile and a shake of her index finger. "Albie is my agent and my friend, nothing more. You just know how you paparazzi people are, making up stories when you got nothin' better to do. Shame on you." She pulled Hannah and Adam closer to herself. "All I was thinking about in jolly old England was coming home to my babies," she said warmly.

"Is Georgia really home to stay?" Nate asked Maddy on the phone an hour later. He hadn't been able to resist calling her.

"You saw us on the news?" Her voice sounded tight, as though she were clenching her teeth. He wanted to drive over there and take her into his arms, soothe her into relaxing her jaw. "The press conference was Georgia's idea. Evidently she's in hot water. The fan magazines got hold of the rumors that she was having an affair with her agent and took her to task. She's so idolized, Nate. Her fans have given her this halo and they don't want it tarnished. There's even some talk that the Japanese leg of her tour might be canceled. So she dashed straight home to refute the stories by making Brennan and the kids and me pose with her for family pictures. She absolutely begged us to do it. Her career was over if we didn't, she said. What could we do?"

"Was she having an affair with her agent?"

"Of course she was. Is."

"She's not really going to stay home forever?"

"She says she is. I give her two weeks, tops. She's done this sort of thing before, Nate. It never lasts. And meanwhile the kids are misbehaving like mad—she brought loads of presents for them, of course—and they are playing her off against me, wheedling her into letting them do anything their little hearts desire. It's not good for them, Nate. I'd be absolutely furious with her, except it's impossible to stay mad at Georgia. Especially when she's vulnerable, as she is right now. I don't think she's been eating right or sleeping properly. She really does suffer over bad press notices. Her fans are very important to her. Brennan can't get angry with her either, even though she's using him, pretending to the media that she's thinking of picking up where they left off, as though that were possible. It's the kids I worry about most, though. They're going to be hurt all over again when she leaves."

"She's staying at the house?"

"God, no. She's at the hotel, but she keeps popping over in a stretch limousine to take her babies places. They haven't been to school, and Hannah had a spelling test today. Her spelling isn't her best feature either, she shouldn't have missed it. And of course if I say anything at all, I'm the world's worst ogre."

"Is there anything I can do?" he asked.

There was a moment's silence, then she very abruptly said, "No," as though she'd just remembered that she was mad at him, as well as Georgia.

"Maddy, I've wanted to call you ever since Sunday night," he said slowly. "I'm truly sorry about making that crack about Hannah and Adam. It was totally uncalled for."

"Yes," she said stiffly.

He wondered if he should apologize again for mentioning Teddie, but decided it probably wouldn't do any good. "I don't suppose there's much chance of seeing you," he said gloomily.

"I'm afraid not. I want to stay pretty close to the children. They need a settling influence right now."

"I understand. Can I call you again?"

She sighed. "Later in the week, maybe." There was a silence, then she said, "I'm sorry, Nate. I was pretty awful to you on Sunday. I guess I must have misplaced my sense of humor. You had suffered at Hannah and Adam's hands, after all. You were only making a joke."

Maybe she'd forgotten about Teddie, he thought hopefully. "I'll call you tomorrow," he said quickly, wanting to quit while he was ahead.

On Wednesday Maddy told him that Georgia had arranged yet another interview, this time with one of the tabloids. She was still telling everyone she was home for good, still hinting that she and Brennan might get together again.

"I thought you said there was no chance of that," Nate said.

"I didn't think there was. Now I'm not so sure. Brennan just drifts in and out in his usual manner. I'm afraid if Georgia sets her mind to it, he might drift back into a relationship with her. She's really frightened this time."

Poor Emma, Nate thought.

"Any chance I could see you?" he asked hopefully.

The silence stretched for so long that he knew her answer before she gave it. "I can't handle anything else right now, Nate. I'm going crazy as it is."

He knew better than to pressure her. "Hang in there, kid," he said gently.

By the weekend his patient load had slackened considerably, and Nate began to feel restless. Emma was moping. Yes, she had seen the stories about Georgia. No, she didn't particularly want to talk about it.

Nate tried Maddy one more time. No, she couldn't possibly get away to see Nate, as long as Georgia was in town. Was she afraid Georgia would suddenly take it into her head to kidnap her own children? Nate wondered, but didn't ask.

On Friday night he impulsively decided to fly up to Seattle to see his folks. Usually he only visited on holidays, but he told himself he needed a break. Probably, he thought on the plane on Saturday morning, he just couldn't accept that without Maddy available, nothing in San Francisco had any appeal for him.

As always his mother was delighted to see him. While he unpacked in his old bedroom, she suggested calling in some of his old school friends, so that they could have a party, but Nate demurred, saying he'd rather spend a quiet weekend with her and Joe at the old homestead on Queen Anne Hill.

"Are you sick?" she asked.

Nate laughed. "I don't have to be entertained all the time, Mom."

"What's her name?" she asked, wandering into her studio.

Nate followed her, wondering as always at his mother's clairvoyance. "Nobody in particular," he said, not wanting to get involved in a discussion of Maddy.

"Uh-uh." Anne absentmindedly picked up a small paintbrush and glanced at the partially finished canvas that stood on the small easel, the photograph of an elderly gentleman in an old-fashioned suit next to it on her worktable. Then she looked at Nate and put down the brush.

"Go ahead," he said. "I like watching you work."

Anne was a portrait painter who worked mostly from old photographs. She always decried the notion that she was an artist. "A copyist creating instant ancestral portraits," she called herself, but her work was in great demand. Somehow she managed to infuse a stiffly posed studio photograph with the personality of the man or woman who had sat for it, bringing the person back to life.

"The girls okay?" Nate asked as she took him at his word, donned a smock and sat down.

"Fine. Babies are growing like weeds. Renny's pregnant again."

She grinned mischievously up at Nate, evidently waiting for him to groan. He obliged, though for some reason he didn't feel as negative as he usually did after such an announcement. "How does Wade feel about that?" he asked, expecting to hear that he was in shock.

"Sticking his chest out as if he alone were responsible," Anne said fondly. "I didn't think he and Renny could get more ecstatic about each other, but I do believe they have."

"Wade and Renny ecstatic? I've been visiting the wrong family. Last I saw they were yelling at each other that it was somebody else's turn to give Deirdre her 2:00 a.m. bottle."

"Babies get parents on edge for a while, honey. It's perfectly normal. It's called lack of sleep. A few hours of shut-eye and everyone's whispering sweet nothings again. There's always some adjustment to be made when babies come along."

"You're telling me Wade and Renny are happily married?"

His mother looked genuinely astonished. "Of course they are, just as Ben and Tess are. Ben's probably more demonstrative than Wade—but Renny doesn't seem to mind." She chuckled. "I guess Wade must be more demonstrative in the bedroom. Another baby, this soon. Ah well, as long as they're happy."

Nate would have sworn both his stepsisters had been on the threshold of divorce last Christmas. Nothing their men did had seemed to please them. Both young women had looked frazzled, worn out. So okay, lack of sleep. But did he really believe in these ecstatic marriages his mother was telling him about? His mother was a realist, he had to admit. She didn't look at life through rose-colored glasses; she always saw things the way they were.

He watched her work for a while in silence, wondering if she was ever going to show any signs of age. Petite and lissome as a girl, Anne Ludlow Spencer had no lines on her face, no sags to her jawline, no gray to mar the dark tangle of curls that Nate had inherited from her.

It was quiet in the upstairs studio, even though the windows were open to catch the warm spring air. "Joe still working in the garden?" she asked after a couple of minutes.

Nate looked out. "He's doing something to the rhododendrons."

"Good. They needed some fertilizer. Going to be blooming soon. Joe prizes those rhodies. And the azaleas."

"How does Joe feel about being a grandpa again?" Nate asked.

"Great. He loves grandbabies as much as I do. I must admit, though, that it's nice to be able to hand them over when they cry. I can enjoy them far more than I enjoyed Tess and Renny. God, I was exhausted when the girls were little."

"You seemed to enjoy them."

"Well, I've always loved babies, but it was hard having two of them all at once."

He supposed it must have been. He hadn't really thought about that before. All his attention had been given to mourning the loss of his mother's constant attention.

"I often think about that time it was just you and me," Anne said abruptly, as if she'd read his mind—which she quite possibly had. "It was a special time, wasn't it?"

"I thought so."

"Much better than those awful years when you couldn't stand poor Joe."

What about poor Nate? he thought.

"I guess I was pretty rough on him."

"You were a monster." She leaned over, putting the final dainty touches on a bushy eyebrow, then sat back and smiled at him fondly. "Good thing for you Joe was such a patient man. Any other man would have beaten you black and blue. God, you used to have storm clouds on your face all the time." She looked at him thoughtfully. "You really hated him, didn't you?"

He nodded. "It's hard to believe now," he admitted, looking out at Joe squatting beside the rhododendrons, his back straight, just as Nate had taught him. Joe wasn't a tall man, though he seemed tall enough next to Anne. He certainly wasn't the bear of a man Nate's father had been.

When had he stopped hating Joe? he wondered. When he'd taken Joe's old Chevy and driven it without permission, and the police had picked him up for not only speeding on the freeway but driving without a license? He had been fourteen years old. "Guess it seemed like a good idea at the time, huh?" Joe had said ruefully when he came to get him at the police station.

Or had the transformation come earlier, when he was thirteen and failing math, and Joe had sat with him night after night, tired after a full day of working on other people's automobiles, but patiently explaining, figuring, explaining again, until the jumble of figures finally made sense to Nate? Or had the change come when his sole dream had been to make the high school basketball team, and Joe had practiced jump shots with him hour after hour at the hoop over the garage?

"We'll be celebrating our twenty-second wedding anniversary October 4," Anne murmured as she cleaned her brush.

"Are you happy, Mom?" Nate asked her.

"Totally," she said without hesitation.

"You and Joe don't fight anymore?"

"Joe and I never did fight."

He looked at her in amazement. "Come on, Mom, where's your memory? You and Joe used to go at it hammer and tongs when you were first married."

She shook her head and grinned at him. "No way, José. You and Joe, yes. Joe and Renny and Tess, yes. Because he wanted you all to do good, to succeed, to be happy, so he pushed you, every one of you, and you resented it. But never Joe and me. Never. He wasn't like your father, Nate. Joe was never jealous or envious, or much of anything except loving and kind."

He was astonished. It had seemed to him that the household had been racked by chaos during the eight years he'd remained at home. There was always somebody shouting at someone. Had all that shouting been coming from Renny and Tess and himself? Possibly. When he put his mind to it, he couldn't think of a single specific argument between Anne and Joe. He had just assumed, he supposed, that they were as unhappy as he was.

"You and Dad used to fight, though," he said, sure of his ground here.

Anne grinned up at him. "Did we ever. Like cats and dogs." She smiled reminiscently, looking younger than ever. "But, the making up, Nate, the making up."

"I guess I didn't get to see much of that."

"I should think not." Applying herself industriously to reproducing the curve of the old gentleman's moustache, she kept her face averted. She was blushing, he realized. Blushing over something that had happened twenty-odd years ago. They must have been something special, those scenes of forgiveness.

"You think you and Dad would have made it to twenty-two years?" he asked. "If he hadn't died in the car crash, I mean."

"Sure we would. We loved each other." There was no doubt in her voice.

"You think that's all you need? Love?"

"If it's strong enough, yes." She glanced up at him. "What's her name, sweetheart? You want me to lay out the tarot, see what's in store for you?"

He laughed. "Her name's Maddy and she's maddening, and you don't need to go making something of it. She's just a really great person and I enjoy her company. We've had a few problems, but I'm optimistic."

"She's nothing like that Leonie person?"

"Nobody's like Leonie."

"Leonie called me, you know."

He hadn't known.

"She told me you were having affairs with all your patients. She said she was gathering information to present to the state board to have you disqualified."

"You didn't believe her, I hope? About the patients, I mean."

"Of course not. Don't I know my own son? Didn't I raise you to be ethical?"

He shook his head. "Leonie was a big mistake, Mom. I'm sorry you got dragged into it. She was really psychotic. Luckily her family finally saw that and got her some help. Last I heard, she was living happily in the Midwest with a farmer."

"You haven't had a serious girlfriend since, have you?"

"I guess Leonie made me gun-shy. I couldn't believe afterward that I'd been so stupid. Made me doubt my own judgment."

"So what's different about Maddy?"

He grinned at her persistence. "I'll bring you up-to-date when there's something to report."

She stood up, came over to him and hugged him. "I want you to be happy, Nate. I'm proud of you. I'm proud of your success. Now I want to stop worrying about your love life."

"Nothing to worry about," he assured her, hugging her back.

Later in the day, when he sat with Anne and Joe at the dining table in the sun porch Joe had built at the back of the house, he paid much more attention to his mother and stepfather than he usually did. For one thing, when he came home for Christmas or Thanksgiving or whatever, Tess and Renny and their families were usually around. This was really the first time he'd been alone with Anne and Joe in years.

Joe had caught and barbecued the salmon they were eating. Anne had never cared much about cooking. It was Joe who had taught Nate how to cook, how to do minor plumbing and electrical repairs, how to set out crab pots, how to fish. Was there anything Joe couldn't do? he wondered, watching his stepfather pad across the kitchen in his stocking feet to fetch a second bottle of wine. "This is an occasion," he said simply when Anne remonstrated. "Here's to you, son," he said, lifting his glass.

"And to you, Dad," Nate responded, suddenly aware of a str10g feeling of love for this simple, quiet man. Young Nate could so easily have gone astray, he thought. He had never been a wild boy, but he'd certainly had a predilection for mischief. But Joe had always been there with the right word at the right time. Often Nate had objected to what he thought of as Joe's lectures, but he'd always come to see that Joe was right.

Joe and Anne were discussing the fishing trip on which Joe had caught the salmon. "I was so sick," Anne confessed. "But I just wasn't about to—"

"Quit," Joe finished for her. "Your mother's not a quitter, Nate. Green face and all, she stuck it out. And she caught—"

"The biggest fish of them all," she added. "Though Joe's was—"

"Pretty close. Give or take a pound or two. Kings—"

"Both of them. Absolute—"

"Beauties. What a day that was."

They didn't even know they were completing each other's sentences, Nate realized. They were smiling into each other's faces, their words tumbling over each other as they relived the good time they'd had on that charter out of Westport on the Washington coast.

"We already ate the one I caught," Anne said. "Joe cooked it too, of course. I never was much for—"

"Cooking. It doesn't matter, love. You do so many other things so well."

He loved them both, Nate thought, when he was back on the plane, returning to San Francisco. Of course he'd always loved his mother, but it had taken him time to come to love and appreciate his stepfather.

Looking out of the plane window at the fluffy clouds below, he decided he should make an extra effort to get Hannah and Adam to like him. The notion came out of nowhere, surprising him. They really were pretty good kids, all in all; he could still see their faces upturned to the stage when he took them to *Beach Blanket Babylon*. Such awe on such small bright faces. And the prompt way they'd owned up to their transgressions. A lot of courage there.

He, of all people, should be able to understand their antipathy where he was concerned. As Maddy hadn't brought in another man to spend time around them, they had to think it was a serious matter. He'd have to tell them that marriage held no appeal for him. Even if it did seem that he might have been wrong about that particular institution.

Odd how he'd developed an aversion to marriage, based on the chaos he'd believed prevalent in his mother's marriages. He had often seen her cry, whenever his father stormed out of the house in a rage. He had seen her wince, when he or Tess or Renny raised their voices to Joe. Yet she insisted that she had been happy with both her husbands and was still happy with Joe. She even believed Tess and Renny were happily married. How about their husbands, Ben and Wade? Would *they* say they were happy?

He thought back to the previous Christmas. All that commotion—babies crying, mothers yelling, fathers— what had the fathers been doing? He had a sudden image of Wade burping his daughter on his shoulder after giving her a bottle, exchanging a satisfied grin with Renny when little Deirdre obliged with a raucous blast of air. And then Ben moved into the picture, smiling at Tess as she bragged how little Jared was now pulling himself to his feet in the playpen.

There's always some adjustment, his mother had said. Were Ben and Wade fully adjusted now? They certainly looked healthy and happy. Maybe marriage wasn't as bad as he'd always thought it. Surely it must be fun to live with someone whose sentences you could finish without even pausing to think. To know someone that well ...

Hell, what was he thinking of? He still had to take statistics into account. How many marriages made it to twenty-two years? How many made it through two? All the same, for the rare ones that did make it, it must feel pretty rewarding to succeed, to have someone you loved, someone who loved you, by your side through all the years of your life....

CHAPTER TEN

WHEN NATE ARRIVED HOME late Sunday afternoon, he decided to go over to Maddy's house rather than call her. If he called, she'd put him off and he missed her, wanted to see her, even wanted to see Hannah and Adam. Maddy's worry about them had been passed on to him by some kind of osmosis, he decided; he wanted to make sure they were weathering the storm Georgia had brought with her.

Hannah, dressed in her usual cotton shirt and blue jeans, let him in and showed him into the living room. Only Adam was in there, sitting on the hearth rug, playing with a toy truck, but Nate could hear voices from upstairs. Maddy and someone else, Georgia no doubt. Quarreling.

"My mom came home," Hannah said, sitting down on the sofa opposite him, evidently in no hurry to leave the room. Maybe she took hostess duties seriously.

"So I heard," he said, testing the waters.

"We were on TV," Adam said.

"I saw you. Hardly knew either of you in those fancy clothes."

Adam made a face.

"Mom brought them from England," Hannah said. "Yucky, weren't they? Especially that ruffly dress. Mom likes that kind of thing. She says a girl should look like a girl." Hannah laughed. "Maddy wanted to know who decided girls had to dress up in bordello window curtains so they'd look like girls. What does bordello mean, Dr. Ludlow?''

"I've no idea," he said, opting for cowardice. He was amazed by the conspiratorial nature of this conversation. When had he and Hannah become such buddies? he wondered. He could only conclude that he was no longer considered a threat. Which was a gloomy thought, if ever he'd had one.

"I heard you had quite a time kite flying," he said.

Hannah grinned. "We almost lost Daddy."

"You should have seen him," Adam said. "It was the funniest thing."

"So Emma told me."

Hannah tilted her head to one side. "We like Emma. She's very..."

"Homey?" Nate finished for her when she seemed lost for a description. He must have caught the habit from his mother and Joe.

Hannah nodded. "She makes you feel as if it wouldn't matter what you did. She would still like you."

"She said you were a great person," Adam said.

Was Emma responsible for Hannah's new attitude? "I think she's great, too. We've been friends a long time."

Hannah had pulled her bear, the famous "drownded" Pookie, from behind a pillow and was straightening the ribbon around its neck. Finally satisfied with the bow, she looked up at Nate from under her feathery blond eyelashes. "We're sorry we took the labels off your cans," she said.

He grinned. "I still can't tell my mushrooms from my tomatoes."

They looked at each other and laughed merrily.
Hannah was going to be as beautiful as her mother
someday, he thought. Then she sobered abruptly and
fiddled with the ribbon again.

"Not to worry, Hannah," he said softly. "I like life
to be interesting."

"Don't you ever get mad at people? We thought
you'd really be mad."

"I get mad sometimes, sure, but not at people I like."

"You like us?" Suddenly they were both sitting up
very straight.

"Sure I do." It was the truth, he realized; somewhere along the way he'd developed a definite fond-
ness for these tough little kids. "I want to tell you
something else," he said, leaning forward. "I'm not
going to take Maddy away from you. I think you've
been worrying about that, and it's not going to happen. Okay?"

Hannah gave him a long, measuring look, then
glanced at Adam. They both nodded solemnly, then
Hannah said softly, "Okay."

"Hello, Nate," Maddy said from the doorway.

He felt like someone who, dying of thirst all the way,
had crossed a desert and just caught sight of an oasis.
She looked cool and composed in a sleeveless, lime-
green linen shirt and skinny white cotton pants that
ended above her bare suntanned ankles. Her hair was
tied back in a French braid. It was a style he hadn't seen
her wear before. It suited her and emphasized her high
cheekbones. He wanted to rush over to her, take her
into his arms and feel all of that coolness against him.
He had the strangest feeling that Hannah and Adam
wouldn't mind at all if he did.

Maddy might, however. There was no welcome on her face. He stayed where he was.

"I hope you don't mind me coming over without calling," he said, getting to his feet. "I missed you, and I was afraid if I phoned, you'd tell me to get lost."

"I called you over the weekend," she said slowly.

"You did? That's great. Does that mean I'm forgiven?"

"Were you spending the weekend in Carmel?" she asked coolly.

So that was the reason for the frosty reception. Was she pulling a Leonie on him, checking up on him, thinking the worst? "I was in Seattle, visiting my folks," he said stiffly.

"Oh." She looked apologetic. "Nate," she said hesitantly, taking a step toward him.

But then a vision in red-and-white gingham, straight off the stage of the Grand Ole Opry, wafted into the room behind her.

"Who's the handsome stranger?" Georgia Malone asked huskily.

"It's Uncle Nate, Mom," Hannah said.

Uncle Nate? He was amazed at how good that made him feel.

Maddy looked startled, which wasn't altogether surprising.

"Howd'y'do, Uncle Nate," Georgia said, coming toward him with her right hand outstretched.

Her hand was small and slender, just as she was, but he felt the blast of her sexuality before she was halfway across the room.

Georgia Malone. Everybody's sweetheart. She was smaller than she appeared on television, a dainty little thing a foot shorter than he was, craning her neck in a

charming manner to look up into his face, her own pixie
face wreathed in the sunniest of smiles. The famous
green eyes were accented by blue-green eyeliner. Layers
of black mascara made her eyelashes spiky, sexy beyond belief. Nate felt about seventeen years old, a
teenage Western groupie who wanted to pull at his
forelock, whatever that was, and say, "Aw shucks,
ma'am."

"How are you?" he managed to stammer, suddenly
conscious that Maddy was eyeing him with a wry
expression.

"Well, I'll tell you, Uncle Nate, I'm plumb exhausted. I've been looking at apartments all day, and
that's no way to spend a sunny Sunday."

"Apartments?" He glanced at Maddy, who had gone
back to lean in the doorway and saw that her expression had become unreadable. He thought she raised her
eyebrows at him a minute fraction, but wasn't completely sure.

"Here in San Francisco?" he asked.

"Close as I can get to my babies," she said, with a
loving smile for Hannah and Adam.

Hannah was still sitting on the sofa. She was cradling Pookie like a baby against her chest, rocking him
gently. When she became aware that he was watching
her, she smiled at him rather tightly and rolled her eyes
in her mother's direction, then started fiddling with
Pookie's ears as though she had to get them arranged
just so.

Nate sat down again opposite her. "Yo, Hannah," he
said conspiratorially. She grinned at him and stopped
pulling Pookie's ears. He felt as if he'd gained a major
victory.

Georgia was still talking about apartments. "Every one of them was so poky you wouldn't believe. Fleas in one of 'em! Fleas jumpin' all over my legs. I got out of there right fast." She sighed and sat down on the sofa next to Hannah, putting an arm around the little girl. "I'm thinking of settlin' for this darlin' house in Pacific Heights," she went on. "I just don't see how I could manage in anythin' smaller. Adam and Hannah need to have plenty of space. You'd like a big bedroom, wouldn't you, honey?" she said to Hannah. "A pretty four-poster in it, with a white eyelet canopy and the softest satiny quilts and lots and lots of dolls."

"Sure, Mom," Hannah said politely, but without enthusiasm.

Nate studied the little girl's face, but couldn't make anything out of her expression. Somehow he couldn't imagine her playing with dolls.

"And your own bathroom, too. Five bathrooms that li'l darlin' has."

"Georgia," Maddy said evenly. "You're doing it again, making promises you don't intend keeping."

"Now, Maddy, honey, don't you go nagging me like that. Nothing wrong with a little daydreamin'."

"There is if the children start believing you mean it."

"They wouldn't do that, surely now?" She looked from Hannah to Adam with wide-eyed innocence. "You all know I'm just funning, don't you?"

"Sure, Mom," Hannah and Adam said resignedly, and Nate saw that they meant it. They had known Georgia wasn't serious. He was the only one who had been taking her seriously.

But how awful that those two little kids should be so cynical at their tender ages. He felt a rush of anger against Georgia Malone. Quite suddenly he could see how disastrous this visit was, not just for Maddy, but for Hannah and Adam who had been sailing right along, doing fine with Maddy's truly loving care.

As though sensing his sympathy, Adam had come to stand next to Nate's sofa. After a moment he let himself lean against Nate's legs. There was something very moving about the warm weight of the little boy's body against him. He put an arm around Adam's waist and pulled him down to sit next to him. The youngster rewarded him with a shy smile, and Nate felt warmth curl around inside him.

He turned his attention back to Georgia. She was gazing apologetically at Maddy, her sunny smile gone. "I don't even know I'm doin' it, honey," she said to her sister in a childlike voice. "I just get carried away with my own imaginin' and it seems so real, so possible." She turned to look worriedly at Hannah and Adam. "I'm sorry, babies. I did look at the house, and it did look so big and pretty and ready for a family, and I just sort of imagined us all living in it. Happy ever after, you know?"

"It's okay, Mom," Adam said. The adult, understanding sound of his voice pained Nate, and he tightened his arm around him. He was only seven years old, for heaven's sake. Such tough little kids, both of them, fighting to keep Maddy, trying to understand the mother who'd deserted them, proud of the father who wasn't often home. He felt a wave of affection for both of them.

"Well, who knows, maybe I'll settle down next year," Georgia said. "Then we'll buy the house in Pacific Heights and—"

"Georgia," Maddy protested and Nate felt a fresh jolt of anger go through him when he saw how tired

Maddy was, how weary she sounded. Then he looked at Georgia again, and to his amazement, his anger dissipated as quickly as it had appeared. Her face was quite drawn and thin, he noticed for the first time. There were faint bluish shadows under the glorious green eyes. Her fingers were trembling. She was really very fragile, he thought. He could almost understand why Brennan and Maddy found it impossible to stay angry with her. Georgia Malone, it was suddenly clear to him, had never grown up. She had no idea of what motherhood was all about. She wanted the children to love her unreservedly and would make any kind of promises to them to get that love, even if she had no intention of fulfilling those promises. It was entirely possible that she *didn't* know what she was doing.

Suddenly Georgia clapped her hands, startling him. "Come on now, babies," she said, smiling sunnily once more. "There's no need for us to sit around feelin' gloomy. How 'bout we sing us a song?"

Hannah and Adam were immediately on their feet, their faces shining with pleasure. Adam went to pull his mother's guitar from its case against the wall and brought it to her. She settled the instrument against her, a child on either side and started to play. The song was one Nate didn't recognize, a country and western ballad about unrequited love. Georgia Malone's voice was as pure and true as the ring of crystal.

He stole a glance at Maddy's face. She was still leaning in the doorway, but the stiffness had left her body and her face had totally relaxed. She was watching Georgia with an expression of love in her eyes, and he remembered her saying she could forgive Georgia anything when she sang. Should there be special rules for people with such remarkable talent, he wondered—or rather, should they be given a dispensation from the rules other people lived by?

When the song ended, Georgia changed the guitar beat and began singing, "Puff the Magic Dragon," which obviously delighted the children. Eager-eyed, they sat watching and listening until their mother gave them the signal to join in; then they sang their little hearts out, Adam more musical, Hannah more intense.

Georgia's voice made magic out of the simple tune. Listening to her, Nate could *see* the dragon frolicking in the mist, see the little boy who loved the rascally dragon, feel the sadness when the dragon went away.

Halfway through, Maddy came to sit next to him, not too close, her back straight, her eyes on the children's flushed and happy faces. He wanted her fiercely.

They both applauded loudly when the song was over. Georgia and the children stood up and bowed, then Georgia cocked her head. Looking first from Nate to Maddy, then glancing at the children she said, "How about cookies and ice cream?"

"They haven't had their dinner yet," Maddy protested, but her words fell on empty air; the children were already gone. "Oh, well, I guess a little ice cream won't kill them," she murmured. "They seem to have recovered from the initial wonder of seeing Georgia," she said to Nate. "They've been behaving much better, and Georgia's been trying harder not to spoil them."

"They're great kids, Maddy. I don't think you need to worry about them at all."

She looked surprised, and he considered telling her how well he and Hannah and Adam had been getting along before she came into the living room. Then he thought, what the hell? Why should he spend this unexpected time alone with Maddy talking about the children? Why should he talk at all?

He reached for her and wound his arms around her so that she couldn't possibly escape, then kissed her hard.

"Nate," she breathed. "The children."

"They're eating cookies and ice cream. They're happy. I want to be happy. Make me happy, Maddy." He kissed her again. "Come home with me," he murmured against her lips. "Let Georgia baby-sit. Let's go to my house."

He thought for a moment she was going to say yes. While he waited for her answer, he painted a minifantasy for himself. First he would unfasten the braid she'd tied her hair in and let the satiny weight of her hair fall forward across his fingers to her shoulders. Then he would gently take off her lime-green shirt and skinny white pants and whatever wispy garments she was wearing underneath. And then he would make mad, passionate love to her without saying a damn word that would get him into trouble. No mention of Teddie or any other female. No wisecracks about Hannah and Adam. No criticism of Georgia. No criticism of Brennan, who was letting down his friend Emma. He was just going to hold Maddy Scott in his arms and love her all through the night.

The word seemed to echo in the stillness of the room as though he'd said it aloud. Love.

"Georgia might do a bunk while I'm away," she said at last with an audible sigh. "Albie's in town. He called her earlier, wanting to see her. She said no, because she knew I was listening. She knows if she's seen with him, all her family appearances will have been wasted, but she's likely to decide to risk it, if I'm not here to keep an eye on her. And she's quite capable of forgetting she was supposed to be watching the kids."

"Okay, let's take the kids with us," he said. "Let Georgia make her own decisions. Hannah and Adam can spend the night at my place. I'll take them to school in the morning."

Maddy looked surprised, which he supposed was understandable. He wasn't sure what had come over him today. He seemed to be *wanting* to involve himself with those two children.

Then Maddy was shaking her head, and abruptly he was furious with her. Taking her shoulders in both hands, he brought her around to face him. "I have never in my entire life walked out on a woman after making love to her," he said angrily. "You were the one who said you didn't want this to be a one-night stand. But that's how you're treating it."

"I didn't exactly walk out, Nate." She looked so sad that his anger withered, as though it had never been.

"Not literally, no, but figuratively," he said quietly. "You withdrew from me, and now you're shutting me out. I've an idea you're using Georgia's presence as an excuse not to see me."

A faint flush spread across her cheeks, confirming his suspicion. "I know I offended you," he said. "I wish I could take the words back, but I can't. I can only apologize for them." She was still looking downcast, and he wanted to shake her. "I can't believe that you'd let a couple of moments of stupidity, my stupidity, ruin what we have, end what we have."

She glanced up at him then, her eyes dark and solemn. "It would have ended anyway. In October."

"What are you saying, Maddy? Talk to me."

"I can't, Nate. Not now. I have to think first, and I can't think. After Georgia leaves, then maybe...."

"You're sure she will go?"

She moved away a little, straightening her clothing, not looking at him. "Oh yes, the signs of restlessness are all there." She sighed. "The children are going to be upset all over again."

Now her eyes were shining with moisture, and he saw that she was close to breaking. Should he press her and hope the break would come down on his side? No, he couldn't take the risk.

Standing up, he looked down at her lowered head. "Will you call me when Georgia leaves?" he asked gruffly. She nodded without looking up.

On Tuesday morning Georgia suggested a "power walk" in Golden Gate Park. "When you get home from work, okay?" She and Maddy had always liked fast walking, even before it acquired a yuppie name.

"Me, too," Adam and Hannah chorused.

"Not this time, darlin's," Georgia said firmly. "Maddy and I need some heart-to-heart talkin'."

Maddy knew immediately from the tone of her voice that Georgia either had something to confess or bad news to impart.

It was a beautiful evening, with a brisk breeze blowing off the ocean. Several joggers were out, families picnicked here and there, flowers were in colorful bloom in front of the conservatory.

"This is great, isn't it?" Georgia said.

"Terrific," Maddy agreed, even though she had been on her feet all day. "What's on your mind, Georgia?"

"Oh, now let's not worry our heads about anything right off. Let's just enjoy ourselves." She glanced up at

Maddy's face, her pixie grin very much in evidence. "I was hoping you'd tell me all about Uncle Nate."

"Nothing to tell," Maddy said.

"That's not the message I got, watchin' the two of you. I swear I could hear wedding bells."

"Not too many men want to marry a woman with two children to raise," Maddy said.

Looking stricken, Georgia stopped dead at the side of the road.

"Did you turn your ankle?" Maddy asked.

Her sister shook her head. "I'm fine. I'm just upset that I've made you unmarriageable."

She looked totally crestfallen—but nonetheless very pretty in her lime-green sweatsuit, her heart-shaped face disguised by large sunglasses, her too-recognizable mane of curly blond hair tamed into a ponytail and tied with a wisp of pink chiffon. She was so tiny, Maddy thought, and so childlike in so many ways that it was hard to believe she was two years older than Maddy herself. Twenty-eight years old, and she looked more like fourteen. Next to her, Maddy felt like an over-grown colt, dowdy in her far more practical gray sweats.

As usual she felt an urge to restore the pixie smile to Georgia's face, to tell her of course it wasn't her fault, but she bit back the words. "I wasn't casting any blame, Georgia," she said instead. "Just stating facts."

Georgia shook her head, still looking mournful, then stepped out again at a good fast clip that soon had them both puffing. "I feel so guilty when I think about you, Maddy," she said after a while. "I did a terrible thing to you, saddling you with my responsibilities."

"I don't feel saddled," Maddy protested. "I agreed to help with the children. I love them, you know that."

"I only meant it to be for a little while. If I'd gone ahead and hired a nanny so they could travel with me, you would have been free."

"We had that particular argument over three years ago," Maddy pointed out. "The children would have been away from their father, they wouldn't have seen much of you, and how could they go to school if they were running around on concert tours?"

"You still don't think I should make some other arrangements?"

"Good God, no! Hannah and Adam are fine as they are. They're settled. Children like to be settled."

"We never were."

"True. Maybe that's why I feel so strongly about it." It was her turn to stop dead. "You haven't gone ahead and *made* other plans for Hannah and Adam, have you?"

"I wouldn't do that without consultin' you and Brennan," Georgia said in a hurt tone of voice. "It was just seein' you with your friend Nate and you saying about not gettin' married."

"Listen, Georgia," Maddy said firmly. "Let me worry about Nate, okay? I haven't even decided if I'm going to see him again. He's not . . . serious enough for me." There was a distinct quaver in her voice; she could hear it herself. She couldn't bear the thought of not seeing Nate again, his teasing grin, those quirky eyebrows, the way his craggy face crinkled with pleasure when he made love. . . .

Evidently Georgia had heard the change in her voice, too—she was glancing curiously up at her face. To distract her, Maddy changed the subject. "I don't mind a bit taking care of Hannah and Adam, and they have their father—at least some of the time—and a stable life. For God's sake, don't go hiring a nanny because you think I've got my heart set on marriage. For one thing, I've no desire to marry any man who wouldn't accept the children as part of the deal. That kind of man would not be my kind of man."

"Nate doesn't want you to keep the children?"

Maddy started walking again. "We're not talking Nate. We're talking generalities."

"Are we now?"

"Anyway," Maddy couldn't resist adding, "you've been saying all week that you're home for good. You'll be taking care of your babies yourself."

Again Georgia looked crestfallen. They were hiking through the music concourse now, cutting over to Martin Luther King Jr. Drive. Georgia was evidently planning a long walk, so there must be more news to come. "How about we catch our breath on that bench by the lake?" Maddy suggested.

They sat in silence for a while, then Georgia said, "You know, what you said about us not being settled got me thinking about when we were growing up, moving around all the time."

"I guess it didn't do us too much harm."

"No, except..." She hesitated. "Did you ever get the feelin' Mom and Dad loved each other so much, there wasn't enough love left over for us?"

"No." Maddy stared at her sister, surprised. "You thought that?"

Georgia nodded. "I used to get jealous sometimes, the way Daddy would fuss over Mom when he'd come home from work. Seemed like we were in the way."

"I don't believe they ever thought we were in the way."

"No? I used to go crazy trying to think what I'd done wrong, what I could do right so they'd love me some more." She fell silent again, then laughed. "I'm rememberin' when you were a baby, no more than a couple of years old, toddlin' around on your fat little legs, picking up after me, puttin' my socks and underwear in the laundry hamper. Mom used to say you were born tidy." Her face was serious now. "Seems like you spent your whole life picking up after me, Maddy."

"You're unusually introspective today, aren't you?"

Georgia was apparently studying a male and female mallard that were picking at the ground at the side of the lake. "I get that way when I'm coming or going," she said finally.

"I see. You're leaving for sure, then. Soon?"

"Tomorrow night. Albie booked me a flight to Tokyo. That was the reason he called. The Japanese tour is still on, after all." She reached over and patted Maddy's knee. "And listen, don't you worry about Albie—I've learned my lesson. I'm not going to jeopardize my career for any man. I'm going to be on my best behavior in Japan, and anywhere else I might go."

Maddy felt a twist of pain, not so much for herself as for Hannah and Adam. She had expected this, had been waiting for it, and was almost relieved that now the household could go back to normal. Yet how could Georgia just walk away?

"We sure are different," Georgia said, as though she'd read Maddy's mind.

"I can't argue with that."

"You're mad at me?"

Maddy sighed. "I just don't see how you can keep leaving Hannah and Adam when you love them—I *know* you love them. But there you were, just a couple of days ago, telling them you were going to settle down and make a home."

"I really wanted to, Maddy. Part of me still wants to." She sighed. "I wish I could explain it to you. I even went to a psychologist once, to see if he could come up with anything."

"When was this?"

"About two years ago."

"You never said a word."

"I was afraid you'd think even less of me when I told you I stopped going to him."

"Why did you stop?"

She shook her head, looking so unbearably sad that Maddy wanted to put her arms around her sister. "I guess I was afraid if I got all straightened out, I wouldn't be able to sing anymore."

"That's..."

"Crazy? Maybe, but I do seem to be single-minded, don't I?" She shrugged. "I did do some figurin' out, Maddy. By myself, mostly, though the psychologist put me on the track. Might not make sense to you, though."

"Try me," Maddy said gently.

Georgia nodded, then leaned back on the bench and lifted her feet, clasping her knees to her chin, looking childlike again, her hair shining in the sun. "'Member what I said about not feeling Mom and Dad loved me enough? Seems I felt that all my life, except with you. I always felt you loved me enough, but there was still this empty hole inside that didn't get filled. Not all the boyfriends I had, all the cheerleading stuff I did, all the good grades I got and the compliments from people on my singing—none of that made me feel completely loved. Not Brennan either—though he tried—nor my babies, except right at first, when I was pregnant and they lived inside me. I felt better then, but I couldn't keep having babies."

"I'm glad you decided that," Maddy said dryly.

Georgia gave her a wry smile. "Anyway," she went on after a moment, "there I was, walking around with this hole inside. Walking wounded. I heard that phrase in a movie once, walking wounded—seemed to fit how I felt." She took a deep breath, then let it out. "Then Brennan had me sing for that benefit." She turned to face Maddy, her green eyes shining, reflecting the lake water. "I'd never sung for that big a crowd before. It was a revelation to me, the way I felt. Right after the first song when the audience applauded, I felt this huge wave of love, coming straight at me from the audience, foldin' itself around me, making me whole. I knew then that I needed that kind of love always. I needed to sing, to make people happy, so that their happiness would come back to me."

There was an intensity in her voice that moved Maddy as much as her words. She had thought she understood her sister, had believed that Georgia's need for applause had been caused by the attention she'd received as a child. She hadn't realized the hunger for love had come first.

Georgia was looking pensive again. "I never would have made a good wife and mother, Maddy. I never could get it right. It was like the instructions for it didn't get programmed into me. I had this yearning all the time, pullin' at me, tearin' at me. The kids knew I wasn't there for them the way I should have been. They were always uptight. With you, they're whole different people."

"Have you talked to Brennan about this?" Maddy asked softly.

Georgia shook her head, the ponytail bouncing.

"Promise me you will, before you leave tomorrow. Hannah and Adam, too. Tell them all of it, just the way you've told me."

"You think they'd understand?"

The little-lost-child look was on her face again, and Maddy put her arms around her. "I don't know, Georgia, but I think you should at least try to explain to them. Make sure they know it's not their fault you can't stay with them. It's not anything they've done."

"Why would they think that?"

Maddy straightened and looked at her sister with loving exasperation. "Didn't you just tell me you thought Mom and Dad didn't love you enough? That it might have been because of something you'd done? You were just a kid. Hannah and Adam are kids, too. Kids often get the wrong ideas."

"Well, I'll surely make it clear they haven't done anything to make me go away," Georgia said firmly, then her voice wavered a little. "But that other stuff, about the yearning feeling, the walking wounded feeling, I don't know if I'm strong enough to talk to them about that. Next time I'm home, maybe."

"Okay," Maddy said flatly.

"I do love Hannah and Adam, Maddy," Georgia said earnestly.

"I know you do," Maddy assured her.

All this talk of love was very distressing, she thought as she and Georgia started walking again. Love itself was distressing, especially when it wasn't reciprocated. If she and the children were ever to return to that settled life she'd just talked about, she was going to have to forget Nate Ludlow. She sighed. Maybe she wasn't so different from Georgia, after all. She had her own hunger for love.

CHAPTER ELEVEN

"HELLO, EMMA," Brennan said.

Startled, Emma looked up from the patient accounts she was getting ready for mailing. Brennan was smiling warmly at her, and her heart skipped at least two beats.

"I didn't know you had an appointment," she said, pulling the book toward her.

"I don't."

He looked tired, she thought, though not as strained as when she had seen him on television with Georgia. *Georgia.* She straightened her spine. "Nate had a pretty busy schedule today, Brennan," she said briskly. "It's just about closing time. Fridays aren't usually this bad, but..."

"I didn't come to see Nate. I'm seeing him on Monday. I came to see you."

"Oh. You're not working today?"

"I worked all night. Some last-minute checking before I finish a paper I'm preparing."

"How's Georgia?"

"Georgia left on Wednesday. She's going on a tour of Japan."

So he thought he could just start in where he'd left off, she supposed, even as her pulse started racing. Standing there in white jeans and a blue Lacoste shirt that matched his eyes, his dark hair tousled over his forehead, he looked so damned attractive. Thinner than

ever, though. He really should eat more.... She broke
off the thought—let Madeleine Scott worry about his
calorie intake.

"I've missed you, Emma."

"I was right here."

He looked sheepish. "I know. I hope you'll understand. Georgia needed help." He took off his glasses,
glanced at them, then put them on again. Without them
he looked defenseless, sad. She always had been a
sucker for sad eyes.

"There was never any truth to the statements Georgia
made about our marriage," he said. "But I had to go
along with her—I still feel responsible for her, and I
still...care about her. She was so young when I married her, and I didn't understand...."

"I don't think you should blame yourself for the
failure of your marriage, Brennan," she said gently.

He sighed. "You are so kind, Emma."

They seemed to have reached an impasse. They
looked at each other in silence for a moment, then
Emma asked how the children were taking Georgia's
departure.

He smiled tiredly. "Surprisingly well. They are used
to her sudden appearances and disappearances, I guess.
They're tough little kids. They'd love to see you,
Emma," he added. "Is there any chance you could
come over, after work perhaps?"

"I'm not sure how your sister-in-law would feel about
that. Maybe she'd enjoy having the house to herself for
a while."

"She's giving a class at the zoo tonight. Some new
volunteers."

"I see." Did he feel he needed help with the children? Was that it? All the same, she had worried about

Hannah and Adam. She would like to see for herself—
rationalizing, she thought, but that didn't stop her from
agreeing to go.

"Brennan's here," she told Nate, putting her head
around the door of his office.

He was shrugging into his jacket, but stopped and
took it off. "Oh, I thought we were through. But that's
okay. Show him in."

"He didn't come to see you."

He raised his eyebrows. "Well, that's good." He
studied her face. "Isn't it?"

"I'm not sure. I'll let you know later."

"He's not having a headache?"

"I don't know. I didn't ask. One headache's gone, I
guess. Georgia left town."

His face became expressionless. "Maddy didn't call
me."

"She only left day before yesterday. Maddy's teach-
ing a class at the zoo tonight, by the way. I'm going
home with Brennan."

"Okay." He smiled wanly. "Good luck, Emma."

The children were delighted to see Emma. They had
to tell her all about their mother's visit and their appearances on television. As far as she could tell, they
had weathered the visit in good shape.

Their baby-sitter also seemed impressed with Georgia's visit. "She was just as friendly as could be," she
told Emma. "No putting on airs or anything. Singing
all the time—not my kind of music, but her voice is terrific."

The baby-sitter's name was Kat. She was a strange-
looking girl, with orange and green stripes in the front
of her hair, far-out clothing and wild earrings that hung

to her shoulders. The children seemed fond of her, however, and she of them.

"Are you a nurse?" she asked, looking at Emma's uniform.

Emma explained her occupation, and the girl's face took on a dreamy expression. "Dr. Ludlow's so *bad*," she exclaimed, which Emma suspected was supposed to be a compliment.

After she'd gone, Emma went into the kitchen and found a thawed chicken in the refrigerator. Brennan unearthed an electric wok and Emma fixed Szechuan chicken, assigning Brennan to shuck the peanuts, Hannah to destring the snow peas and Adam to help her time each step of the stir-frying. Hannah and Adam had a great time with their chopsticks, and Brennan pronounced the meal delicious. Digging in a cupboard, he came up with a bag of somewhat stale fortune cookies. Hannah's said she was going on a long journey, Adam's, that he needed to keep his affairs in order, which puzzled him no end. Brennan's made him laugh and he didn't want to show it, but the children insisted. "You are going to meet the woman of your dreams," it said.

"What kind of woman do you dream about, Daddy?" Hannah asked.

He didn't answer. He just looked at Emma, and she felt a warm glow suffuse her entire body. "What's your fortune?" he asked.

She read it and laughed wryly. "You will be a contest winner."

"Have you entered a contest?" Adam asked innocently.

"Not lately," Emma said, then glanced at Brennan and wondered if that was strictly true.

They all worked together to clear away the dishes, laughing when they got in one another's way. "How about an after dinner drink?" Brennan suggested and when she nodded, he looked at the children and proposed that they might like to watch television in Maddy's bedroom for a while. They argued a little, but then went off docilely enough.

Brennan poured Kahlua into two small glasses and led the way into the living room, but just as he set the glasses on the coffee table, the telephone rang in the hall. "I'll be right back," he promised.

Emma sat back on the sofa, one of two that bracketed the fireplace, and glanced around. Maddy Scott was a good housekeeper, she decided; the room looked comfortable but tidy and extremely clean. Nate was a neat person also, so that was good. She laughed and took a sip of her drink. Was she seriously considering that something would come of this romance between Nate and Maddy? Yes, she was; she'd never seen Nate quite so agonized as he'd appeared lately. There were no personal phone calls coming through the office for him, either—he'd evidently severed all connections with his other female acquaintances. It would be the greatest of ironies if Nate, who wasn't exactly crazy about children or marriage, was to marry Madeleine Scott, while she, who was crazy for both...

"I'm sorry, Emma," Brennan said, coming back into the room.

She thought he was apologizing for leaving her, but one look at his face told her there was more to it than that. "What happened?" she asked.

He sighed. "One of the mice has developed rather alarming symptoms. I have to go into the lab."

Her disappointment was out of all proportion to the news, but she stood up at once. "I quite understand. It's lucky I drove over myself. Don't worry— Oh, the children!"

He nodded. "I'll call Kat."

"No, don't do that. I'm here. I'll stay with them until Maddy gets home."

"You're sure you don't mind?"

Actually she did, but what could she do about it? "You go ahead, Brennan."

"Thank you, Emma," he said, turning to go. Almost at the door, he stopped, turned to look at her and seemed to make up his mind about something. Walking back, he put his hands on her shoulders, then kissed her gently on the lips.

Emma felt her whole soul go up to meet his mouth. That kiss felt so right. It moved her tremendously. No wonder she had never liked Gary's kisses; she had been waiting for one like this.

Brennan's arms moved around her, hers around him. "Emma, I think I might be falling...."

She stopped the words with her fingers. It was too soon for any declarations. She wanted to think about his kiss for a while, then she'd see.

After he'd gone, she could have kicked herself for not letting him finish. But after all, here she was, babysitting. If all Brennan Malone wanted was a full-time baby-sitter, he could hire one. Sighing, she picked up her Kahlua and drained the glass, then, after a moment's reflection, drank Brennan's too.

Time moved along slowly. She and the children played a couple of rousing hands of Go Fish at the kitchen table. They were very good. She didn't have to pretend to lose; they wiped the floor with her, which put them in very good moods.

"How old are you, Emma?" Hannah asked unexpectedly as Adam painstakingly shuffled the cards.

"I'm thirty-four," she said without hesitation. There had been a serious note in Hannah's voice. This was not just idle curiosity.

"Daddy's thirty-six," Hannah said thoughtfully, then asked, "Do you like working for Uncle Nate?"

"Uncle Nate?"

Hannah grinned. "We've decided we like him. We did the most awful things to him, but he never got mad and he was always on our side when Maddy yelled at us." She frowned. "Anyway, do you like working for him? Do you want to work for him forever and ever?"

"Yes, to the first, no to the second."

"What do you want to do then?"

"Get married and have children," Emma answered truthfully. She was a little afraid of Hannah's reaction. Would the child feel threatened? Would she and Adam start playing tricks on her as they had on Nate?

She could almost see the wheels spinning in Hannah's mind. "Do you like our daddy?" she asked after a while.

Yes, she was putting it all together.

"Very much," Emma said, then added for Hannah's benefit, "I don't know him well yet, of course."

Hannah nodded. "You're an awfully good cook," she said thoughtfully.

Somehow Emma managed to keep her face straight. "Wait until you taste my chili."

"Is it real spicy?" Adam asked. "I love it when it's spicy, with lots of onions."

"Piles of onions," Emma assured him.

"Do you like housework?" Hannah asked. Her face was still very solemn. "Mom detests it. Maddy hates it too, but she does it anyway, because she likes a clean house."

"I enjoy keeping a house clean, yes," Emma admitted. "I like the smell of furniture polish, too." She smiled at Hannah, who had come around the table to stand beside her. "I even like the sound of a vacuum cleaner." She laughed. "When I was a baby I had colic, and my mom used to run the vacuum cleaner so I'd sleep. I guess I found it soothing."

"You like children too, don't you?" Hannah said, ignoring Emma's attempt to lighten things.

"Very much."

Hannah nodded. "That's good. Very good."

Emma felt as if she'd just gone through a tough job interview. Had she passed? she wondered, looking at Hannah's frowning face. Evidently Hannah wasn't going to enlighten her. Suddenly scowling at her brother, she said, "Are you going to take all night shuffling those cards, Adam Malone?"

Later, when Emma put the children to bed, they each allowed her to hug them good-night. Adam's answering hug was enthusiastic. Hannah held back a little. Obviously she hadn't yet made up her mind.

Emma sighed when she returned to the living room. She was coming to love those two children. They were tough little kids in many ways, vulnerable in others. But one way or another, they were beginning to wind themselves around her heart.

"And Brennan?" she asked herself softly. "How do you feel about him, Emma Fieldstone?"

Before she could formulate an answer, someone unlocked the front door and came into the hall. A moment later, Madeleine Scott walked into the room.

She looked startled to see Emma, which was hardly surprising.

Emma stood up and introduced herself. A curious expression appeared on Maddy's face. "Hannah and Adam told me all about your kite flying expedition," she said. "I understand we almost lost Brennan."

"It was close," Emma agreed. There was a moment's awkward silence, then Emma explained her presence. "Brennan invited me over for dinner. He was called to the lab, so I volunteered to stay with the children until you returned."

"Brennan cooked dinner?"

"No, I did."

Maddy laughed. "You had me worried there for a minute. Brennan in the kitchen is something of a disaster." She smiled warmly at Emma. What a gorgeous smile she had. "Thank you for staying," she said. "That was very nice of you."

"My pleasure." She supposed she should go now. She'd hoped Brennan might come home again, but it didn't seem likely, and it would look pushy if she hung around waiting for him.

Maddy was friendly, she thought, but a little distant. Was she worried about Brennan falling into the wrong hands? Should she put in a word for Nate as long as she was here? No. Nate would have to work out his own problems, just as she would have to work out hers.

MADDY PREPARED FOR BED puzzling about Emma. Brennan had never brought a woman to the house, and as far as she knew, he never saw any women other than colleagues. He had told her he liked Emma, of course, when he met her in Nate's office, and she had evidently encouraged him to talk about his work, which was the quickest way to Brennan's heart at any time. He'd said she was intelligent. She seemed nice enough, certainly as unlike Georgia as she could be—there was something very likable about her—her smile was warm, the sort that made you want to smile back. The children had liked her too, when they all went kite flying. What was Brennan up to? She'd had a long talk with him after Georgia left, telling him he had to try to make more time for Hannah and Adam, because they needed him. Was bringing in another woman his solution? It was all rather worrying. But she just wasn't up to worrying about Brennan. She had to make up her mind what to do about Nate Ludlow. She had promised to call him when Georgia left, but hadn't done so. What was the point? Wouldn't it be better to end it now, while there was still some distance between them, than to go on and have her heart broken when he dropped her?

EIGHT DAYS LATER on a Saturday afternoon, she had to conduct the new group of volunteers on a tour of the zoo. They convened at noon at the zebra train depot. It wasn't a real train, just a series of trolley cars on wheels, painted in zebra stripes of black and white. As she checked off the names of the volunteers on her clipboard, she became aware that someone was hovering close behind her. Too close. She turned abruptly.

"Hi, Maddy," Nate said softly.

There ought to be a law against letting physically perfect men out of the house in soft gray sweatshirts and brief white shorts, she thought.

She took a deep breath to still the sudden racing of her pulse. "What are you—?" She broke off. It was obvious what he was doing here. He was confronting her, forcing her to make a decision. "I can't talk now, Nate," she said. "I'm about to conduct a tour."

He smiled. "I know. I managed to get myself invited along." He raised an eyebrow. "Did I ever tell you one of the leading lights of the zoological society is a patient of mine? She was delighted when I expressed an interest in becoming a member. I've paid my twenty-five-dollar fee and everything." He held up an Animal Express card and beamed at her. "Sheila said she was sure it would be okay for me to join your tour, so I could familiarize myself with the zoo. I hope you have room for me."

Sheila was one of Maddy's closest friends. Maddy had seen her earlier and had wondered at the sly, almost conspiratorial smile she had given her. Now all was clear. She considered telling Nate the train was full, but one glance at the empty seats would be enough for him to see she was lying. In any case, she was glad to see him—the whole day seemed to have taken on a sparkle around the edges. Surely the sun hadn't been shining quite that brightly when she reported in for work?

She became aware that the group of volunteers was watching both herself and Nate with great interest. "I'll deal with you later," she murmured.

"I'll look forward to it," he said with unmistakable pleasure.

Naturally he managed to get a seat right behind the driver. As she gave her commentary on the various exhibits, she was conscious of his admiring gaze on her face. Whenever she invited questions he was first in line. "Why is that mandrill picking at his foot with a piece of stick?'' he wanted to know. ''Is it the African elephant that has bigger ears?''

He appeared vitally interested in the entire zoo, amused first by the strong odor of jungle that hung around the lion house, then by the rhinos trotting in single file around their enclosure as though they were marching to music, by the cheetah running very fast along his fence, easily outstripping the train, and finally by the enormous orangutan who always posed for pictures when a group of tourists came by.

''Do all bears hibernate?'' he inquired as they passed the bear exhibit, and when she didn't answer, he lowered his voice and asked, ''Are you going to hibernate forever?'' which brought him a sharp glance from Thomas the driver.

She found herself growing breathless, making mistakes, talking about ruffed lemurs when she meant patas monkeys, and generally losing control of the whole tour. She was relieved when it was over.

''Next stop Tiburon,'' Nate said as he insisted on helping her down from the train.

''Tiburon?'' she echoed.

''I called Hannah, and she told me you'd said you'd be home by two-thirty at the latest. I asked if she and Adam would like to go on the ferry to Tiburon with us. She seemed quite taken with the idea.''

''She would. She loves Tiburon. There's a shop there that absolutely fascinates—'' She broke off. ''You invited the children to go on a ferryboat? Aren't you afraid Hannah will push you overboard?''

''I'll take my chances.''

''You had no business promising them a trip without consulting me,'' she grumbled. ''What if I don't want to go to Tiburon? Will you take them by yourself?''

He shook his head. "We'll just have to disappoint them, I guess."

It was a form of blackmail, of course, but he was quite unrepentant when she pointed this out. An hour and a half later she had changed into her own shorts and pulled on a sweatshirt over her cotton work shirt, and all four of them were climbing aboard the ferry for Tiburon, the children excitedly running ahead to claim seats on the upper deck.

It was incredibly windy on the water, so much so that they couldn't talk; the wind snatched the words from their mouths as soon as they opened them. Maddy's hair blew straight out from her head, and even Hannah's braid was horizontal most of the time.

Boats were not Maddy's favorite places to take the children, but for once they stayed pretty close. They did try climbing onto the rail a couple of times, but Nate hauled them down immediately. It was nice having someone else to help with them for a change, she thought, wondering at the docile way they obeyed him. There seemed to be a whole new atmosphere between the children and Nate. Probably Hannah had set aside her hostility for the sake of a trip to her favorite place, she decided.

They walked around the quaint little town for a while, ending up in Hannah's favorite store. Maddy managed to dissuade Nate from buying her a photograph frame she had her heart set on—an expensive ceramic with a bathing beauty, complete with parasol, stretched out across the base—but she did allow him to pay for a crystal pendant that caught Hannah's eye, and a bathroom plunger with a carved pig topping the handle that Adam decided was a perfect gift for Kat. Afterward Adam marched ahead of them with the plunger over his shoulder, chanting, "Pig plunger," and drawing amused glances from passersby.

They ate grilled turkey and avocado sandwiches on the deck at Sam's, hanging on to their napkins in the wind. Hannah and Adam fed crumbs to the sea gulls, who already looked far too fat. It was a happy time. Maddy decided that since the children had come along, there wasn't much point in worrying about her relationship with Nate; she'd just enjoy herself and worry again later.

But that evening when they took the children home, they found Brennan all dressed up in his best suit, ready to leave the house. When Maddy asked where he was off to, he said he was going out with Emma.

"Your mouse is okay now?" she asked. He had been worrying about that particular mouse for over a week now.

He nodded. "We've even begun the controlled trials in the hospital. It looks good." He left a minute later, beaming. In anticipation? Maddy wondered.

"Is this thing with Emma getting serious?" Maddy asked Nate while the children were taking their baths.

He had seated himself on one of the living-room sofas and was looking hopefully up at her, probably expecting that she'd fall into his arms now they were alone. He smiled. "I certainly hope so. I'm not sure Brennan would want to brave the madness of matrimony, but Emma's likely to. She wants nothing more than a husband and children. Earth Mother, that's Emma."

She stood with her back to the empty fireplace, looking at him with narrowed eyes. "You *hope* it's serious? Why? Because that would solve the problem of the children, where you're concerned?"

He seemed surprised, but Maddy was running with the idea now and didn't give him time to answer her question. "You introduced them, didn't you? You even suggested Brennan should come into your clinic. Did you have this in mind all along? What did you do? Tell Emma it would be helpful if she took the children off your hands until October?"

"October? What the hell does October have to do with anything?" He leaned forward on the sofa. "Listen, Maddy, I have no idea what you're talking about. Did Emma say something to you? She told me she'd met you."

She continued to gaze at him suspiciously, and he began to look uncomfortable. "Okay. I did say to Emma in the beginning that she might suggest to Brennan that he think seriously about finding a new mother for Hannah and Adam, but that was before she ever met him." He grinned, as if hoping to placate her. "It was just a joke, Maddy."

"This whole thing is a joke to you, Nate Ludlow," she said flatly. "The children got in your way, so you had to find a way of...disposing of them. Is that it?"

"That's not it at all." Sighing, he stood up and came toward her. She stiffened, but he paid no attention to her signals and put his arms around her, anyway. "Brennan looked like a lonely guy to me, but it didn't cross my mind that he and Emma might get along until I saw them together. When Brennan came into my office, they started talking, and I didn't *have* to do anything to push them together. The only contribution I made was to stay out of sight. They like each other, Maddy, and Emma's a fine person. You must have liked her?"

"She seemed very nice," she said grudgingly.

"You know what the problem really is, don't you?" he said.

She looked at him warily.

"You're afraid if Brennan and Emma get together, you'll have to give up the children."

"I told you I was prepared to do that," she said stiffly.

"In theory, yes, but if push comes to shove, what then?"

She looked so bleak that he tightened his arms around her in a hug, then set her away so he could peer into her face. "Is there any reason you can't share them?" he inquired.

"They aren't toys, Nate. Face it, you know nothing about children."

"Sure I do. I used to be a child myself. And I learned to share my mom with my stepfather and stepsisters. It took me a while, but eventually I found out there was more than enough love to go around." He shook her a little. "Isn't this premature, anyway? This is Brennan and Emma's first real date. Do you really need to worry if it's serious or not?"

She sighed. "I guess not." She gave Nate an exasperated smile. "You are the most persuasive man...."

"I know." His expression was pensive. "Could I persuade you to come over to the sofa and sit down?"

"I have to check on the children," she said.

Now it was his turn to sigh, but he let her go.

When she came back into the room a half hour later, he had leaned back his head on the sofa cushions and gone to sleep. His face looked as young, as vulnerable as when she had looked at it on the pillow in Carmel.

Carmel. She had been so furious with him. Now she could hardly remember what she had been furious about. It had been much easier to stay angry when she wasn't seeing him, she thought as she left again and went down the hall to put the children to bed. For once they didn't argue. The windy trip each way on the ferryboat had tired them.

Nate was still asleep when she returned. But as soon as she sat down beside him, he awoke instantly, smiling. "Am I still in the doghouse?" he asked.

She shook her head. "I guess not. I can't seem to stay mad at you, but I am worried about Brennan and Emma."

"They're both adults, Maddy."

"I know that, but Brennan is so devoted to his work—I don't think he can sustain a relationship."

"That's for him and Emma to work out."

She sighed. "What about the children?"

"They like Emma." He laughed. "She told me Hannah conducted an interview of her when she was here, asked her all kinds of personal questions, as if she was applying for a job."

"Is she applying?"

"She likes Brennan. A lot." He sat up and looked at her directly. "I'm more worried about Emma than Brennan. She's such a patsy. She seems to attract men who take advantage of her. Is Brennan just looking for a mother for his children?"

"He doesn't need to. He's got me."

"Then perhaps he needs to satisfy other needs." His wickedly innocent grin appeared. "I know how that is."

She couldn't help laughing. He always made her laugh.

He took advantage of her weakening, pulling her into his arms.

"The children might wake up, Nate," she protested, making a half-hearted effort to push him away.

"They ought to sleep like logs. All that fresh sea air." She had taken off her sweatshirt, and he leaned over to kiss the spot where her shirt gave way to satiny-smooth breasts.

He heard her catch her breath, then felt her hands moving down his back, pulling him closer. With his mouth, he pushed aside the cotton fabric of her shirt, and then his tongue was circling the tight nipple that was clearly outlined under her bra. His lips closed on it through the lacy fabric, tugging slightly, and he moved his hands down her lovely slender body, seeking the places that would urge her toward him, pressing his palms roughly over her bare thighs toward the part of her that was arching toward him, stroking and teasing her, while his mouth continued its tender ministrations to her breast.

"Oh, Nate." She was laughing breathlessly, fondly. "You're impossible."

"Wrong. I'm very possible. Try me." Lifting his head, he took the hand that was clutching the back of his sweatshirt and brought it around to a far more satisfying place. He saw her eyes darken and leaned forward to kiss her again.

"I want to make love to you, Maddy. Now," he said against her lips.

"The children," she protested again.

"Don't mommies and daddies make love when the children are asleep?"

"We're not Mommy and Daddy."

"Let's pretend," he suggested with a leer.

She laughed again. He truly was impossible and she wanted him. And a part of her mind was telling her that there was no reason she couldn't enjoy him until October. Who knew when she'd find someone she'd want to make love with again? Shouldn't she stockpile these occasions against the lonely winter nights ahead?

"My bedroom door does have a lock," she conceded.

He was on his feet instantly, dragging her up with him.

MADDY HAD THOUGHT it would be impossible for her to relax completely, even with her bedroom door locked and the knowledge that the children's bathroom was between their bedrooms and hers. Once asleep, the children usually didn't wake up until morning, but there was always the possibility of an exception.

But once she and Nate were lying together, naked and warm, she was able to assign the children to a place in the back of her mind that was always alert, but still far enough away from present happenings not to interfere.

In Carmel, Nate had proceeded at a leisurely pace, making her wait as he explored every part of her body, but tonight he had set patience aside and she was glad of it. Too much time had passed since they had first made love. She wanted him quickly and telegraphed her need for haste to him with mouth and hands. His kisses were hard and hot on her face, her throat, her breasts. Her hands reached for him, found him, held him as she guided her body over him. They were both breathing raggedly. They fell still for a moment as he entered her, then moved in a frenzy until they climaxed together.

After a few minutes more, Nate rolled with her until he was over her, then laughed softly. "So there, Maddy Scott," he said.

She smiled against his bare shoulder. "Wham bam," she murmured. "Am I supposed to thank you now?"

"Couldn't hurt. But the expression is 'Thank you *ma'am*,' I do believe. And I do. Thank you."

He lifted himself on his hands. With the heavy draperies closed, it was dark in the bedroom. She could see only a silhouette above her, but could feel his warm breath on her face. "You are a remarkable lover, Nate Ludlow," she murmured. She felt rather than saw him smile.

"You have your moments yourself, Maddy Scott," he replied.

He lowered his mouth to hers and kissed her tenderly. To her astonishment she felt herself quickening again. Her lips parted to his insistent tongue and her hands pressed against his back, pulling him down. "I'm too heavy for you," he protested, but she made a negative sound against his lips and he relaxed his body over hers. She thought for a moment he was drifting into sleep, but then felt an unmistakable sensation. He was growing again inside her; she marveled at his ability to regenerate.

It was an entirely new sensation to just lie there beneath him, allowing passion to build again without doing anything to encourage it. They stayed like that for a long time, not speaking, not kissing, just breathing quietly together, and then he very carefully, very gently rolled over onto his back, still holding her tightly.

Then she was above him, his hands were cupping her breasts and she was moving slowly, teasing him, easing herself away, bringing herself back over him. He murmured incoherently, and though she could not understand the words, she knew she was bringing him pleasure and thrilled to the fact. Sex with Nate Ludlow was an adventure, she decided, a shared adventure. He could initiate moves and positions, or she could. There was a heady sense of exploration, not just of each other's bodies, but of each other's feelings. She could tell immediately when she was doing something that he found exciting.

His hands had moved around her now and were stroking her back as she moved on him, then they tightened and he instigated another change of position, with himself over her, his body moving against hers, thrusting gently, slowly. Her hands and hips urged him to more speed, but he kept up his measured pace and she learned that resistance was more exciting than compliance. That sweet, remembered pressure was building again inside her, and she was conscious of nothing but the man above her. Her mouth sought his, held his, parted to his, her pulse rushing in her ears like the muffled roar of the ocean, rushing, stilling and rushing again as he lifted her, then moved against her. The world first shrank to their own small part of it, then disappeared as her body arched to his and exploded against him. *I love you, Nate Ludlow,* she wanted to cry—and had to clamp her mouth shut to keep the words hidden.

Afterward he slept for a while and she lay awake, gazing upward, though she couldn't see the ceiling, remembering an article she'd read in some popular magazine. The writer had stated that most women made the mistake of confusing terrific sex with love. It was possible, the writer had insisted, to have great sex without love, but not so possible to have great love without sex.

It was all very confusing.

Then she found herself remembering Nate—on the zoo tour, teasing her with his supposedly earnest questions, his hands gently massaging the ache from Barbara Oates's stiff shoulders, his laughter at the children's mischief. Somehow he seemed to have learned the secret of how to extract the most joy out of life. She loved the *whole* man, she thought, sighing; there was no doubt about that.

"That bad, huh?" Nate murmured into her ear. He had heard her sigh, she supposed.

"Just breathing," she said.

"You've got breath left? Guess I didn't do my job right."

"You did good," she assured him.

He kissed her. "I thought so, too."

She sighed again. "You have to go, Nate. Brennan..."

"Lord, yes, that would be embarrassing. I'm not sure Brennan is aware such things go on."

"He's such a dear," Maddy said.

He was pleased to discover that he no longer felt jealous when she spoke fondly of Brennan. And she seemed to have recovered from her jealousy of Teddie. Their relationship was maturing as it should.

And what of the future, Ludlow? he asked himself as he was driving home. But almost immediately he shook his head. It wasn't his way to try to forecast the future. All the same, he couldn't help thinking of how Maddy had looked when he left, lying in the tumbled bed, her satiny brown hair spread on the pillow, her dark eyes glowing. Somewhere in the back of his head a voice said, *It isn't going to get any better than this, Ludlow. This is the best.* The thought terrified him.

HIS BEDSIDE TELEPHONE woke him at 6:00 a.m. Maddy. For one second he thought she'd called to whisper sweet nothings, but then he realized her voice had sounded upset.

"What's up?" he asked, sitting up and raking a hand through his hair, trying to blink himself awake.

"It's Georgia. Albie called us from Japan a couple of hours ago. Georgia's very sick, Nate. She went swimming at some air force base and then got sick and they thought she'd just taken a chill from swimming, but she got progressively worse and now her temperature's up around 106°."

He whistled under his breath.

"Albie says she's asking for us, for Brennan and the children and me. She says she has to see us right away. They don't know if she's going to live, Nate. They don't know what's wrong with her. Her fever isn't coming down. And she was having such a terrific time. The Japanese loved her. She was getting rave reviews in all the papers over there. The kids and I had a postcard and she said her voice had never sounded so good. It was the humidity, she said. They were having a freak hot spell. I guess that's why she went swimming."

Her voice was rising and she was talking very rapidly. Nate made his own voice very calm, hoping to steady her. "You're going to Japan? Is there anything I can do? Can I help you pack?"

"We're packed already. There's a plane at seven-thirty. Albie's arranging tickets for us. Luckily our passports are up-to-date—Brennan had a conference in Sweden last year, and I took the children to France to visit my folks a couple of years ago, before they went to Saudi Arabia—my parents, I mean. Oh, I should call them. I've got the children up and Brennan's dressing them. I just told them their mom's sick and misses them. I don't want to worry them until I have to, *if* I have to." She took a deep breath and made an obvious effort to speak more slowly. "I just wanted you to know...and Brennan wants you to tell Emma. He didn't want to wake her. Evidently they were out pretty late last night.''

"I'll tell her," he assured her. "If there's anything I can do..."

"I'm so worried, Nate. I thought Georgia seemed drawn when she was home. I should have arranged for her to have a physical, but she's always been reluctant to see doctors, ever since she was a little girl. I should have insisted.''

"It's not your fault she got sick, Maddy," he said firmly.

She made a sound that was halfway between a laugh and a sob. "I know. Listen, Nate, I have to go. We may have to get some shots. We're not sure what's necessary.''

"I'll be rooting for you," he said. "And for Georgia.''

"Thank you, Nate." She hesitated, but evidently changed her mind about what she was going to say. "Thank you," she said again.

CHAPTER TWELVE

EMMA WAS LATE getting to work. Jamie had shown in two patients, and Nate had already taken care of one before she arrived. One look at her face and he decided Brennan must have called her, after all. But when he asked her, she looked blank. He invited her into his office and closed the door.

"I'm sorry I'm late," she said. "I had to go see Gary."

"I thought Gary was history."

She nodded, tight-lipped. "Late and unlamented." She looked sheepish. "I didn't tell you, Nate. I figured you had enough on your mind. Lately I've been missing stuff out of my fridge and larder. I thought I was having memory lapses at first, then I remembered Gary still had a key to my apartment. I asked old Mr. Rosini and he said sure, Gary had been coming in and out right along. It had never occurred to me that he'd do that, Nate. I felt so stupid for ever trusting him."

"He was helping himself to food? What a rat! Did you get the key?"

"He said he couldn't find it."

"Change the locks." Nate was incensed. "That does it," he said. "I was thinking of ordering another security system from him, but damned if I'll contribute another dime to the Gary Conrad retirement fund."

"He needs the money, Nate," Emma demurred.

"He's the kind who'll always need money, Emma. Giving it to him just perpetuates the problem."

He suddenly remembered that he had to deal her another blow. Gazing at her sympathetically, he said, "Listen, Emma, I've got to tell you something and I don't have much time. Mrs. Rodriguez is waiting for me."

"Her shoulder's acting up again?"

"She will carry that damn shoulder bag. Puts everything into it but the kitchen sink. Damn things should be outlawed." He took one of her hands in his. "Maddy called me early this morning."

Her round face lighted up. "Brennan told me you were over there last night. Oh Nate, we had such a super time. We went to Harry's Bar and ate fettucine and sourdough bread and sat there the longest time, talking and talking until the place finally closed. I can see why his marriage didn't work out—he's absolutely devoted to the work he does. Georgia just wasn't the right type for him. He needs someone who understands what he's trying to do. He's such a—" She broke off, her gaze sharpening. "What happened? Did something happen to Brennan?"

She looked stricken. *Yes, Maddy, it's serious,* he thought as he shook his head. "Georgia's sick. In Japan. Evidently it's pretty bad. She sent for Brennan and Maddy and the children. They're flying out this morning."

Her face showed a complete roster of emotions before it settled on a questioning expression. "Maddy's sure this is the real thing? Georgia didn't just get in trouble again and send for them to bail her out?"

"She has a fever of 106°."

"God, what happened?"

He told her the facts he knew, then added, "I thought the same thing myself, that she might be exaggerating, but evidently it was the agent who called, and he stressed that she's very, very ill. The doctors have no idea what it is. They're doing tests, of course."

She pulled away from him and turned her back, picking up a letter opener on his desk and fiddling with it. "I guess Brennan had to go," she said in a small voice. "She is the mother of his children. He does care about her. I guess I shouldn't resent him going."

"Resent away," he advised. "I resent the hell out of Maddy going. I know that's a selfish attitude, but we're only human, Emma. We both got dumped for Georgia a short time ago, only natural we'd get fed up with it."

"No, it's right for them to go," she said in a stronger voice, turning to face him. "If she's really sick, if anything happened, they'd never forgive themselves for not being there. Brennan talked a lot about Georgia last night. He does feel responsible for her. They are still linked by the children after all, and by Maddy."

"You going to be okay?" he asked.

She nodded, then smiled wanly. "How about you?"

"Hell, yes, I'm a patient man. Maddy will be back. Things are looking up, Emma," he added on a lighter note. "The kids call me Uncle Nate now."

She raised her eyebrows.

"Don't you go getting ideas, Emma Fieldstone," he warned as he started for the door.

And who's to stop me? she asked herself as she followed him out.

IT WAS RAINING HARD in Japan. From the taxi window, as they drove to the base hospital, Maddy watched men and women and children hurrying along the sidewalks, all of them clutching umbrellas, the rain slanting down in definite lines—looking like a woodblock print by Hiroshige.

Maddy had visited Japan once before while she was still in college, when her father was working on a project there. She remembered him telling her that Japan was the most honest country in the world; you could leave anything anywhere and it would not be stolen, unless it was an umbrella and the weather was wet.

The streets were much more crowded with traffic, she thought, and there were even more high rises. But the Kanji lettering on the signs on stores and offices still looked like artworks and made the atmosphere unmistakably Oriental. There was still a prevalence of western dress, much to the children's disappointment. They had expected everyone to look like the Japanese dolls their grandparents had sent them years ago.

Hannah and Adam were excited about the journey, but subdued, worried about their mother. Brennan was subdued, too; she had no idea what he might be thinking. It seemed impossible that less than twenty-four hours ago she had been lying in Nate's arms. Dear Nate, he had wanted so badly to help in some way. He really cared about her, she was sure. If only...

She shut off her thoughts. She had to concentrate on Georgia. Poor Georgia, to get sick when she was enjoying life again. She hated being sick, always had. She liked being cared for, but missed the attention she'd get if she was out there entertaining everybody.

You have to get well, Georgia, she thought fiercely. *We love you, all of us, even if you do exasperate us. You are special, unique, and we can't bear to lose you.*

Georgia was unconscious, the doctor told them. After one glance at the children's worried faces, he took

Brennan into another room and kept him there for a while. When Brennan came back, he looked pale. "Her fever's still high," he told them. "They've found out what it is, though. It's Japanese encephalitis B. They're guessing she got bitten by a mosquito while she was at the base pool."

"That's serious, isn't it?" Maddy said quietly.

He nodded.

"Is Mom going to be okay?" Hannah asked in a tight little voice that made Maddy want to cry.

"We don't know, honey," Maddy told her. She never lied to the children.

"They have her packed in ice to get her fever down," Brennan said. "They're doing everything they can. All we can do is wait. And pray."

They waited for hours. A very nice air force major came by and introduced himself as Jed Allen. He brought them coffee and soda for the children. After a while he insisted on taking them to the officers' club for dinner. He had been with Georgia at the pool, he said; in fact, he'd invited her to go swimming and felt responsible. He remembered her saying she thought a mosquito had bitten her, but hadn't thought anything of it. He'd thought she was coming down with a cold, or maybe flu. She'd started shivering and said she was aching all over, so he'd brought her into the hospital and called her agent at her request. She was supposed to appear on television that night and had worried about missing the show.

"She would," Brennan said with a shaky little laugh.

"Her tour was going very well," the major said. "She was interviewed by all the media, and everyone was so impressed by her. She's so nice to everyone, so down-home. And her voice..."

There was a note in his own voice that was more than admiring. Maddy studied his face for a minute. He wasn't a handsome man, but he was striking, gray-haired, strong featured, maybe forty years old. Judging by the look on his face, he was smitten with Georgia Malone. Well, he certainly wasn't the first, Maddy thought resignedly, and wouldn't be the last.

Major Allen arranged for them to stay the night in the hospital. They were allowed one quick glance at Georgia, who was tossing and turning amongst her ice packs, muttering to herself, occasionally shouting something that was unintelligible. An intravenous drip hung by her bed, the needle entering the back of her left hand. She looked diminished, Maddy thought, so tiny and flushed in the white hospital bed, her hair so slick with perspiration that it had lost its curl and its shine. Looking at her sister, she was convinced she was going to die. She had promised her parents she would call them again as soon as she saw Georgia, but didn't have the heart. She'd wait until tomorrow, she decided.

Tomorrow brought no change. They sat together in the waiting room, Maddy reading to the children, walking the hospital corridors with them when they became restless. Every time anyone came near the waiting room, they all looked up, not sure whether to be hopeful or frightened. But hour after hour no one came in. They could still hear Georgia shouting, so they knew she was alive, but that was all they knew.

And then at four o'clock on the morning of the third day, Brennan came into Maddy's room and woke her from a fitful sleep. "She's turned the corner," he said. "Her fever's on the way down. They think she might pull through it."

Maddy offered up a brief thanksgiving, then glanced at Brennan's tired face. "Might?"

He nodded heavily. "That's what the doctor said."

A couple of hours later they were allowed to see her. She was conscious, but very weak. "Hey, Maddy, Brennan," she said softly. "Did you bring my babies?"

Maddy nodded and pushed Hannah and Adam forward. They seemed reluctant, even frightened to approach the weak-looking woman with the straggly hair. But then Georgia managed a smile and they flung themselves at her with such vigor that Maddy was afraid they'd dislodge the intravenous needle. "It's okay, Maddy," Georgia said as Maddy reached to pull the children away.

Georgia looked up at Hannah and Adam as they gazed down at her. "I'm okay, babies. I'm going to be just fine, I can tell. Take more than a li'l old mosquito to keep Georgia Malone down."

"We were scared, Mom," Adam said gruffly.

"Me, too, sweetheart," Georgia admitted with a faint attempt at her usual radiant smile.

"I think you'd better come home, Mom," Hannah said briskly. "Maybe we should get that house in Pacific Heights. I'll take care of you."

"Sweetheart, there's not going to be any house in Pacific Heights," Georgia said weakly. "I hope you don't think that means I don't love you."

Hannah shook her head, but looked unconvinced.

"You know what," Georgia said. "Every once in a while I see a little girl with a long blond braid like yours and I get a real bad stomachache, thinking of my Hannah. And then I see this little boy with hair that stands up at the back, like my Adam, and I get to thinking how much I miss you and I cry. But it's just no use, babies. If I tried to live back there with you all again, I'd treat you all wrong and mess up your lives, and before you know it, I'd go crazy with the yearning again, the yearning to sing and to go places, and there I'd be, off again. So you just mind Maddy, okay, and help her all you can, and I'll come visit you whenever I have a chance. Okay?''

They both nodded vigorously and she smiled, then settled back into her pillows. "I'm thinking I need a nap," she told them. "Maybe we can talk some more later." As they turned to go, she added, "You might just ask that nice Major Allen to come in. I've an idea he's blaming himself for me gettin' sick, and I can't have that now, can I?''

Maddy was laughing as they all filed into the waiting room again. "Georgia's going to be just fine," she assured Brennan.

He grinned at her, looking as though a huge weight had been taken off his shoulders. "I think so, too," he said.

Hannah's face showed strong disapproval. "Has Mom got something going with Major Allen?" she asked.

"Well, I think maybe they're friends," Maddy said discreetly.

Hannah snorted.

"I like Major Allen," Adam piped up; Hannah snorted again and started picking through the magazine rack.

After they'd all settled into their usual seats, Brennan murmured, almost to himself, "I wonder where I can buy a postcard around here."

Maddy smiled at him gently. "To send to Emma?"

He flushed. "You think maybe I shouldn't write to her?"

"On the contrary. I think you should." She glanced at the children. They had made themselves comfortable on a vinyl-covered sofa on the other side of the room and were occupied with a children's magazine, trying to find the hidden animals in a large picture. "You care about her, don't you?" she said softly.

He didn't answer directly, but behind his glasses, his eyes had acquired a soft, almost nostalgic expression that she hadn't seen before. "Emma *listens* to me," he said. "I can discuss my work with her. I've never really been able to do that with anyone but a colleague before. Emma truly enjoys discussing my work. Other women, well, they might pretend an interest, but after a while their eyes glaze over and I know they are tuning me out."

Maddy felt guilty, knowing that she too had led him along with an "uh-uh" and a "really?" from time to time, when his conversation went over her head.

"She seems to understand what my work means to me," Brennan went on, still with that same dreamy expression on his face. "She'd have gone to medical school herself if she could have afforded it, but her father died when she was still in high school and there wasn't any money, so she settled for medical services instead. But the interest is still there—she's done a lot of reading about medical research. She's remarkably well-informed." He hesitated. "She likes Hannah and Adam," he added after a moment.

"They like her, too," Maddy offered. "But this all sounds a bit one-sided, Brennan. I can see the benefits of this relationship where you're concerned, but what about Emma? How will she feel when you get so wrapped up in your work that you forget you have a date with her?''

''That's a funny thing,'' Brennan said, sitting forward and raking his fingers through his dark hair, looking so earnest that Maddy felt a rush of affection for him. ''I find myself thinking about Emma even when I'm working. There's something so warm about her, so caring, sometimes I want to be with her more than I want to work.''

He sat up even straighter. ''Not that I'd ever neglect my work,'' he hastened to say. ''But the last few days, watching Georgia so close to death, I did some thinking about my own life. I'm beginning to see things aren't as urgent as all that in the long run, and I need to spend more time with the children, as you've been telling me all along. Maybe if I do spend some time with them and with Emma, I wouldn't feel the need to be at the lab all the time.''

He grinned at Maddy. ''Anyway, it's not all as one-sided as you seem to think. Emma's had some bad experiences with men. She's so warmhearted, people take advantage of her. I would never do that. She talks too, you know, and I enjoy her stories about her widowed mother, who's something of a character, an English war bride from Yorkshire, evidently very outspoken, spends most of her time cooking, but never gains an ounce because she attacks life on the run. Unfortunately, according to Emma, she didn't inherit her mother's metabolism, so she spends most of her time with her trying not to eat. She wants me to visit. Mother would have a great time putting meat on my bones, she thinks.''

''You do listen to her, don't you?'' Maddy teased.

Apparently he was still thinking about Emma and didn't hear her. "I'm easier around the children when I'm with Emma," he said, as though Maddy hadn't spoken. "What I mean is—" He frowned, worrying his hair with fingers again as though trying to forcibly straighten out his thoughts. "I don't mean I only want to be with Emma because she's so good with Hannah and Adam. I mean when we're all together it's like we're a whole family."

His grin had turned sheepish. "It's a good feeling." He raised his eyebrows. "Do you mind, Maddy? That I...like Emma? You don't think I'm being unfair to the children, or to Georgia? I still care about Georgia, you know, I guess I always will, but it's not the way it used to be—it doesn't hurt anymore. I was worried, of course—I'm fond of Georgia, and I think I finally understand her but—"

"I don't think you owe Georgia more than you've given her, Brennan," Maddy interrupted when he seemed to be floundering. "As for the kids, they don't seem threatened by Emma at all, not the way they've been by Nate. Children pick up signals from people. They've obviously sensed that Emma truly cares about them, and about you."

She glanced again at the children. Adam had dozed off against Hannah's shoulder. Hannah was still concentrating on the magazine, and neither Maddy nor Brennan had raised their voices. All the same, Hannah had probably heard every word—there was something unnatural in her posture.

"Well," Brennan said, following her glance. "There's lots of time, I guess. Emma doesn't seem to want to rush into anything, and I guess that's the best way, to take it one day at a time."

A young and very pretty Japanese nurse opened the door abruptly and looked in. Maddy and Brennan stiffened, but she just smiled warmly and said, "Everything okay, *okusan* sleeping, no worry," and closed the door again. Hannah had looked up too, Maddy realized. She was fully alert, no doubt about that.

She and Brennan were silent for a while, then Brennan stirred. "Should I get a postcard for you, too, to send to Nate?" he asked with an innocent smile.

Maddy grinned at him. "You really haven't been quite as buried in your work as usual, have you?"

"Let's just say I've sensed a certain atmosphere between the two of you."

Maddy laughed, then sighed. "I'm afraid the atmosphere is all on my side, Brennan."

"Didn't seem that way from where I sat."

"Well, maybe atmosphere isn't the right word. What I'm saying is—" She broke off and darted another glance at Hannah, who hadn't turned a page in a long time. The child's head was lowered as though she were studying the design on her T-shirt—perhaps she was asleep. "Nate isn't interested in anything long-term," she explained.

"Are you sure?"

"He made it crystal clear right from the start."

"Does he know how you feel?"

"Are you serious? There's no way I'm going to tell him anything, as long as I know the ax is going to fall come October."

"October?"

"Nate doesn't feel any relationship can last more than six or seven months. Our seven months is over in October."

"But you do feel something, right?"

"Right." She sighed again. "I don't think we should discuss this at the moment, Brennan," she added, inclining her head towards Hannah.

"Okay, but I think you may be doing Nate an injustice. I'll admit Emma told me pretty much the same thing—that his relationships don't usually last. But I've seen him look at you, Maddy, and given time, I think he may discover he feels pretty strongly himself."

"The point is, he isn't going to give me time," Maddy replied.

"Uncle Nate likes you a lot," Hannah said abruptly.

Maddy shook her head. "I knew you were eavesdropping. Since when did you become Nate's champion, anyway?"

"Uncle Nate's okay," Hannah said stoutly. "He's always on our side. He doesn't get mad at us like you do, Maddy."

"I never get mad at you."

"Sure you do. You have to. You take care of us." Hannah gently moved Adam's head to the side of the sofa, stood up and came over to lean against Maddy. "I didn't mean you were ever nasty to us, Maddy. We always know you love us, even if you're grounding us or making us wash dishes."

"Well, I'm glad to hear that," Maddy said, hugging the little girl close. "And I'm delighted you've found out how nice Nate is, though I'm still amazed at this Uncle Nate business."

"We had a talk," Hannah explained. "Uncle Nate told Adam and me he didn't get mad at us when we played tricks on him, because he doesn't get mad at people he likes."

Maddy felt a bubble of pure happiness grow inside her. Was it going to work out after all between Nate and herself? That last night together had been so gloriously exciting, yet so tender. Nate was a wonderful man. If he really did like the children, then surely...

"He knew we were worried he was going to steal you away from us," Hannah went on happily. "He knew that's why we acted as if we didn't like him. And he said we weren't to worry. There was no way he was going to take you away."

The bubble didn't so much burst as somehow change form, becoming a shaft of pain.

"Are you okay, Maddy?" Brennan asked.

"Sure I'm okay," Maddy said irritably. "I just need for people to stop talking for a while, that's all."

She hated herself for snapping at Brennan and Hannah, especially when Hannah looked hurt and went back across the room to her magazine. After all, Hannah had only confirmed what she'd always known. Nate Ludlow wasn't in this for the long term. Of course he could swear truthfully that he wasn't going to take Maddy away from the children. How could he be a threat to the children when he was going to decamp in October?

She gritted her teeth to hold back the despair she could feel building inside her, and after a moment felt anger growing in its place. She would send Nate a post-card report on Georgia's progress. Yes, she owed him that, but that would be the finish. "I'm damned if I'm going to stick around, waiting for the ax to fall in October," she announced.

"Huh?" Hannah inquired.

"Never mind," Maddy said grimly.

THE POSTCARD CAME on Friday. *Georgia on the mend,* it said. *Everybody fine.* Nothing more. Nothing about when they might be coming home.

Nate studied Maddy's handwriting. He hadn't seen it before. It was as elegant and neat as she was herself, the letters rounded and completely legible. He wished she'd included a little more information, but decided she had probably been rushed and would write again, maybe the following day.

But Saturday's mail brought no more information, and he spent a frustrating weekend, wondering why he felt so totally useless when Maddy Scott wasn't around. He had no appetite, no energy. For a while he tried to convince himself he was coming down with a cold, but knew he was just fooling himself—he missed Maddy Scott, he needed Maddy Scott, he loved Maddy Scott.

He sat down hard on one of the leather sofas in the living room. Having made the admission, he wasn't sure if he felt better or worse. It wasn't as if he hadn't been in love before. He had loved several women, for a while. But even while he loved them, he had known it was a temporary affair. This thing with Maddy Scott was different. He literally could not imagine going on like this, day after day without her. He found himself trying to remember the words of an old song that kept going through his mind—something about getting along without someone before and being perfectly capable of getting along without them now—but somehow the words didn't seem to convince him.

On Monday, Emma had no more information either. She'd received a brief note from Brennan, which she *thought* said everything was okay. "His handwriting's like any other doctor's," she said flatly, with a meaningful look at Nate.

Leaving the clinic that evening, Nate ran into Casey Dixon in the elevator. "Karen wants you to come to dinner," Casey informed him. "She's complaining we haven't seen you in a long time. She wants to show the midget off to you."

Casey's newest offspring was a girl, Sarah, born two weeks earlier. Nate had sent Karen flowers and received in return a picture of a red-faced little monkey wrapped in a blanket. Sarah had been nicknamed the midget, Casey told him, because she weighed only seven pounds, two pounds lighter than her brother and sister had weighed at birth. She had been premature, but was doing fine.

"I'd like to see her," Nate said, surprised to discover that this was true. New babies usually made him nervous; they seemed so breakable. Perhaps he was looking for something to occupy his mind.

"Come home with me now," Casey suggested.

At first Nate demurred. "Karen doesn't need guests along with a new baby."

"You kidding, man?" Casey said. "For one thing, what's one more person, when you've already got five? For another, that woman gets more energy out of having babies than Jane Fonda gets from aerobics. Besides, she's got grandparents falling all over themselves to help. She'd love to see you, Nate. For some reason she thinks you're a sexy man, says you decorate the environment."

A half hour later, Nate found himself sitting in the Dixon's living room, gingerly holding the latest addition to the Dixon clan. "She's so incredibly small," he said wonderingly, holding her stiffly and looking at the tiny, perfectly made infant. Such impossibly small fingers, each tipped with a perfect little fingernail. A nose that was no bigger than the tip of his own finger, a diminutive rosebud mouth. Flat, tight, little black curls all over her small round head.

"That's just because she's such a contrast to the two monsters I had before," Karen said serenely. She was still generously curved, though she had lost some weight with the baby's birth.

"She looks like an elderly guru who's wandered too far from her Himalayan mountaintop," Nate said.

Casey beamed at his newest offspring. "Looks just like her beautiful momma," he argued.

Karen smiled at him, her love for him evident in her eyes.

How did they do it? Nate wondered as he watched Casey walk over to her and kiss her gently on the cheek. Casey had told him that he still got chills up his spine when Karen walked into a room; his heart still bumped around in his chest when she smiled at him. But right now, the two older children, Melanie and David, were squabbling in the kitchen over a flat-footed puppy Nate hadn't seen before, each wanting to hold it. Their voices were growing increasingly shrill, but Casey and Karen seemed able to shut them out while they enjoyed their own romantic world.

Even as he thought this, Casey yelled, "Hold it down, kids. We've got company, remember?" Melanie and David came out of the kitchen, David holding the puppy, both of them beaming at Nate.

"You like our new baby?" David asked.

"Isn't she a princess?" Melanie offered.

No sibling rivalry here, Nate thought.

He enjoyed dinner with the Dixons. There was a lot of talk, a lot of noise, especially with the new puppy joining in once in a while, but there was so much

He grinned and looked over at the baby, who was still slung over her mother's shoulder. "You ever hear that on your mountaintop, Sarah?"

The baby burped loudly.

"*I* said it to you," Karen reminded him amid the general laughter.

Casey grinned. "Whoever. Anyway, it made me stop and think. Maybe it's time for you to stop and think, old friend. How does this going on alone look to you?"

Nate thought about Maddy looking at him when he made love to her in Carmel, Maddy's expression when she looked at Georgia while Georgia was singing, Maddy's face when he surprised her by arriving for the zoo tour. He thought about how he felt when he saw her, and how he felt when she wasn't around. How his condo had seemed so empty the last few days. Lonely. "Like looking at the bottom of a barrel," he answered honestly.

"So what do you have in mind for Maddy Scott?" Casey asked.

"Could I hold the baby again?" Nate asked Karen.

She passed over the milky-smelling bundle, and Nate stared for a few moments into the wise little face. Such a warm little bundle, he thought, feeling a definite tug at his heart. "What I have in mind scares me to death," he said finally.

"Which is?"

He took a deep breath, then let it out and grinned at the two people watching him. "That maybe, just maybe, I want to marry Maddy Scott."

As Casey and Karen cheered and exclaimed, he amended the statement, looking down again at the baby's cherubic face. "No maybes about it," he said.

AFTER MAKING this momentous declaration, it was hard for Nate to believe his eyes when he saw Brennan coming into the clinic two days later. As it happened, he was in Emma's cubicle, checking on appointments for the following day, thinking he might get in nine holes of golf in the evening. He needed to do something more than mope around the condo, waiting for Maddy to come back to town.

Emma had already left, wanting to check on Muggsie, who hadn't been feeling too well the past couple of days.

The thing was, if Brennan was home, why hadn't Maddy called him?

Brennan seemed agitated. "Do you know what happened to Emma?"

"Emma went home half an hour ago," Nate said.

Brennan took off his glasses, looked at them and put them back on again. "Something's not right," he said. "I went to Emma's apartment first, on the off chance she'd be there. Some old man who lives in the next apartment—Mr. Rossi?"

"Rosini."

"Yes. He said Emma had come home and left again. Something about her dog getting out."

"Mr. Rosini let Muggsie out?"

"No. He said he'd taken her out earlier, but had put her right back in the apartment. That was around two o'clock. He told Emma the same thing, and evidently Emma was mystified, then she looked at Mr. Rosini and said, 'Dammit,' and ran out and got in her car. I thought maybe you might know something about it."

"Gary Conrad," Nate said at once. "He's been going into Emma's apartment, helping himself to food when she's at work. He must have taken Muggsie. Just the sort of thing he'd do."

"Why?"

Nate was tidying up, switching on the security system. "We'll go over there. He lives on the corner," he told Brennan. "I don't *know* why he'd take the dog, but it's the best idea I've got."

As they waited for traffic to clear, so they could cross the street outside the clinic, he asked about the Japanese trip.

"We got in last night around eleven," Brennan said.

"Maddy, too?"

Brennan nodded. "I spent most of the night in the lab, didn't get through until noon, then I fell on my face and slept a few hours. Jet lag."

And what was Maddy's excuse? Nate wondered. "Georgia okay?" he asked.

"Just about fully recovered. She's going to recuperate for a while, then carry on with her tour."

"That's great."

"Yes."

So why hadn't Maddy called him?

GARY CONRAD LOOKED as if he hadn't shaved in days. He was wearing a grungy navy-blue sweatshirt and rumpled tan pants. Obviously he hadn't been making too many sales calls. "Where's Muggsie?" Nate asked, as soon as Gary opened his door.

"How am I supposed to know?" Gary asked in return, with a curious glance at Brennan. "I've already told Emma what happened. It wasn't my fault the dog ran out, the minute I opened the door. She never did that before."

"Muggsie's having bladder troubles," Nate said.

"Well, she was haring off down the street, last I saw."

"You didn't go after her?"

"I looked around, but I couldn't see her."

"So you just left her locked out?"

"What the hell else could I do? I *told* Emma...."

"Where did Emma go from here?"

He shrugged. "Home, I guess. What's it to you?"

Nate had an overwhelming urge to punch the man's stupidly belligerent face, but repressed it. "Did you give Emma her key?"

Gary frowned. "Her key?"

"Give it over," Nate said, holding out his hand.

"I'm not sure I know..."

Nate's hand became a fist. "Now."

Gary fumbled in his pants pocket, pulled out a bunch of keys, removed one from the ring and passed it to Nate. "No need to get so steamed up," he said sullenly.

"You come anywhere near Emma or her apartment again, and I'll be back," Nate said tightly. "Then you'll see how steamed up I can get, when I really try."

"That goes for me, too," Brennan added grimly.

"All this fuss about a damn dog," Gary said, then slammed the door in their faces.

"I should have hit him," Nate said, clenching his fists.

"I thought you were going to."

Nate shook his head wonderingly, as they started back to the clinic. "I've never thought of myself as a violent man, but I sure came close." He grinned wryly. "It felt good, too." He shook his head. "Obviously Emma went looking for Muggsie. How about we drive around her neighborhood and see if we can find her? Maybe we can help.''

They drove separately. Emma's car was parked in front of her apartment building now, but when Brennan ran up the stairs to check on her, there was no answer to the doorbell. She must have decided to look for Muggsie on foot. They drove around, scanning the side streets.

Nate saw her first and signaled to Brennan. She was sitting on the curb, a couple of streets away from her apartment building, holding the little gray dog in her lap. Even before he got out of his car, Nate could see the blood that was streaking Emma's white uniform.

Brennan got to her before Nate and sat down next to her on the curb. He put an arm around her. "I'm sorry, Emma."

She looked up at him. "Gary let her out," she said dully. "She must have been killed by a car. I found her lying by the side of the road. She must have been killed instantly. She couldn't see very well, you know, she was so old.''

"I know."

"I've brought your key," Nate told her, holding it out.

She took it from him, looking puzzled, but didn't question him. Her soft brown eyes were shining with tears that were almost ready to spill over. Nate felt his own throat close. She had loved that old dog so much. Nate remembered her saying only a week ago that she was dreading having to make the decision to put Muggsie to sleep. As long as she wasn't in pain, she wouldn't have to make it, she'd said.

She attempted a smile that didn't come anywhere near succeeding. "Thank you for coming, Nate." She glanced at Brennan, seeming to see him clearly for the first time. "You just got back? Is everything all right? Are the children okay? Georgia?"

"Everybody," he assured her.

"You didn't want to stay with Georgia?"

He stroked her hair gently, tucking it back behind her ears, then shook his head. "I don't feel quite so responsible for Georgia anymore, Emma. She's a grown woman, after all." He smiled rather wistfully. "In any case, there's usually someone around to take care of her."

"You still love her, don't you?" Emma said softly.

"The way I love the children. Not as a man loves a woman, Emma."

Their eyes met and held. To Nate the look on Brennan's face was very clear. He loved Emma Fieldstone. Perhaps he'd realized it on seeing her just now, so distraught over her little dog. And judging from the expression in Emma's brown eyes, she was aware of it, too. She looked as though she wasn't sure whether to believe, but oh, how she wanted to believe.

"I made a decision while I was gone, Emma," Brennan said. "Looking at Georgia when she was so close to dying, I realized how necessary it is to make the most of life. I'm going to work on rearranging my priorities, making more time for Hannah and Adam, more time for a personal life."

For "personal life," read Emma Fieldstone, Nate thought. This was no place for him, he decided. These two extraordinarily nice people had some sorting out of emotions to do, and he was in the way. "We can't stay here, Emma," he said quietly.

She nodded, then looked down at the little dog in her lap, one hand very gently touching the soft gray hair. "I know," she said, her voice tight. "I've just been sitting here, trying to decide where to bury Muggsie. I don't have a yard."

Brennan reached out with equally gentle fingers to cover Emma's hand with his own. "We can bury Muggsie in our yard, Emma. The backyard is very sunny and nice."

The *look* on her face. "She liked to lie out in the sun," she said softly.

Brennan nodded, tightening his grip around her shoulders, helping her up. "Let's go home," he said. She nodded, and they walked off together toward Brennan's car, Emma still cradling the dog, heedless of the blood on her clothing, heedless of Nate, standing there, watching them go.

NATE CALLED every evening for the next three days. Maddy was at a meeting. Maddy was conducting a class. Maddy had gone somewhere with her girl-friends. She didn't call back. He couldn't imagine why. They had parted as friends, as lovers—what had happened to make her back off again? He was conscious of a feeling of panic. Had he messed up in some way? Had he held out for too long against admitting how much he loved her?

Emma had no idea why Maddy was avoiding him, she told him; she could only repeat what she'd heard from Brennan. Maddy was working long hours at the zoo, making up for her time away. "She could have made time for a phone call, too," Nate protested.

Emma nodded, giving him a sympathetic look. He wanted to suggest she pump the children, but it was obviously impossible to get Emma to concentrate on his problems right now. Though she was still grieving for

Muggsie, she was walking around as if her feet didn't quite touch the ground. Which was all very well, Nate thought grudgingly, but he wanted his share of happiness, too.

On Saturday he decided it was time to force whatever issue there was. He called the Malone household from the clinic and spoke to Hannah. Maddy was at work, she informed him. So was her father.

"Did you and Maddy have a fight?" she asked.

"Not that I know of. Why do you ask?"

"Maddy's awful grouchy. She got grouchy at the hospital in Japan and she's been grouchy ever since. When we got home and I asked her if you were coming over, she grouched at me and said it wasn't any of my business."

"What made her get grouchy?"

"I don't know." She hesitated. "We were talking about you. She wanted to know how come I was calling you Uncle Nate all the time, and I told her we had a talk, and about me thinking it was pretty good that you didn't get mad at Adam and me."

"Was there anything else, Hannah?" Nate urged. "Think hard."

"Well...she said she was happy we'd found out how nice you were. That doesn't sound like she was mad at you, does it?"

"No."

"Oh, and I told her what you'd said about not taking her away from us."

"And what did she say then?"

"*That's* when she got grouchy. She went real quiet for a while, then she said there wasn't much sense hanging on, waiting for the ax to fall in October. She wouldn't tell me what it meant."

"In October, she said?"

"I think that's what she said."

Maddy had made several obscure references to October before. He couldn't imagine... Light suddenly dawned, and he couldn't think how he'd been so stupid. Our first real date was in March, he'd told her—and October was seven months after March. Seven months. And he'd laid out his usual plan of action for her right at the start. *Six or seven months, and the newness is gone. Time to break it off.*

So if she got grouchy thinking of October, didn't that mean she didn't want their relationship to end? Quite suddenly the sun seemed to be shining in through his office window much more brightly than it had in days. It was a beautiful day, a wonderful day in May. He might burst into song any second.

"What time is Maddy due home?" he asked Hannah, thinking fast.

"Five o'clock," she said. "Maybe a little after."

"How would you and Adam like to go to the marina?" he asked.

She squealed. "With you? Yay!"

He thought through his schedule. "I'll pick you up at three-thirty," he said.

But when he arrived at the Malone house, he ran into unexpected opposition from Kat. "I'm not supposed to let the children go with anyone without permission from Brennan or Maddy," she said firmly.

"Kat," he said, smiling into her heavily made-up eyes, calling on every scrap of charm he possessed. "This is a matter of the heart. It's very important that I kidnap the children. You have to tell Maddy I won't bring them back. She'll have to come and get them at the marina beach."

"Kidnap?" She shook her head, her earrings swinging wildly. "Forget it, Dr. Ludlow."

"We could call Daddy," Hannah suggested excitedly.

Luckily Brennan was available and gave his permission at once. "Good luck, Nate," he said with a laugh. Nate couldn't remember ever hearing Brennan laugh in quite such a carefree manner. *Good for you, Emma,* he thought.

He passed the telephone to Kat, so that she could get the message personally, then rehearsed her on the part she was to play. "I also want you to be available to baby-sit from around eight o'clock or so," he told her.

"Whatever are you up to, Doc?" she asked, grinning.

"Just keep your fingers crossed," he told her. "I'll fill you in later. You might even hear my shout of glee all the way from the marina."

"WE HAD A LONG TALK with our mom," Adam told him as they sat side by side on the beach blanket Nate had picked up at his condo. He'd also taken time to change into a sweatshirt and shorts, superstitiously remembering that that was how he'd been dressed when he last saw Maddy.

"That's good," Nate said cautiously.

Hannah was watching the sailboarders. There was a good stiff breeze, and a lot of them were out today, some of them really catching air. Normally Nate would have been one of them, but he had no desire to be out there, frolicking around on the water right now. He had important business to take care of; afterward there'd be time for play.

He became aware that Adam was talking again and made himself concentrate on what the little boy was saying. "Mom said she was sorry she wasn't a better mother. She had this yearning, you see," he added seriously. "She's always had a yearning, to sing and to go places. The yearning won't let her be, she says."

"She's going to write a song about it," Hannah said. "We're going to be in it too, with our names and everything."

"That'll be fun," Nate said.

"Do you have a yearning for Maddy?" Hannah asked, gazing directly at him with her clear round blue eyes.

"I sure do," he said wholeheartedly.

"I used to hope Maddy would marry Daddy," she said after a moment's silence. "I wanted it so badly, Uncle Nate. We could have been a family again, you know?"

"It would have solved a lot of problems," he agreed, "but if it isn't there for two people, there's no way to make it happen." He hesitated, then reached out to twitch Hannah's braid affectionately. "You are a family, anyway. You all love each other." He grinned at her. "When I used to complain to my mom about her loving too many people and not having enough left for me, she said love was like eating an artichoke. You always seemed to end up with more than you started with."

He looked from Hannah to Adam, then decided it was time to lay his cards on the table. "I love Maddy," he said. "I want to ask her to marry me. Today. But if you don't approve, if you aren't ready for me to do that, I'll wait awhile. Remember though, you wouldn't be losing Maddy, you'd be gaining me."

Hannah screwed up her face against the sun as she looked at him. "You suppose you could love Adam and me, too?"

"No problem there," he assured her, hugging her close. "Depending on how many more tricks you play on me, of course. It's hard to love somebody when they turn a hose on you."

Hannah and Adam both giggled, then Hannah sobered again. "I guess it looks like Emma and Daddy might get married, too, huh?"

"Daddy's going around whistling all the time," Adam offered.

"Is he now? Well, then I suppose it's possible they might get together."

"So Adam and I don't really know who we'll end up with."

"Hard to tell," Nate agreed. "Especially as everyone is going to want you."

The two children exchanged a delighted glance. Evidently the thought pleased them. "Looks to me as if you might finish up with four parents," Nate told them.

"Five parents," Hannah corrected him at once. "You're forgetting our mom. She's around some of the time."

Adam nodded solemnly.

Nate was moved by their loyalty. Including the small boy in his hug he said, "We'll work it out between us. Maybe through the week you'll live with Maddy and me, and spend weekends with your Dad. With adjustments as necessary and Kat to fill in. Just think, you can shuttle back and forth while everyone spoils you."

Hannah shook her head. "Maddy won't let anyone spoil us," she said flatly. "It's not good for us."

MADDY DROVE to the marina, pondering Nate's cryptic message. He'd kidnapped the children; he wouldn't give them back until she came to get them. He was forcing another confrontation, of course. He was good at that.

"Brennan gave his permission," Kat had insisted.

Thanks a lot, Brennan, Maddy thought dryly. Now she had to make a decision whether to break things off herself or wait to be discarded in October. She knew what would happen the moment she saw Nate Ludlow in the flesh. The word brought a vivid memory of Nate lying next to her, naked, holding her, and she began to feel excited at the thought of seeing him. Fine holdout she was.

The children were burying Nate in the sand when she arrived. He was lying back, his hands behind his head, while they covered him up to the waist. None of them saw her for a minute, and she let her gaze move greedily over Nate's profile, feeling love welling up inside her until she thought she'd explode with it. Make it be all right, she prayed under her breath.

"You aren't afraid they'll bury all of you?" she asked aloud, taking a couple of steps forward so that she could look down at Nate.

Something blazed in his face when he heard her voice, something that made her heart leap inside her breast, but all he said was, "Hello, Maddy Scott," in a gentle voice.

Hannah sat back on her heels, scowling up at Maddy. "We don't play tricks on Uncle Nate anymore," she said indignantly. "Especially now he's going to be one of the family."

"So much for the power of surprise," Nate groaned.

"What's going on here?" Maddy asked, not daring to come up with any interpretations.

Nate grinned. "It's a complicated story. Sit down and we'll tell it to you."

"Love is like an artichoke," Hannah chimed in. "Everyone has a yearning." She and Adam and Nate exchanged laughing glances that seemed to be full of hidden meanings.

"A yearning?" Maddy queried. She had no idea what artichokes had to do with anything, but she associated the word yearning with something Georgia had said, though she wasn't sure what it had to do with this situation.

As she sat down on the blanket, she looked from Nate to Hannah and Adam, amazed by the affection she could feel burgeoning among them. She realized quite suddenly that the pain in her jaw that had flared up over the last few days was completely gone. She touched her face wonderingly, and Nate asked with immediate concern, "TMJ bothering you?"

"No," she said slowly. "That's what I'm amazed about. I don't have any pain at all, and it's been hurting for days."

"You've been clenching your teeth again?" he asked. His gaze hadn't left her face since she sat down. His eyes shone green in the sunlight, and a smile played around his mouth. She wanted to lean forward and kiss him, but didn't quite dare until she found out what this was all about. Unable to meet his direct gaze, she looked instead at the sailboarders skimming over the water, some of them jumping waves. So many strong-looking bronzed young bodies, male and female. None of the men quite so perfectly formed as Nate Ludlow.

"You ready for another lesson tomorrow?" he asked.

"Maybe," she said cautiously, then forced herself to turn back. He was still smiling. "You look very pleased with yourself," she blurted out.

"I have reason to." He grinned at her. "Are you clenching your teeth now?"

She shook her head.

"So don't you think that means you're pleased with yourself, too?"

"Maybe," she said again.

"No maybes about it," he said, then grinning as though the words had some secret meaning for him.

"Aren't you going to ask her, Uncle Nate?" Adam burst out.

Nate looked at him with a rueful grin. "How can I? You've made it impossible for me to get down on my knees."

"Guys have to get down on their knees to ask ladies to marry them?" Adam asked.

"Absolutely."

"Yuk," Adam exclaimed.

"Nate?" Maddy asked weakly.

He turned his head and looked at her directly; the something she'd seen in his eyes earlier was blazing at her again. "Here it is, then—this is the moment when pride is humbled, as the once arrogant Darcy confesses his love."

"Darcy? *Pride and Prejudice*? The movie with Laurence Olivier and Greer Garson? What on earth are you talking about?"

He beamed at her. "Damned if I know. I got it off a calendar that illustrated old movies. It seemed to fit."

He took a deep breath. "I love you, Madeleine Scott. Will you please marry me?"

"But what about October?" she asked faintly.

He spoke to Hannah without turning his head. "Give Maddy the thing from my duffel bag there, will you, honey?"

Hannah rummaged around, then passed Maddy a large square pad. A calendar. She looked at it, mystified, then suddenly hazarding a guess, she thumbed through the pages. The entire month of October had been torn out.

She gazed at him, letting all her love for him show now. "Oh Nate," she said shakily. "Are you sure?"

"I had the hardest time figuring out what all those cryptic references to October meant," he told her. "You weren't to know, of course, that I almost failed math in junior high. How was I supposed to guess you were adding seven months to March?"

"But you said . . ."

"I said a lot of stupid things. I've been discovering lately that I was wrong. I was wrong to be gun-shy about marriage, wrong to be nervous around children. . . ."

"You were nervous around us, Uncle Nate?" Adam asked, his eyes wide.

"Scared to death. With cause, I might add." Nate brought out his hands from under his head and supported himself on them. "Well, are you ever going to answer my question?" he demanded.

"I love you, Nate," she said softly.

Behind her a wet and burly young man in a very brief swimsuit pulled up his sailboard onto the beach, then flung himself down next to his girlfriend. "That's big-league stuff on the other side of the buoy," he declared.

"This is big-league stuff too, Maddy," Nate said. "However, I figure if I'm ready for it, you *have* to be ready for it. You're a much braver person than I am. So what do you say?''

"I say yes," she said breathlessly, then finally allowed herself to lean over to kiss him. He put his arms around her as their lips met, losing his balance, so that both fell back onto the sand. But neither of them noticed; they were too busy exploring the new, extraordinarily enhanced sensations that this first "committed" kiss was bringing them. Maddy was reveling in the feeling of Nate's mouth against her own. Surely their mouths had been sculpted to fit together, she thought. Nate was thinking that holding Maddy in his arms might just be the best hobby he'd ever come up with, a hobby to last a lifetime.

It was a while before Maddy noticed that Hannah and Adam were busily covering her own legs with sand, trapping her in Nate's burrow.

"Let them have their fun," Nate murmured into her ear. "I've hired Kat for the evening. We can just lie here a while and think about what we're going to do when we get to my condo."

"You going to watch old movies, Uncle Nate?" Hannah asked. What sharp ears she had.

"No, Hannah," Nate answered patiently, without moving his gaze from Maddy's face. "We're going to make a new movie together."

THE SUN WAS SHINING in a cloudless July sky as Maddy and her father walked up the steps to the small church. She stumbled on the hem of her long white gown as she reached the top, and her father steadied her. "You okay, darling?" he asked.

''More than okay,'' she said with a smile. He looked wonderfully distinguished in his tuxedo, she thought—Spencer Tracy in *Father of the Bride*.

Her parents had flown in two days earlier after visiting Georgia, who was solidly booked for the month in one of Hawaii's major hotels. By coincidence, they had told her, exchanging rueful glances, Major Jed Allen had recently been transferred to Honolulu's Hickham Air Force Base.

The church was banked with enough flowers to stock a major conservatory. Georgia had airlifted in orchids and anthuriums and birds of paradise to make up for her absence. The church was crowded with people, too. Many of Maddy's colleagues had come from the zoo, her girlfriends were there, and there were several people from the nursing homes and schools she visited. Even Barbara Oates was there, sitting erect in her wheelchair in a side aisle. Nate's side of the church was just as crowded with patients and friends. His gorgeous friend Teddie was also present. Teddie turned and winked at Maddy as she waited with her father for the signal to walk down the aisle. No doubt she hadn't been able to resist coming to see this newly domesticated Nate one more time, Maddy reflected.

At the front of the church she could see Nate's parents sitting side by side. She had met them a month ago, when she and Nate had flown to Seattle to deliver their wedding invitation personally. Nate's sisters and their families sat next to them—they had all attended the rehearsal yesterday—a noisy but attractive crowd, all of them obviously crazy about Nate.

Her own mother had been escorted to her seat in the front moments before, drawing many admiring glances.

And there was Nate, waiting beside Casey, not yet aware that she had arrived, looking absolutely breathtaking in a white tuxedo that fitted perfectly across his muscular shoulders, standing straight and tall with his eyes on Hannah and Adam. Hannah stood proudly in her slender pink gown, rosebuds twined into her braid, while Adam, in white pants and shirt, was as erect as Nate, the rings wobbling slightly on the cushion he was clutching.

Even as Maddy noticed the cushion's dangerous slant, Emma was there beside Adam, setting it straight, lightly touching his hair where it always stood up at the back, then going back to her place beside Brennan. The little boy flashed her a grateful smile over his shoulder.

Hannah evidently caught the smile and turned to see who was receiving it, grinning nervously at Emma in her turn.

The children were going to be just fine, Maddy thought thankfully, letting her gaze return to Nate.

Then the organist nodded her head, lifted her hands and brought them down, and Maddy started the long slow walk down the aisle. Nate had turned at the first chord and was watching her approach, his eyes blazing love at her. Even before her father released her to Nate, it seemed to Maddy that everyone else in the church had disappeared—friends, family, minister, everyone. There was no one else in the world but Madeleine Scott and Nate Ludlow smiling deeply into each other's eyes, while the organ played somewhere in the background with just a hint of balalaikas.

The others didn't come back into focus for some time, not until the minister asked, "Who gives this woman in marriage to this man?'' and Maddy's father answered, ''Her mother and I do.'' Very distinctly, Hannah and Adam, and perhaps even Brennan, added, ''So do we.''

Harlequin Superromance®

COMING NEXT MONTH

SWEEPSTAKES RULES & REGULATIONS

NO PURCHASE NECESSARY TO ENTER OR RECEIVE A PRIZE

1. To enter and join the Reader Service, check off the "YES" box on your Sweepstakes Entry Form and return to Harlequin Reader Service. If you do not wish to join the Reader Service but wish to enter the Sweepstakes only, check off the "NO" box on your Sweepstakes Entry Form. Incomplete and/or inaccurate entries are ineligible for that section or sections(s) of prizes. Not responsible for mutilated or unreadable entries or inadvertent printing errors. Mechanically reproduced entries are null and void. Be sure to also qualify for the Bonus Sweepstakes. See rule #3 on how to enter.

2. Either way, your unique Sweepstakes number will be compared against the list of winning numbers generated at random by the computer. In the event that all prizes are not claimed, random drawings will be held from all entries received from all presentations to award all unclaimed prizes. All cash prizes are payable in U.S. funds. This is in addition to any free, surprise or mystery gifts that might be offered. The following prizes are offered: *Grand Prize (1) $1,000,000 Annuity; First Prize (1) $35,000; Second Prize (1) $10,000; Third Prize (3) $5,000; Fourth Prize (10) $1,000; Fifth Prize (25) $500; Sixth Prize (5,000) $5.

   * This Sweepstakes contains a Grand Prize offering of a $1,000,000 annuity. Winner may elect to receive $25,000 a year for 40 years without interest; totalling $1,000,000 or $350,000 in one cash payment. Entrants may cancel Reader Service at any time without cost or obligation to buy.

3. Extra Bonus Prize: This presentation offers two extra bonus prizes valued at $30,000 each to be awarded in a random drawing from all entries received. To qualify, scratch off the silver on your Lucky Keys. If the registration numbers match, you are eligible for the prize offering.

4. Versions of this Sweepstakes with different graphics will be offered in other mailings or at retail outlets by Torstar Corp. and its affiliates. This promotion is being conducted under the supervision of Marden-Kane, Inc., an independent judging organization. By entering this Sweepstakes, each entrant accepts and agrees to be bound by these rules and the decisions of the judges, which shall be final and binding. Odds of winning in the random drawing are dependent upon the total number of entries received. Taxes, if any, are the sole responsibility of the winners. Prizes are nontransferable. All entries must be received by March 31, 1990. The drawing will take place on or about April 30, 1990 at the offices of Marden-Kane, Inc., Lake Success, N.Y.

5. This offer is open to residents of the U.S., United Kingdom and Canada, 18 years or older, except employees of Torstar Corp., its affiliates, subsidiaries, Marden-Kane and all other agencies and persons connected with conducting this Sweepstakes. All Federal, State and local laws apply. Void wherever prohibited or restricted by law.

6. Winners will be notified by mail and may be required to execute an affidavit of eligibility and release, which must be returned within 14 days after notification. Canadian winners will be required to answer a skill-testing question. Winners consent to the use of their name, photograph and/or likeness for advertising and publicity in conjunction with this or similar promotions, without additional compensation.

7. For a list of our most current major prize winners, send a stamped, self-addressed envelope to: Winners List, c/o Marden-Kane, Inc., P.O. Box 701, Sayreville, N.J. 08871

If Sweepstakes entry form is missing, please print your name and address on a 3" × 5" piece of plain paper and send to:

In the U.S.	In Canada
Sweepstakes Entry	Sweepstakes Entry
901 Fuhrmann Blvd.	P.O. Box 609
P.O. Box 1867	Fort Erie, Ontario
Buffalo, NY 14269-1867	L2A 5X3

LTY-H89
© 1988 Harlequin Enterprises Ltd.

Your favorite stories have a brand-new look!

HARLEQUIN
American Romance

American Romance is greeting the new decade with a new design, marked by a contemporary, sophisticated cover. As you've come to expect, each American Romance is still a modern love story with real-life characters and believable conflicts. Only now they look more true-to-life than ever before.

Look for American Romance's bold new cover where Harlequin books are sold.

ARNC-1R

Harlequin American Romance®

Gull Cottage

SUMMER.

The sun, the surf, the sand...

One relaxing month by the sea was all Zoe, Diana and Gracie ever expected from their four-week stays at Gull Cottage, the luxurious East Hampton mansion. They never thought they'd soon be sharing those long summer days—or hot summer nights—with a special man. They never thought that what they found at the beach would change their lives forever. But as Boris, Gull Cottage's resident mynah bird said: "Beware of summer romances...."

Join Zoe, Diana and Gracie for the summer of their lives. Don't miss the GULL COTTAGE trilogy in American Romance: #301 *Charmed Circle* by Robin Francis (July 1989), #305 *Mother Knows Best* by Barbara Bretton (August 1989) and #309 *Saving Grace* by Anne McAllister (September 1989).

GULL COTTAGE—because a month can be the start of forever...
